MW01140933

The Clash of Sabers

RANDELL WHALEY

Copyright © 2020 Randell Whaley
All rights reserved
First Edition

PAGE PUBLISHING, INC.
Conneaut Lake, PA

First originally published by Page Publishing 2020

ISBN 978-1-6624-3277-4 (pbk)
ISBN 978-1-6624-3278-1 (digital)

Printed in the United States of America

CHAPTER 1

Life in the South

Jim leaned forward and laid his left forearm on his horse's neck to urge her forward faster. He never wore spurs while riding Blue Bonnet. She wouldn't tolerate it. Blue Bonnet was a very sensitive mare and really went all out to please her rider. But Jim's father had learned when she was just a filly, while breaking her to the saddle, that she would go berserk anytime anyone touched spurs to her ribs. All you had to do was loosen the reins, and she was off like a shot out of a cannon. And Jim had learned that if you wanted her to really go all out, just lean forward and put your forearm on her neck.

Jim was fifteen years old, about to turn sixteen. He was exercising Blue Bonnet today to keep her in shape. She was an excellent foxhunting horse. But Jim wasn't foxhunting today. He hadn't been on a fox hunt since before the war started, and his father and older brother went away. He lived on their plantation in South Carolina with his mother and sister. His father and older brother, Jonathon, had gone off to war to fight the Yankees.

They came to the creek, which ran along the length of their plantation, and Jim stood up in his stirrups and tightened his knees while Blue Bonnet started her jump and cleared the creek. She cleared the creek easily like she always did.

Jim Bennett had wanted to go off to war too, especially when he got the news of his father's death. Captain Jonathon Bennett Sr. had been killed in action last fall at Fredericksburg. The family got the news in the middle of December. He had wanted to take a horse and go join up with General Jeb Stuart's cavalry right then. But his mother went into hysterics at the very thought of his doing so.

"But you're still just a boy!" she exclaimed through her tears and grabbed him and hugged him. He was already taller than her by then, and he hugged her back and tried to comfort her. He resisted the impulse to tell her he was not a boy. He was a grown man, and he knew it. He just had yet to convince anyone else of that fact.

When Jim was twelve years old, he started shooting up in height and was five feet, ten inches tall by the time he was thirteen. But he grew in height first and looked skinny as a scarecrow with his height advantage and scant frame. He had filled out since then, and his shoulders had grown broader, and his leg muscles, while still slender, had grown hard and firm from riding Blue Bonnet so often. He had blue eyes and dark-brown hair.

They had arrived at the northern boundary of their estate by now, and Jim reined up and halted Blue Bonnet. She objected as usual, but he knew she'd run herself to death if he didn't rein her in and let her blow for a few minutes. She loved to run and loved to jump and just couldn't contain herself when he let her go like he was doing today. While he was making his mare rest and catch her breath, he looked up toward the north. He could see the cotton fields of the neighbor's plantation, and beyond that he could see the distant forests. Somewhere up there General Lee's army was fighting Yankees, and he knew he belonged up there with them.

When Jim got the news of his older brother's death in February, he made up his mind. Second Lieutenant Jonathon Bennett Jr. had died of influenza, but Jim knew he was weakened by a wound he had received the previous fall when hit by a piece of shrapnel from a cannon blast—injured in the leg. The privations of insufficient rations and inadequate protection from the cold were more than his weakened system could handle, and Jim knew that was the real cause of his death. So Jim Bennett made up his mind; he was going to go join up with Jeb Stuart's cavalry come spring. It was now April of 1863. His only problem was figuring out how to break the news to his mother. Sis would object too. But then getting away from wailing women would be one of the advantages of going. His mom had loved him with all the love a mother could possibly give to a son as long as he could remember. And his sister, Joanne, just two years younger, had been a pretty good sister as far as sisters went.

He turned Blue Bonnet back toward the plantation home quarters. He let her run again on the way back. It was Sunday, and the field hands had the day off. The slave quarters were located to be near the fields to minimize the walking time to and from work. It was plowing time. So the plow horses were getting their day of rest too. He reached the stables and dismounted and unsaddled Blue Bonnet. He could have had Jamie unsaddle her. Jamie was the stable keeper. But his father was emphatic about making sure each of his sons learned how to saddle and unsaddle their own horses.

"What if you were out somewhere and you didn't have a stable hand handy to do it for you?" he'd ask. "The servants have a purpose. They work for us, and we feed and clothe them and give them a roof over their heads. But it wouldn't be good for us to grow into a helpless race of people who couldn't do for ourselves." So if the stable hand wasn't nearby, he'd always saddle and unsaddle his horses himself.

He walked up toward the house, a beautiful Southern mansion. Supper should be ready by now. He had to figure out a way to tell his mother of his decision, but not today. He'd put it off another week or so.

He walked in, and Emma saw him.

"Now you remember to wash up, and you barely made it back by suppertime," she told him in her reprimanding voice. You'd think he was the servant instead of her. But she had been his mammy when he was a baby, and she had never gotten used to him being grown up. She still fussed over him and reminded him of every little thing he was supposed to do without giving him a chance to remember it on his own or even get credit for remembering it if he did. But he was mainly just amused by her. He knew this was her way of expressing affection. That was why she was chosen as the family mammy; she loved babies and kids so ardently. She was very fat and black as the ace of spades. She had nine kids of her own, most of whom were field hands by now though her oldest son was the butler for the mansion.

He sat down at the table: chicken and dressing, mashed potatoes, black-eyed peas, and hot biscuits—delicious food. Emma was always at her best in the kitchen. She was the family cook. She was proud of her talent and showed it off three times a day. They started the meal mostly in silence as had sort of become the custom after the bad news had arrived from the front of Papa first and then Jonnie.

"Blue Bonnet jump okay today?" Joanna asked, mainly to break the silence.

"Yes, she jumped fine and ran fine, just like always," he replied. Joanna was fourteen and just growing into womanhood. She had beautiful long, black hair and a beautiful smile to match. She had been kind of skinny too, just like Jim until during the past year or so, and then her young figure had started filling out. She had beautiful blue eyes. He had grown closer to her since she had sort of gotten out of her silly childishness that he figured every girl must go through.

"Are you gonna ride Blue Boy again tomorrow?" she asked; he knew it was mainly to keep the conversation going.

"Yes." Blue Boy was Blue Bonnet's colt. He had turned two years old the previous fall, and Jim had started breaking him to the saddle. Jonathon Sr. wanted all his sons to become excellent horsemen and firmly believed that no one was truly a horseman unless he could break his own horses. So he had taught both his sons to break horses as soon as it was practical after they had learned to ride. But Jonathon used the "gentle breaking" method. With Jon's method, you gentled the horse down with frequent handling from the time he was a baby colt. He was so used to being touched and curried and being led around by a halter so that when he was old enough to start being broken to the saddle, it was merely another transition for the horse to go through. Papa always explained that if a horse was broken properly, he'd never buck a single time. He wouldn't even learn how to buck. Papa was into foxhunting, and any foxhunting horse had to know how to jump. So learning to jump had to be part of any colt's training before Papa considered him to be a completely broken colt.

Jim hadn't taught the colt to jump yet. But he saddled him and rode him every day except Sunday. He figured a colt deserved a day off on Sunday just like the field hands and plow horses.

He didn't dare mention the war, nor did anyone else at the table. He didn't want his mother to go into another fit of crying, which she was very prone to do ever since she got the news about Papa. And Jonnie had been her favorite son though she never would admit it. Two heavy losses within months of each other had aged her terribly. She looked more like sixty rather than her forty-two years.

After dinner, Jim got out his mandolin, and Joanne sat down at the piano. All the household servants were permitted to gather around and listen to their music. Jim could easily forget all his troubles while playing his mandolin. And Joanne did an excellent job of accompaniment on the piano. Mama would sometimes sing when they played a song with words she knew. It would even lift her out of her depression for a few moments while she was singing. Jim deliberately played every song he could think of that his mother knew. Many of his songs were instrumentals and didn't have words. But he stuck to the ones with words this night. Even then it wasn't until the third song that Mama finally sort of came out of her shell and started singing. Mama had such a beautiful soprano voice. And Joanne would sometimes sing harmony to her. It made him feel all warm inside from head to foot just to listen to it. Music seemed to be the anecdote that healed all ailments—emotional ailments, at least. He'd deliberately play sad songs at times like now because they were the ones that Mama was most likely to sing. But they seemed to cheer her up a little. He wondered why sad songs seemed to cheer someone up when they were already sad. He figured there must be a reason. But music and horses—they seemed to be the two things that could provide a body with an uplift.

CHAPTER 2

Plans

The next day Mr. Jones came in after breakfast as usual. Abe, the butler, went to the door and let him in. Mr. Jones was the tutor for Jim and Joanne. He was Jim's math and grammar teacher as well as Joanne's music teacher. The only musical instrument he taught was the piano. Jim had learned the mandolin on his own. Papa had played the fiddle, and Jim had learned the fiddle. Then he found out that playing the mandolin was very similar to the fiddle as far as hitting the notes were concerned, and he just took more to the mandolin than to the fiddle. Since his father's death, he totally lost interest in the fiddle. It depressed him to even see a fiddle.

They had school as usual. He did his math problems while Mr. Jones taught Joanne music. Then he studied his grammar assignment. School was over at noon. Then after dinner he went out to ride Blue Boy.

Jamie had Blue Boy all saddled up for him as usual. Jim did wear spurs when riding Blue Boy. At first he didn't. He expected he'd probably be high-strung like Blue Bonnet, but he found out shortly after he'd got him used to being ridden and had taught him to neck-rein that Blue Boy had a stubborn streak and would sometimes balk just to express his feelings about being ridden and controlled by someone other than himself. So Jim had taken to wearing his spurs, and one jab with his spurs would always be enough to remind Blue Boy that the rider on his back was the boss after all. It had gotten so he rarely had to jab him with the spurs. Just having them on and hearing their occasional jingle were enough in most cases.

Papa used to say, "Two things are important for any boy to learn. And that's riding and shooting." The reason we were an independent country today was because during the Revolutionary War the American colonists knew how to ride and shoot. Jim had read in the history books provided by Mr. Jones that most of the battles during the American Revolution were fought by infantrymen. But he didn't correct his father. Jim's grandfather had fought in the American Revolution, which was a fact of which Papa was very proud. So Jim was taught to shoot a rifle, and Papa took Jonnie to the nearby mountains each fall to hunt deer, and then when Jim was old enough, he was allowed to go along too. They didn't really hunt on horseback. They just rode the horses to the mountains. The long Pennsylvania rifles they used were too long to use from the back of a horse. But they'd kill several deer every year. They'd bring along some servants to field dress the deer. They'd bring them home, and the blacks would skin them out and cook and eat them. Mama and Joanne didn't like deer meat, so they allowed the slaves to use all the meat. The field hands loved venison. But Emma would go and cut a couple of steaks and cook them just for Jim and Jonnie. She admitted that she spoiled them.

Jon had also kept milk cows and chickens. He had many times remarked that to stay a free country, you needed to be as self-sufficient as possible. Milk cows had calves, and calves grew up, and a grown calf could be butchered, so the slaves as well as the family had plenty of beef. And during the late summer when the chickens, raised by the setting hens, were the right size, they had fried chicken. This time of year they never had fryers, only stewing hens. They'd cull the hens in the spring, and the ones that didn't lay would go into the stewpot. Papa had said many times that one of the flaws in the South's way of doing things was depending on raising cotton alone for its livelihood. Jim could agree. So they had cows and chickens, and the servants raised a vegetable garden each year.

So Jim kept up his routine and didn't tell Mama or Sis about his plan. He decided to keep it a secret until it came time to leave.

Jim's sixteenth birthday came on a Saturday. That would mean that Mr. Jones wouldn't come and, therefore, no school. So he decided to go out and ride Blue Boy. After breakfast he notified Mama and Joanne of his plans.

"Can I come with you?" Joanne asked.

"Sure," replied Jim. She knew she didn't have to ask. He always liked having her along. He went and told Jamie to saddle Blue Boy and also Lady, Joanne's mare. Joanne told Emma to start packing them a picnic lunch. Mama didn't complain about being left home alone, which was unusual. But Jim had given up on Mama's predictability a long time ago and went out to the saddle room in the stable barn and got some saddlebags. He brought them in so Joanne could have Emma pack them a picnic lunch and put them in the saddlebags.

They left the plantation headquarters and headed north along the path Jim normally used when exercising Blue Bonnet. There was a spot along the creek that was fairly narrow. He thought maybe Blue Boy's training had come along well enough that maybe he could try jumping him. He knew Lady could clear it easily. He told Joanne his plans, and she wholeheartedly agreed. There were beautiful trees all along the creek bank and green grass and rocky places. It was really a beautiful creek. They reached the spot that he had told Joanne about, and he told her to jump Lady across the creek first. He held Blue Boy in check while he watched Lady get her run and then jump. He figured having him watch another horse do it would help Blue Boy to figure out in advance what he expected of him. Lady cleared the creek with her jump easily. Joanne rode her beautifully. Joanne was an excellent rider. Then he headed Blue Boy toward the creek and touched his spurs to his ribs—down, down, down, toward the creek. When they reached the creek, Jim gave him his head and stood up in the stirrups, holding his knees tight. He felt Blue Boy's muscles bunch up, and he jumped and cleared the creek and landed okay on the other side.

"Whoopee!" yelled Joanne. "He did it!" She could really get excited over the simplest things. But that was Blue Boy's first jump. He guessed it *was* an occasion. They just rode up and down the far side of the creek for a couple of hours and enjoyed the beautiful cool spring weather. It was May 5, 1863.

At about noon they found a good place to eat lunch. Jim tethered the horses at a place where there were lots of grass, loosened their cinches, and took the bits out of their mouths so they could graze during lunch. There were steak sandwiches this time, an apple, some potato salad, and a piece of cake and a jug of lemonade. It hit the spot.

The following Monday morning Jim finished making preparations for his departure. All his preparations had been made secretly. Mama and Joanne had given him a surprise birthday party when he and Joanne had returned from their ride Saturday. He hated birthday parties. It was mostly boring though he and Joanne did play music, and that part he enjoyed. He always enjoyed playing music. There was no one to attend the party outside the immediate family. All the boys who lived nearby who were near Jim's age had already gone off to war.

But for now he had to make preparations for his leaving. He took his rifle out to go squirrel hunting one afternoon and left it in the barn, also some powder and ball. He had smuggled a couple of blankets out there one morning before anyone had gotten up. He had managed to smuggle some salt pork and flour out there one morning the same way. Tin plates, some tin cups, a coffeepot, and skillet were already out there that they had always taken along on hunting trips. He knew he'd also need money. Since Papa and Jonnie had left, it was usually his job to take the buckboard and go buy supplies occasionally. He had been saving back some money each time and had built a war fund that way. He didn't consider it stealing since it was family money, and he was a member of the family. Besides that, since he was using it to further the cause of the human race, you couldn't say he was taking it for selfish reasons.

He decided to leave on Tuesday, the following day. Before breakfast he went out and told Jamie to have Blue Boy saddled by the time breakfast was over. He also showed him the pack of supplies he had prepared and told him to put a packsaddle on a packhorse and pack them too.

"Going huntin'?" Jamie asked.

"Yes," Jim replied. It wasn't too much of a lie. He was going hunting after a fashion. After that he simply told his mother he was leaving and walked out into the yard.

"Oh no!" Mama screamed and followed him out into the yard. He turned to face her, and she grabbed him and hugged him. He put his arms around her and stroked her hair. "No! No! No! You're my baby, you can't go!" she wailed. He gave her a big hug and then released her. She held him tight as if she were holding on to him for dear life. Joanne stood a little behind Mama and to her right. Big crocodile tears were streaming down both sides of her face.

"You can't go, Jim," said Joanne, not quite as hysterical as her mother. "You have to stay here and take care of things. You're all we've got now."

Jim took his mother by the arms to move her away from him. She only clung to him even tighter. He paused a moment and then moved her back so he could take Joanne in his arms and hug her.

"You can't go, Jim," she said. "We can't afford to lose you too. First, Papa, then Jonnie, and now you. You *can't* go!"

Jim gave her three big hugs and then took her by the arms and pushed her back, took the reins from Jamie, and swung up into the saddle. He took the halter rope of Chugger, the packhorse, and touched his spurs to Blue Boy's ribs and hurried out of the yard.

While this was going on, Emma was staring out the window with big tears streaming down both sides of her face. Her huge body trembled heavily while she sobbed convulsively. She had known this was coming all along. But now that the moment had arrived, she felt her heart breaking. When little Jimmie was three weeks old, Mama had come down with the fever. Emma had a nursing baby at the time and gave more milk than her own baby needed, so she had nursed little Jim with her own breast. It had caused a bonding that made her think of little Jim as her own child. It was as if she had a little, white baby of her own. His little, white face had made such a contrast against her huge, black breast. She had never loved even her own kids as much as she had loved little Jimmie. When Mama recovered from the fever and her milk came back, she resumed nursing little Jimmie herself, but the bonding Emma had developed for little Jimmie never went away.

When Mama and Joanne started back toward the house, Emma quickly went to the kitchen and dried her face on a dish towel and started making some coffee cake for their midmorning snack. She didn't want anyone to see her crying. Just lose herself in her work was what she'd do. That was how she kept her sanity—by burying herself in her work. But why wouldn't the aching in her heart go away?

Jim rode Blue Boy out of the yard and onto the road. When he was past the trees that hid the house from view, his own tears started. He sobbed convulsively for several minutes. Then he took out his handkerchief and wiped his eyes and blew his nose. It was downright disgraceful for a grown man of sixteen to cry like that. He was glad no one could see him. But he had to go. Why couldn't they understand that? He just had to.

After riding for a while, he started feeling jittery and nervous. *What is this?* he thought. *Why am I jittery? Is this a premonition—a foreboding of something to come?* There had been reports of an increase in robberies since the war started. That was probably it. He halted Blue Boy and pulled Chugger up so he could untie his rifle from Chugger's pack. He had left it loaded. He took out his powder horn from one of the compartments of the canvas pack and reprimed the priming pan. He checked the flint and made sure it was okay. Then he held the rifle across his saddle and continued riding. He felt better now. Any robbers who came along would have his .45-caliber Pennsylvania rifle to deal with now.

Then he started feeling angry—Papa and then Jonnie. He'd show those Yankees. Papa was worth any five Yankees. So to even accounts, he'd have to kill five Yankees for Papa and then another five for Jonnie. Then the score would be even. He knew he was doing right. That part was for sure. He knew he was doing right.

Jim didn't know it at the time, but he had just shed the last tears of his boyhood. He'd never cry again. There would be times when he probably should and maybe wished he could. But he had now started his career as a man.

Joining Up

The Bennett plantation was seven miles south of the town of Florence, South Carolina. Jim had headed north, of course. At noon he reached back to one of his saddlebags and got out a piece of ham and took a bite out of it. He finished eating the piece of ham and then reached back again and got out a cold biscuit and started on that. After having lunch on the run, he took his canteen from the saddle and took a big pull of water from it. Shortly after that he came to the Pee Dee River. He came to the ferry and got out some money to pay the fee for himself and his horses. Old Jeb limped up.

"You leaving home?" he asked.

"I'm going up to join General Jeb Stuart's cavalry," was Jim's reply.

"But you're just a boy," said Old Jeb.

"I'm not a boy!" Jim almost yelled.

"Okay, okay, you're not a boy," conceded Jeb. Jim offered him his money, but Jeb rejected it. "Nope, if you're going up to join Gen'l Stuart's cal'vary, you get to ride free. Soldier boys don't have to pay nothin'."

Jim didn't argue, but boarded the ferry with his two horses. He debarked the ferry at the other side of the river and continued his journey. Toward nightfall he started feeling a little weary—just like on hunting trips. If you weren't used to riding all day, you'd get tired. Blue Boy was in pretty good shape since he'd been riding him regularly. He wasn't accustomed to going all day with a rider on his back either, however. But the youthfulness of horse and rider both increased their endurance. Jim could tell that Chugger was more tired than either himself or Blue Boy.

When he found a likely camping spot, stopped to make camp, and unsaddled and tethered the horses, he remarked to Chugger, "Not in shape, huh?" He tethered the horses next to a creek where they could get some good grass and could drink in the creek. "Eat your fill," he said to both horses. "It'll be another long day tomorrow."

He built a campfire and boiled some coffee. He made some biscuits from the flour moistened in water from the creek. Then he put a piece of cold ham in a skillet and warmed it up. He had brought some spare bacon grease to fry the biscuits in. He kept the spare bacon grease in a tin can with a lid on it so it wouldn't spill in the saddlebag—just like on hunting trips. He knew just what to do. After supper he laid his oilcloth on the ground just like Papa had taught him years before to keep his blankets off the damp ground and unrolled his blankets on top of it. He then rolled up in his blankets and went to sleep. His body felt exhausted, and he was asleep almost instantly. He would have felt loneliness had he not been so exhausted. But the fatigue made the quiet repose of the cool evening feel like heaven.

He awoke just at dawn. When he rolled out of his blankets, he felt the stiffness of his muscles—just like on hunting trips. He knew it would take several days to work the soreness out—the same for the horses. After about a week it would start getting easier. He had brought corn along for the horses. He knew they had to have grain to keep going all day, day after day like this. He took two feed bags out of the pack and put some corn in each and went and put them on the horses.

Then he sliced off another piece of ham and fried it and then made some more hardtack. He made enough hardtack so he'd have enough for noontime without having to stop. He also brewed a pot of coffee. After several cups of coffee, he cleaned up the tin cups, plates, and pots and pans, washing them with sand from the creek. Papa had taught him a lot. He then felt a twinge of grief as he thought about how he'd never see Papa again. Camping out reminded him about how much he missed him—him and Jonnie both. But he was just starting to realize the value of the training Papa had given him. After the horses had finished eating, he took the feed bags off, repacked everything, and saddled up, ready for another day's travel. He noticed his sore muscles again as he swung up into the saddle.

On the fourth day, he noticed the soreness getting less. They had been making about twenty miles a day. That was about all he figured the horses could handle until they were in better shape. On Sunday morning he decided to let the horses rest a day as was the custom back at the plantation. That was why he rode Blue Bonnet on Sundays instead of Blue Boy. He normally had been riding Blue Boy every day because he was breaking him to the saddle. He didn't ride Blue Bonnet every day, so she got her day of rest every day or two anyway. He had camped near water again, so he decided to see if he could find any squirrels. The diet of hardtack and jerky was already getting tiresome. He did see a gray squirrel after a couple of hours and went down to one knee so he could make a head shot. As soon as he squeezed the trigger, the squirrel fell instantly and tumbled to the ground. He went up to check his prize and found the squirrel's head blown to bits, only the ears and some fur still attached to its shoulders. A .45 ball would ruin too much meat unless you made a head shot. Even then some of the shoulder meat would be blood shot. He took out his belt knife and skinned out and cleaned the squirrel right then. Then he carried the unloaded rifle back to camp. He washed the squirrel in the creek and took a piece of string and tied it to a lower tree limb to let it drain. Then he put some water on to boil to clean his rifle—something else Papa had taught him: "Powder is very corrosive, and you should wash the bore of your rifle with soap and water after you fire it—that is, if you don't expect to be shooting it again that day. Makes the barrel stay accurate longer." He didn't have any soap, but he did rinse out the barrel with hot water and wiped it clean with a piece of cotton swab that he wound around the tip of the ramrod. When he had wiped it clean and dry, he ran another patch soaked in meat grease up and down the barrel, and he then reloaded and reprimed it. He figured it was better to keep your rifle loaded all the time, just on general principle. He used grease rendered from fresh pork, so there wasn't any salt in it.

It was a couple of hours before noon by now, so he arranged the squirrel on a spit he had whittled from a piece of tree limb and placed it on two forked sticks he had driven in the ground on each side of the fire. He sprinkled the meat with salt and sat on a log, waiting for dinner to cook.

Half an hour or so before he thought the squirrel to be done enough to eat, he cooked some more biscuits. Then he had a delicious meal: fresh squirrel meat and bread. It tasted really good.

Squirrels grew pretty big in South Carolina, so he could only eat half of it. He put the other half in a stewpot and covered it with the lid. He'd save it until suppertime. It wouldn't spoil now that it was cooked. So he just leaned back against a tree stump and watched the horses graze and rested his tired muscles. He felt a contentment he hadn't felt since before Papa and Jonnie went off to war two years previously. He knew his feeling of contentment was because he was doing right. To go and join up with the Army was his duty, of course, and he knew his duty.

After two weeks, he reached the town of Raleigh, North Carolina. He stopped at the stable and turned his horses over to the hostler. He decided they needed a couple of day's rest. He was nearly out of corn, so he decided he'd better buy some more grain. When you worked horses all day long every day like he'd been doing, they had to have grain. And he decided he'd better buy some food supplies for himself too. A diet of hardtack and jerky had turned out to be pretty grim in spite of the occasional squirrel he had managed to get for his campfire. Also he decided to do something with his rifle. It was just too long to carry on horseback. To carry it across your saddle all day was just too much strain, and when he left the road for any reason, like to make camp or let the horses drink, he'd catch the barrel on tree branches.

He pulled into the stable. He left instructions with the hostler to feed and curry his horses and went to find a gunsmith. He found a good gunsmith and told him he wanted him to saw the barrel off to about twenty inches or so and refix the front sights. The gunsmith had apparently had many similar orders recently. Jim asked if he could have it ready the next day. The gunsmith told him, "You'd better come for it Thursday, I can't get to it until then." This was Tuesday, and he figured his horses needed two days' rest anyway, so he said that would be fine.

"I also need a saddle boot for it," said Jim.

"I don't make saddle boots," replied the gunsmith. "I just do gunsmith work. But there's a leather-making shop two doors down."

Then he went back to the stable and put all the things he needed for his two-day stay in a canvas sack and went to find a hotel with a bathhouse. He decided two weeks without a bath were long enough. The tub of hot water really felt good, and he decided to just soak awhile before soaping up. His muscles had hardened considerably during his two weeks of continuous travel. He had never before ridden a horse all day long every day like the way he'd done for the last couple of weeks. But he had now—that was, with the exception of letting the horses rest one day each week. He must be starting to get accustomed to it because the past several days it had been getting easier. The soreness and stiffness he had felt that first week were gone. Getting the trail dust off really made him relax. He soaped up and rinsed off. He had dropped all his clothes off at a laundry except for his riding habit, which he didn't wear on the trail. He had worn his riding habit while leaving the plantation but, the following morning, had put on hunting clothes made from rough cloth he had brought along, which seemed more natural to wear while riding day after day. So his riding habit wasn't very dirty and would be more appropriate to wear in town anyway.

CHAPTER 4

After he dressed, he found a mirror to comb his hair and noticed he had peach fuzz on his face! Now that wouldn't do! He couldn't ride up to one of Jeb Stuart's cavalry units with peach fuzz on his face. And he didn't want to listen to the remarks a barber would make. Besides, he needed to use what little money he had left sparingly. So he went out and bought a straight razor and some shaving soap. Then he went back to the hotel and lathered his face and shaved. He cut himself in two places. He guessed this would take some practice. He held his handkerchief to the cuts until they stopped bleeding. Then he washed his handkerchief in cold water and laid it on the table to dry. He had another handkerchief and put it in his pocket. Then he went to a store and bought some paper and envelopes. He figured he'd better write to Mama and Joanne. They'd be expecting to hear from him by now.

He went back to the hotel room and wrote Mama and Joanne each a cheerful long letter. He described all the beautiful scenery he had ridden through and the squirrels he shot. He made it seem like there had been an abundance of game for camp meat, which was only partially true. He explained how Blue Boy and Chugger both had benefited from the excellent exercise and that Blue Boy was in excellent shape from being ridden every day. He tried to paint a picture of all sunlight and roses for them. Then he went down to the hotel lobby and asked the clerk if there was a place he could mail his letters.

The clerk said, "Yes, do you need stamps?"

Jim hadn't thought of that. He would have mailed them without stamps. But, of course, he knew they had to be stamped. He had written to Papa and Jonnie to answer their letters and knew he had to put stamps on them. So he bought a stamp from the hotel clerk and mailed his letters. He put them both into the same envelope since they were going to the same place. Then he went out to find a restaurant and find something to eat. He was starved and eager to eat some decent food. He found a restaurant and had a meal of steak and potatoes and black-eyed peas and hot coffee. Now that was good.

It was nearly sundown by then, and he was exhausted. He dropped by the stable to check on his horses first, and they seemed to be doing okay, chewing hay. So he went up to his hotel room and went to bed. He was asleep almost immediately.

He got up the next morning and went to the same restaurant for breakfast—eggs and bacon, hot biscuits and gravy, and hot coffee. The coffee really tasted good. He seemed to get a pickup from coffee. Then he went to the general store again and bought a pipe and some tobacco. Papa always used to enjoy his pipe. And when Jonnie joined up with the Army, he started smoking a pipe too. When he left the store, he packed the pipe, got out a match, and lit it. The fragrant smell of the tobacco was very pleasing, so he kept on puffing the pipe. After a few minutes he felt a kind of numbness all over—a very pleasant feeling. So that was why Papa and Jonnie enjoyed their pipe smoking so much! Then he started feeling nauseated. *What's wrong now?* he thought. Maybe breakfast disagreed with him—been too long without really good food, and his stomach just couldn't handle it. Yeah, that must be it. But he decided he didn't want any more of the pipe for now. He knocked the tobacco out against a hitching post like he'd seen Papa do and put his pipe in his pocket. The nausea cleared up, and he decided to just walk around town and stretch his legs.

Then it occurred to him that he didn't even know where General Jeb Stuart's cavalry was. Sure, he knew it was up north, but that was all he knew. He figured, well, he could just ask someone. He saw an old man sitting on a bench on the wooden sidewalk and went up to him and said, "Hello."

"Hello, kid," the old man replied. He was puffing on a pipe. Jim started to yell, "I'm not a kid," but stopped himself. He wanted information. Jim sat down on the park bench too.

"Do you know where General Jeb Stuart's cavalry is at?" he asked, rather bluntly.

"Well, now if you find General Lee's army, you'll find General Stuart's cavalry because his cavalry is part of General Lee's army." Jim didn't know that, or he hadn't thought of it. Papa and Jonnie had always talked about General Stuart's cavalry as if it were an army all by itself. Though they did talk about the infantry. He had just assumed that the infantry must be part of General Stuart's cavalry too. But, of course, if they were infantry, they couldn't be cavalry. And come to think of it, they had also talked about cannon and artillery. So it apparently took all three to make an army.

"Well, can you tell me where General Lee's army is?" he asked.

"Yep, it's up around Chancellorsville and Fredericksburg. General Jackson just got through whipping the Yankees at Chancellorsville and put General Hooker's army on the run."

"Who's General Hooker?" followed up Jim.

"For a man who's off to join General Stuart's cavalry, you've sure got a sight to learn, son," the old man replied. "General Hooker's the general in command of the Union Army."

Now, how did he know I'm off to join General Stuart's cavalry? Jim thought. *I didn't tell him.* Then he asked, "And General Jackson whipped him? What about General Lee and General Stuart?"

"You sure don't know nothing at all, nothing at all, boy. General Stuart and General Jackson fight for General Lee. At least Jackson did till he got himself killed. He whipped the Yankees at Chancellorsville, but got himself wounded during the battle and died from his wounds two days later. General Jackson was in command of Lee's infantry, and General Stuart is in command of Lee's cavalry."

"But you said General Jackson whipped General Hooker. Does that mean the war is over?" He felt a tinge of panic. The war mustn't be over when he hadn't even got there yet. He had to get in on at least some of the fighting. He had to kill at least ten Yankees to pay them back for Papa and Jonnie.

"No, no, the war's not over. They just whipped General Hooker in that one battle. General Hooker and his army retreated—is all. General Lee will follow him and force him into another battle and whip him again. Don't you read the papers, son?" Papa would always buy a newspaper when he was home whenever he went to town, but Mama said they were too depressing, so he had to admit he hadn't read a newspaper since Papa went away.

"Where can I get a newspaper?" Jim asked.

"Down the street there's a newsstand." The old man pointed with his pipe. "And if you're going off to join General Stuart's cavalry, you'd better get a map so's you'll know where you're going. But if you take my advice, you'll just be content to be a boy for a few more years, and by then the war will be over."

"Thanks," said Jim and got up to leave. He knew he wouldn't take his advice, but he figured he didn't have to tell him that. He did think maybe he'd better hurry up to Virginia. If the Confederate Army was whipping the Yankees, the war might be over before he got there.

He went down to the newsstand and bought a newspaper and asked them if they had a map he could buy.

"A map of North Carolina?" the newsstand clerk asked.

"No, a map of Virginia."

"Sure." The clerk found him a map. Jim paid him for the newspaper and the map. He took his newly acquired intelligence documents up to his room to study.

He read the newspaper first—mainly, stuff he wasn't interested in. It told him the same things the old man had told him about General Jackson defeating General Hooker at Chancellorsville and General Hooker's retreat across the Rappahannock River. But he looked up Chancellorsville and the Rappahannock River on the map and felt like he did have a better picture of what was going on now.

He then went to a restaurant for supper and back to the hotel again. He went to bed that night with a better sense of direction. And he was glad he had written to Mama and Joanne. For the first time since he had left home, he missed them. He had been so busy traveling and doing things until now that he hadn't had time to miss them. He especially missed Joanne and her piano. And he wished he had brought his mandolin along though the reason he left it at home was because he was afraid it would get lost or busted or something.

The next morning after breakfast he walked past a saddler's shop. While there was nothing wrong with his saddle, he decided he had some time to kill and went to browse awhile. He liked looking at new saddles and bridles and such. He saw a pair of spurs that he wanted, but the spurs he had were working fine, so he resisted the impulse to buy new ones. The money he had was being depleted fast enough. Then he saw something he did need. There were several saddle boots, designed for carrying a saddle carbine, and after having his rifle converted to a carbine, he definitely needed one of them. The storekeeper wanted to know if he needed any help, and he said no, but that he'd be back later with his carbine to see if he had a saddle boot it would fit.

He went to the general store then and bought his food supplies. This time he bought bacon, cornmeal, potatoes, and beans. He decided he'd have to live on a soldier's diet soon enough. He was definitely sick and tired of a diet of warmed-over ham and hardtack with only an occasional squirrel for variety. He also bought coffee and a sack of oats for the horses. The storekeeper told him oats were actually better than corn to improve a horse's endurance on day-after-day riding. That was something Papa always said too, but the reason Papa always fed his horses corn was because corn gave a better yield per acre than oats. The oats didn't cost any more than the corn at this store, so he bought a hundred pounds of oats. After paying for it, he took his groceries and put them in the canvas sack he used for this purpose, hoisted them up over his strong young shoulder, and told the storekeeper he'd be back in a couple of minutes for the sack of oats. He carried the groceries across the street to the stables and laid them down next to his saddle and other gear. He told the hostler he'd be back in a little while to pack up and go. The hostler said that was fine. He walked back to the store, hoisted the hundred pounds of oats over his shoulder, and carried it across the street and deposited it with the rest of his gear too. He felt a tinge of pride to show off his strong muscles in public that way and secretly hoped some girl had seen him, but no such luck.

He then went to the gunsmith to collect his rifle and took it to the saddler's to find a saddle boot to fit. Then he went back and saddled up Blue Boy, fixed the saddle boot and carbine in place, loaded the pack on Chugger, and swung up in the saddle. He had put on his rough hunting clothes this morning, so he was all ready to continue his long ride up to Virginia and General Lee's army.

CHAPTER 5

He felt especially proud as he rode out of the town of Raleigh. His carbine was where he could get to it in a hurry, so he didn't have to worry about carrying it across his saddle except when he expected to use it right away. As soon as he got clear of town, he did take his carbine out and rode off into the woods a little ways to see if his problem of raking the barrel against tree limbs was solved. *Much better,* he thought as he rode along, in and out of the trees with his carbine all handy to shoot an enemy if one happened along. He then put it in its boot and pulled it back out a few times just for practice. Then he replaced the priming powder in the priming pan. He didn't know if he'd encounter any robbers or not, but it didn't hurt to be ready. And he knew from deer hunts in the past that stale powder in the priming pan could cause a misfire—not that you could be sure you wouldn't have a misfire anyway. But with fresh powder in the priming pan, he had always been able to just pull the hammer back and try again, and it would nearly always fire the second time. He wished he had one of those cap-and-ball rifles he'd heard about. Jonnie had told him that was what they used mostly at the front.

Traveling was easier now, with horses and man in good traveling condition, and the improved food rations did seem to help decrease the fatigue at the end of a hard day's travel. He was able to travel about twenty-five to thirty miles per day while he had averaged only about twenty miles a day on the trip from South Carolina to Raleigh.

He arrived at Richmond after six days' travel, but this was because he halted outside Richmond to rest the horses for a day. He decided he couldn't handle hotel bills and stable bills with what little money he had left. He did ride through Richmond and stopped to buy a newspaper. He found out from the newspaper that General

Stuart had set up a cavalry recruiting station at Culpepper. It was May 30, 1863. It was about a two days' ride to Culpepper.

He arrived on the outskirts of Culpepper on June 1. He noticed some mounted horsemen in Confederate gray, drilling just out of town. He felt a surge of excitement. He needed to find out where the cavalry recruiting station was. He thought about riding over and just asking, but some instinct told him he'd better not interrupt them while drilling. He rode on into town and saw many of the men walking along the sidewalk wore Confederate gray uniforms! He stopped and asked a Confederate soldier where the recruiting station was. He simply told him to ride through town and look for a Confederate flag on a flagpole. The tent under it would be the recruiting station. He was filled with a combination of excitement and nervousness as he rode through town. He found the recruiting station and saw some men standing in line. He saw some horses tied to a long hitching post. He rode up and asked one of the men if this was the recruiting station. He told him yes. A man in Confederate gray walked up.

"Planning to join up?" he asked.

"Yep," replied Jim as calmly and nonchalantly as he could. "My two horses and I are joining General Stuart's cavalry."

"You're at the right place. Just hitch your horses to the rail over there, and loosen their cinches. Then go to the back of the line." It was about 10:00 a.m.

Jim noticed several of the men in line were smoking pipes. That made him think about his pipe. He hadn't thought about it since he left Raleigh after his first smoke. It was still in his pocket—tobacco too. This made him think of his peach fuzz, and so his hand went up to rub his face—nope, no peach fuzz. Apparently, that one shave was going to last him awhile. The sun had tanned his skin, and he stood six feet tall with his boots on. With his broad shoulders he wouldn't be mistaken for a kid. Come to think of it, the only people who called him a kid were old men—old men and Mama. Maybe he didn't look like a kid after all. Well, for now, he got out his pipe and packed it and lit up. He was glad he had bought the pipe now. He was one of the men having a smoke while waiting in line. After several puffs, he got the tingly, halfway-numb feeling again. He didn't inhale, but enough of the nicotine from the smoke would have entered his bloodstream from his salivary glands to cause him that sensation. He didn't know that, of course. He didn't feel the nausea this time, so the nausea that first time he smoked must have been caused from breakfast not agreeing with him. He felt proud as a peacock now, standing among a crowd of men and smoking a pipe just like they were doing.

After about an hour and a half or so, it came his time to go into the recruiting tent. There was an officer there who asked him his name and where he was from. He asked him if he had any horses with him. He answered the officer's questions and explained that two of the horses outside were his.

"Fine," replied the officer, "that makes you eligible for the cavalry. Go with Corporal Smith here, and he'll fit you out with a uniform and saber." Wow, he was going to get a saber!

Corporal Smith took him to another compartment of the tent and gave him a shirt, gray short coat, and trousers. "Here's some boots, but I recommend you put your own in your saddlebags, and save 'em for later. Boots wear out, and we don't always have new ones in stock. Here's a saber that looks like will fit you. You're in the Army now, so go ahead, and put your uniform on. Report to the parade ground south of town tomorrow morning. That's where we train new recruits. Be sure and have your uniform and saber on, and have your horse with you. Any spare horses you have, turn them over to Corporal Day. The Army can use them for teams pulling supply wagons and artillery pieces."

So he had to go over his pack and see what would fit in his saddlebags and what to leave behind. He put his tin cup, tin plates, coffeepot, and pans inside his blankets and rolled them up and tied them behind Blue Boy's saddle. He got all the food he had left to fit in his saddlebags. He had about twenty-five pounds or so of grain left. He kept it in a canvas sack, which he took and tied behind his saddle. He put his powder horn and pouch of round balls over his shoulder. He then put his razor and shaving soap in his pocket. After that he went over to where Corporal Smith said Corporal Day would be behind the tent, leading his horses. He handed over the lead rope to Chugger's halter and mounted Blue Boy. It looked like he had the rest of the day off.

Corporal Day looked at Chugger and said, "Fine-looking horse. Looks good and strong. He'll go to the artillery." Jim saw no problem with that. He figured Chugger would do a good job for them there. He never had panned out much as a saddle horse because he wasn't fast enough. That was why they always used him for a packhorse.

Private Jim Bennett rode his horse down through the town again, this time sporting his new uniform complete with hip boots and saber. He still had his rifle in his saddle boot. He was glad he brought his rifle since it seemed like the saber was the only side-arm he was going to be issued. He noticed several saloons on both sides of the street, and most of the soldiers who had just come from the recruiting tent stopped and tied their horses to a hitching post and went into one of the saloons. He'd never been in a saloon. He remembered Papa told him they were bad and that he should stay out of them. He was hungry by now, so he just rode out of town and found a place where he could start a campfire and cook some bacon and biscuits and hot coffee. He was in the Army now.

After having dinner, he got out pencil and paper and wrote to Mama and Joanne. He told them where he was and about his new uniform. He told them about the beautiful country so green with grass and trees. He told them about the beautiful creek running by the town where he was camped. A lot of the new recruits had made camp along the same creek though most of them were in town, enjoying their freedom while it lasted. He made both letters as cheerful as he could. Then he put them both in the same envelope and sealed it and wrote the address on it. He put his return address on the envelope so they'd know where to send their letters to him. The corporal had told him what his mailing address was when he checked out his uniform and outfit. He just wrote "soldier's letter" in the upper right corner of the envelope. The corporal explained he didn't have to use stamps now that he was in the Army.

He got up and walked into town to mail his letters and noticed a photographer on one of the wooden sidewalks, taking pictures. He found a place to mail his letters and then decided to get his picture taken. There was a line of new recruits waiting to get a picture taken of themselves in their new uniforms. So he joined the line.

After getting his picture taken, he paid the photographer and gave his military address. He walked back to the outskirts of town where he had camped and checked where he had tethered Blue Boy. The photographer said his picture would be ready in about four or five days and that if his unit moved out, he'd mail them to him.

Blue Boy was cropping the lush tall grass along the creek. It was good; he was getting a chance to rest his horse. He didn't know how the Army handled things, but he was sure they knew the importance of resting horses every few days after using them hard. A horse would just drop over dead if you ran him or worked him too many days in a row without adequate feed and rest. He decided he'd put the feed bag on him that night and give him some more grain. He'd given him his daily ration of grain that morning, but he figured it was important to have his horse in as good a shape as possible in preparation for what was ahead. He hoped the Army was in the habit of graining horses. Papa had taught him how you could keep a horse in good shape by graining him every day and giving him one day of rest each week when without the grain after a few weeks he'd just fall over dead from exhaustion. With grass only, a horse had to have about three days' rest or so after each half a day's hard riding to keep him in good shape. And even then the horse wouldn't be in quite as good a shape as the grain-fed horse. Jim believed in feeding grain to horses—part of what Papa taught him.

Toward evening a soldier rode up and looked at Blue Boy. "I'm Lieutenant Hanson," he said.

"I'm Private Bennett, sir," he replied. He hadn't been taught to call officers *sir* yet, but with his upbringing, he had been taught to call every man *sir*.

"I'd be willing to buy that horse from you, Private."

"He's not for sale, sir," was Jim's reply. "I have to have him so I'll be eligible for the cavalry."

"Oh, I'd trade in my horse to you."

"No, sir," insisted Jim. "I couldn't think of selling him, sir."

"Well, okay," said Lieutenant Hanson. "But think it over. I'll give you fifty dollars and my horse if you decide to trade."

"I understand, sir, but I can't give up my horse, sir. No way I could sell him, sir."

The lieutenant finally tapped spurs to his horse and moved on. He was glad he was gone—*sell* Blue Boy? Was the lieutenant out of his mind? There was no way he would ever sell Blue Boy.

CHAPTER 6

Mock Combat

Jim was up at the crack of dawn, cooking breakfast. He heard a bugle call, but he didn't know what it meant. After breakfast he cleaned up and broke camp and either packed his stuff in his saddlebags or tied them up behind his saddle. He mounted Blue Boy and rode over to the drill field where he saw mounted soldiers forming up. This was where the recruiter told him to be this morning. He didn't tell him what time.

"You're late!" yelled a sergeant in an angry voice.

"I am?" queried Jim.

"Don't give me any back talk!" yelled the sergeant. "And get off your horse. And stand at attention. You stand to the left of your horse, and you hold the reins of your horse in your left hand! No! No! Hold the reins behind your back!"

So this was the Army. Jim wasn't actually as taken aback by the sergeant's manner as he let on. This was the Army, wasn't it? Weren't sergeants supposed to be grippy? So Jim started his first day of drill. After taking roll, they learned to come to attention and how to mount and dismount on command, then they were told to water their horses and tether them down near the creek that ran by the town where they could graze on the lush green grass. Apparently, the main reason they had to bring their horses that first morning was so they could prove that they had a horse and were, therefore, eligible for the cavalry.

They were then divided into groups with a corporal in charge of each group. They practiced coming to attention, parade rest, about-face, left face, and right face. Then they learned the manual of arms with the saber. On the command, "Prepare to draw swords," they lifted up their scabbard and drew the saber out about eight inches. Then on the command, "Draw swords," they drew the sword, pointed it skyward, and brought it back to the port arms position, which was arm straight at your side with the point of the saber, resting against your right shoulder. Then they were taught to salute with the sword and that they were to salute only commissioned officers, not sergeants. And they always called commissioned officers *sir*. Jim had been taught to call any man *sir* from the time he was very small, so this was nothing different to him. Then the sergeant explained what the officer's insignia looked like so they'd know whether to salute him or call him *sir*, etc.

At noon they were dismissed and told that rations were being distributed by the commissary. About ten men were assigned to each mess. A man from each mess was sent to go pick up their rations. Corporal Marion told Jim and another man to start a campfire. There was a stack of cordwood that had been chopped by someone that they were apparently supposed to use. The man helping Jim start the fire turned out to be Private Joe Williams, also from South Carolina. He had grown up on a plantation too. By the time they had the fire going, another soldier came up with a huge canvas bag of something. It turned out to be beef. Someone had been slaughtering cattle that morning. A fourth man had set a huge coffeepot on the fire. The man who set the coffeepot on the fire introduced himself to Jim as Private Sam Blake, and the man who had brought the beef was Private Pete Simmons. Joe was about Jim's height, but slenderer. Sam was maybe an inch or so shorter than Jim, but a little heavier. He had a slight bulge to his waistline though not a lot. Sam and Joe appeared to be only a year or two older than Jim, but Pete looked like he was thirty or so. Jim was starving.

A fifth man came up with a sack of flour and rolled out an oil-cloth on the top of a wooden box for a roll board and started mixing a batter to make biscuits. Corporal Marion was about six feet tall with blond hair and a slightly broad nose. He had a medium build for his height. He came and told Jim and Joe to take a couple of axes and go cut some more firewood to replenish their supply. Neither Jim nor Joe had ever used an ax before, so they didn't know what to do, but they each one picked out a tree apiece and started hacking on it very ineffectively.

Pretty soon a soldier who looked like he was about fifty years old came over and said, "Give me that ax. Now stand back." Then he chopped the tree down very skillfully and made it look easy. Then he handed the ax back to Jim and said, "Now trim the branches off, and cut them in pieces about so long" and showed the length by touching a branch with the ax in one spot and then touching it again about three feet down the branch.

So Joe and Jim thus received their first lesson in how to chop wood. Neither of them had ever worked a day in their lives before unless you could call riding horses work. But they managed to chop off the branches and cut them into the sizes specified by the old soldier. The old soldier's name, they were to learn later, was Monday Mane.

After Joe and Jim had finished replenishing the stack of wood, they noticed that the man who had been making bread dough had placed a huge Dutch oven in the fire and had started the biscuits to cooking. The coffee was done by then, so Joe and Jim both found their gear and got out their tin cups and tin plates and went up and filled their cups with coffee. Sam shortly came and joined him with his cup steaming with coffee. Joe learned that the man cooking the biscuits was Private Zeke Dally, who had been a mountain man from West Virginia before the war. His biscuits were superb, and he wouldn't let anyone else in their mess touch the flour or Dutch ovens, but himself. Zeke looked even older than Monday. He had a slender frame and shaggy, gray hair. Jim guessed him to be sixty at least.

Zeke finally announced that the biscuits were ready, so the men all got in line. They got three biscuits apiece and a large piece of boiled beef. Jim and Joe took their plates and cups and went over to a log and sat down to eat. Sam joined them shortly.

Joe was telling Jim about his brother, Corporal Arnold Williams.

"And they rode all the way around General McClellan's army and captured twelve thousand horses and then rejoined the main force."

Jim thought that was very interesting. "Where was this?"

"Up at Chambersburg, Pennsylvania, deep in Yankee territory. About a year and a half ago. I went and visited my brother last night. He's camped with his regiment over there," Joe said, pointing to a huge array of tents to the west of the town. "They really gave them Yankees hell, attacking their supply lines from behind the lines! You can bet the Yankees didn't know what was going on. They thought the Rebel Army was in front of them, which they were, actually, but they sure had them guessing." Sam was silent during this portion of the conversation.

"Do you have any kinfolks in the Army?" Joe asked him, to include him in the conversation mainly.

"Did have. My brother was killed at Manassas."

"I'm sorry. I didn't know," replied Joe.

"It's okay. What's done is done. I figured I'd join up and get the Yankees back for it." It struck Jim that Sam's motives were the same as his own. He didn't tell them about his father and brother. Sam's reply had sort of brought home to all three of them that they were playing for keeps. They finished the rest of their meal in silence.

After dinner, they returned to the drill field. A man with a bugle was standing in front of the formation of men.

"It's time for you to learn the bugle calls," explained the sergeant. They learned there was a bugle call for getting up in the morning called reveille, and the call to retire for the night was called taps. There was a bugle call named tattoo, which meant, "Unroll your blankets, and prepare for bed." Then there was a bugle call named boots and saddles that meant, "Saddle up, and get ready to move out." There was another for *charge* and one for *retreat*. It was almost as if everything you did was done by a bugle call.

Then he learned his unit was called a troop and that a squadron was made up of two or more troops. A regiment was made of squadrons, and a brigade was made up of regiments. He was told who the commanding officer was at each level. He knew there was no way he could remember all this. Then they were divided into details and practiced drilling some more. He had been on his feet all day long with the exception of their brief respite at dinner. He was not accustomed to so much walking. He had grown up in the saddle. Why all the walking? Every soldier must learn the fundamentals of marching, he was told.

When evening finally came and they were dismissed, rations were drawn from the mess wagon again, and each man in the mess participated in preparing the meal again as they did at noon, each man performing his assigned tasks. Jim and Joe were put to chopping wood again. This time the rations were cornmeal and dried black-eyed peas and ham and lots of coffee again. Zeke cooked the corn bread. It looked like Zeke's job was to cook the bread because other men cooked the peas and ham and coffee. But Zeke's specialty was making bread. And his bread was second to none, Jim decided.

Jim went to check on Blue Boy after supper. He still had plenty of grass and looked okay. He had tethered him where he could drink out of the creek whenever he wanted. He put a feed bag on him and gave him some more oats. He figured he might as well keep him in as good a shape as he could while he had some oats left.

He came back and found out the other men were sitting around the campfire. He found that Joe and Sam had hung their canteens and personal gear on a tree nearby, so he hung his canteen and saber on the same tree.

After supper they got out their pipes and had a smoke. Then Joe got out his mouth organ and started playing music. Now Jim hadn't thought of that. A mouth organ would fit in your pocket! He had been afraid he'd bust or lose his mandolin. He had never played a mouth organ though.

Joe played sad songs. But since it matched the mood of most of the men who had already lost loved ones in the war, it seemed to cheer them up. Sam would even sing to some of the songs. Jim sang along too on any of the songs he knew.

Then Zeke sang a couple of songs he knew, and Jim was impressed with his singing voice. After Zeke had sung one verse, Joe started doing little things with his harmonica to provide background for Zeke's singing. It really sounded good!

Then they heard tattoo being played on the bugle, so they unrolled their blankets and prepared for bed. Then sure enough, just like they'd been told that afternoon, in a few minutes they heard taps being played. It had a rather sad tone to it, but the bugler, apparently, was good at his job; it sounded pretty. They rolled up in their blankets and went to sleep. Jim had completed his first day of Army life.

Jim was tired, but he lay awake a little while, thinking about Mama and Joanne. He understood why they didn't want him to join the Army. But they didn't understand why it was something he had to do. He would have liked it better if they could have understood him in return. The night was cool, and he looked up at the stars. It was a clear night, and the stars were bright though there was no moon. He finally drifted off to sleep.

CHAPTER 7

Then Jim awoke and heard a bugle playing. *Hey, that's reveille,* he thought. He recognized it as one of the tunes that was played during the demonstration out on the drill field the day before. He rolled out of his blankets, shook his boots out, and put them on. He then rolled up his bedroll and started a fire. Joe and Sam were up by the time he got started on the fire. Joe started the coffee, and Sam started slicing bacon into a skillet. Zeke had already started a batch of biscuit batter. Apparently, the rations for breakfast must have been drawn the night before. Within minutes, the men all had a steaming cup of coffee in their hands. Breakfast was bacon and baked biscuits sopped in bacon grease. It was a gourmet meal to Jim. They went and formed up on the drill field.

"Where the hell are your horses?" the drill sergeant yelled. "You men wanting to join the infantry?" Sergeant Adams was as grippy as ever. So the men fell out and went and got their horses and saddled them. They spent the morning drilling with horses this time.

"Prepare to mount!"

"Mount up!"

"Prepare to dismount!"

"Dismount!"

"Prepare to mount!"

"Mount! Forward… Ho! Detail, halt!"

That was all they did all morning. That afternoon they formed up as a troop and rode off toward the east of Culpepper. The drill field just outside Culpepper was for raw recruits who had never drilled before. Since men and horses were coming in daily by the hundreds, it was necessary to move out the newly formed troops to make room for the initial indoctrination of new recruits. When they arrived at their new camp in a meadow a few miles from Brandy Station, they halted. Then Lieutenant Hanson gave them a speech. Jim remembered his face. He was the same officer who had tried to buy Blue Boy that first day. He welcomed them to the Army of North Virginia and told them they were now a member of the greatest fighting outfit in the world. After Lieutenant Hanson's speech the entire troop marched under Lieutenant Hanson's direction. Part of the time Lieutenant Hanson would give the marching commands himself. Part of the time he'd turn the detail over to Sergeant Adams, and he'd observe while Sergeant Adams drilled them.

The bugle was also used for drilling commands. They learned to charge when *charge* was blown on the bugle and withdraw when the bugle played *retreat*.

The following day they formed up as a troop again, and Captain Wilson, the troop commander, reviewed the troop and drilled them awhile himself. It was more difficult to hold the formation in all the various maneuvers with a body of mounted horsemen of that size, Jim noticed, and the troop orderly sergeant was screaming at them almost constantly most of the afternoon. They had learned to move as a column and to do flanking movements and to dress their line and cover down in their column. That afternoon they practiced mock cavalry charges with wooden sabers they had made from tree limbs.

The fourth day they formed up as a squadron, all four troops. Jim learned that the squadron commander was Lieutenant Colonel Thompson. Two hundred and fifty mounted men were on parade. They passed in review and had to come to present arms with their sabers, which Jim had already learned was one form of salute. That afternoon they did mock cavalry charges, first as a troop, then three troops were formed up as a squadron, and they did several mock charges as a squadron to the bugle. The bugle would blast for both *charge* and *retreat*. It got so that the horses recognized the bugle calls too and would anticipate the next move just by the sound coming from the bugle.

After a week both men and horses had learned to respond to the commands and bugle calls by instinct. The seventh day of their training they were to form up the entire brigade, which, Jim learned, included two regiments of three squadrons each. The brigade commander was Brigadier General McClinton.

They drilled awhile on horseback as a regiment, and then they drilled to the sound of the regimental band. They rehearsed passing in review. Then they rehearsed a mock charge as a regiment. Then they were told that after lunch they would be putting on a show for the town of Culpepper. That was what this week of intensive drilling was all about, to get ready for it. They loosened their saddle cinches and tethered their horses and found out that enough cattle had been butchered to make a barbecue for the entire regiment, and the women of Culpepper had all come out to prepare a feast for them. The beeves had been divided up among the squadrons, and after watering and tethering their horses, they all got in line to be fed. The squadron had formed in about a dozen lines or so to get their beef and biscuits. When Jim arrived at the head of the line, he saw this beautiful little, blonde girl, who looked a couple of years younger than himself, serve out for him a big portion of broiled beef, some black-eyed peas, and several biscuits with gravy. She looked up at him and flashed him a beautiful smile, showing off her dimples. She couldn't be more than fourteen—same age as Joanne.

"What's your name?" he asked, trying to be casual.

"Vickie!" she said almost too eagerly.

"I'm Jim," he said, and that's all he could think of to say. He felt a tingly sensation all over. He'd never felt that way before.

As he moved on to find a place to sit and eat with his friends, she called after him, "Enjoy your meal." She had such a fine feminine voice. It was like listening to music. He turned and smiled back at her and wondered if she could sing.

He didn't taste the food. He had been starving, as usual, before the meal, but now he'd forgotten all about being hungry. The picture of her dimpled smile still had him spellbound. But as soon as he finished eating, the sergeant started yelling, "Get your horses, and form up!" So it was back to the task at hand.

They put on a show for the town. First they formed up in a line. Twelve thousand mounted horsemen all lined up in one long line. Jim could not see the end of the line on either side of him, but saw where they disappeared in the trees. Then they started the parade with the Confederate flag and regimental colors waving in the breeze. The regimental band played "Dixie," "The Girl I Left behind Me," and a few other tunes. Marching to the music caused shivers to run up and down his spine. Then they passed in review for the entire town. When they passed in review and presented arms with their sabers, he caught a glimpse of Vickie's beautiful smile again. He caught her eye for a moment, and she smiled bigger and waved. He had never seen a girl that pretty before. He smiled back and nodded ever so slightly. He hoped no one saw him—all those generals on the review stand that way. He saw one big, bearded general whom he thought was probably General Jeb Stuart. The general returned the salute of each regiment that passed and was holding his salute now with his saber pointed to the ground. To salute with a saber, you first held the tip of the sword skyward and held the haft to your forehead, then swung the point toward the ground. Then you lifted it back up to the present arms position with your hand at your side and the point resting against your shoulder.

After each regiment had passed in review, they then made a mock cavalry charge as a regiment—each regiment in turn. When it came Jim's regiment's turn, Blue Boy responded to the bugle call on his own like he'd learned to do during the previous week, and Jim held his saber high like he'd been taught, pretending to be ready to slash at an enemy cavalryman whom he pretended was coming toward him. The noise was deafening as the entire regiment screamed their battle cry.

After the show they put on for the town, Jim found out there was going to be a ball in a clearing just outside the town of Brandy Station. They cooked supper more hurriedly than usual this time. Jim took his soap down to the creek and took off his uniform jacket and shirt and washed up as well as he could. He then watered Blue Boy and tethered him on some lush grass, and then he heard the sounds of General Jeb Stuart's band. Joe and Sam had already gone, so he just followed the sounds of the band. Now that was real corn-shucking music he heard. He secretly hoped Vickie would be there, but he knew it would be hard to find her in all that crowd of people. He'd never been to a ball with this many people before—thousands upon thousands.

He found Joe and Sam and walked up to them and said, "Hi." They each had a drink in their hand.

"Want something to wet your whistle?" asked a young soldier Jim didn't know.

"Sure," said Jim and accepted a tin cup. He took a drink of it and choked and coughed. It was like it was liquid fire!

The soldier laughed loudly, a derisive, mocking laugh, and Jim hit him. It was a solid blow on the chin, and it knocked the soldier down, and he almost rolled under several other soldiers nearby. Joe and Sam both immediately grabbed Jim, one on each arm, and dragged him away from the crowd.

"What do you want to do? Start a brawl?" Joe hissed.

Jim coughed and wheezed some more and finally caught his breath. "Well, he shouldn't have laughed at me," Jim answered.

"So he laughed at you. He was just being friendly, offering you a drink of his corn liquor. He just meant to be friendly!" said Joe emphatically.

"Well, he just shouldn't have laughed at me," was all Jim could say, and he coughed again.

The ball was held in a big clearing, and the middle of the clearing was being used as a dance floor. He started walking around, and all of a sudden he saw Vickie. He recognized her instantly in spite of the dim light. It stunned him momentarily because he didn't really expect to see her, but was secretly and desperately hoping he would. He walked straight toward her.

"May I have this dance?" he asked when he saw she had noticed him walk up.

"You can leave now or immediately," he heard a male voice at his elbow. He turned and saw a soldier who appeared to be in his twenties. "I'm taking this dance and the next and the next," he added.

Jim drew back his fist and started to hit him, and Vickie grabbed his arm and dragged him out to the dancing area. "I accept," she said.

They blended in with the crowd of dancers very quickly. "He's been trying to get me to dance with him ever since I got here, and I refused to. I tried to tell him he's too old for me, but he wouldn't listen."

"Looks like he's at least twenty-two or twenty-three," Jim agreed.

"Yes, he's an old man," confirmed Vickie.

The dance was a waltz, and Vickie moved to the sound of the music so beautifully. Jim had been made to take dancing lessons as a boy. He resented it at the time. He had to have dancing lessons partly because he was being raised as a gentleman, and it was considered mandatory that he learned to dance, and the other reason was that Joanne had to have a partner for her dancing lessons. He was glad of it now.

After the dance they moved over to the side and talked until the music started again. Jim danced every dance with Vickie until the ball was finally over, well after midnight. He learned her full name was Victoria Marie Allen and got her mailing address so he could write to her. He gave her his address, which amounted to his troop, squadron, and regiment, with just "Army of Northern Virginia" rather than any city or state.

Then Vickie's parents came to get her. She introduced her mama and her papa to Jim, and he escorted her to their carriage. Her mother's first name was Louise, and her father's, Abe. Then he walked back to camp with his feet touching the ground maybe once every dozen steps or so. He floated to his bedroll and couldn't think of going to sleep right away. He got out his pipe and had a smoke. After smoking his pipe out, he finally rolled up in his blankets and tried to go to sleep. He lay awake a long time, thinking of blue eyes and blond hair and dimples and that beautiful smile. He just never had seen a girl that beautiful before.

It was June 8, 1863.

Battle of Brandy Station

Jim finally got to sleep at about 3:00 a.m. He awoke at dawn to the sound of cannon fire. *What is this?* he thought. He had heard cannon fire the day before because the artillery fired a twenty-four-gun salute as part of the show. But it wasn't even daylight yet. And he hadn't heard reveille sounding. Then he heard Sergeant Adam's voice.

"Everybody up! The Yankees are attacking. Get saddled. Move it!"

Barely awake, Jim quickly pulled on his boots and rolled up his blankets and oilcloth. He took his canteen and tin cup from where it hung on the nearby tree and his tin plate and stuffed them in his saddlebags. He grabbed his saber where it was hanging on the tree also, and along with it he grabbed up his blankets and saddlebags in one hand and his saddle and bridle in the other; he hurried down to where the horses were tethered. He bridled and saddled Blue Boy and tied on the saddlebags and blanket roll behind his saddle and fastened on his saber. He had already found that his saber got in his way, and he didn't like to wear it except when mounted up. He heard the bugle blowing boots and saddles just as he swung into the saddle. *Bugler must have overslept,* he thought. The cannon fired continuously while this was going on. He reined Blue Boy over to where he saw his troop forming up and got in line. Sergeant Adams took a muster and gave the muster report to Lieutenant Hanson.

Then the regimental commander, Colonel Atkinson, said, "Forward" followed by "Squadron" from the squadron commanders, then "Troop" by the troop commanders, then "Ho!" came from the original voice, the regimental commander. Then Jim and Blue Boy were moving in a mass of mounted horsemen. It seemed like a sea of horse's heads and cavalrymen's caps moving in the dim, early-morning light—no breakfast, not even time for coffee. The cannon fire continued steadily, but the sound of it grew lighter as they rode. *What is this?* he thought. *Why are we riding away from the sounds of battle?* Then he figured it out. They were moving south and were maneuvering to attack the enemy's left flank since the Yankees were attacking from the east. He reached over and felt his saber. Yep, it was there. He reached down and touched his rifle in his saddle boot. Yep, it was there too. Other than his empty stomach, he was ready.

Jim felt no fear, only excitement and anticipation. He felt the eagerness and exhilaration and total unawareness of danger that was only possible in the very young whose childhood had been completely sheltered from harm—well, almost completely sheltered. Some would say there's danger to riding horses, especially breaking horses, but Jim had learned at an early age that knowing how to do something and being proficient at it removed the danger. So he was not aware of any danger this day, only excitement and enthusiasm and a feeling of being very much a part of this tremendous mass of men and horses. They moved as one organism. It was like the regiment was one huge body, and the squadrons and troops were arms and legs, and each mounted trooper was just an individual living cell of this huge living thing.

After crossing a vast meadow and going between two wooded areas, the regiment made a left turn and started heading eastward. It was daylight by now. Then all of a sudden he saw a huge mass of horses coming toward them, each carrying a blue rider—a sea of blue riders against his own sea of gray!

"Draw sabers. Prepare to charge!" came the regimental commander's voice. Jim immediately drew his saber. Then the bugle sounded, and Blue Boy was off like a shot at the sound of the bugle that he had been trained to respond to so well during the past week.

He saw the troops in front meet with the enemy and saw them hacking and slashing at one another with their sabers. Then he heard small arms fire and saw men falling from their horses and horses rearing and, in some cases, falling, spilling their riders. Some of the enemy were using revolvers instead of sabers! How could that be fair? Then he was among them himself and saw a blue rider with saber held high and an angry look on his face, charging toward him. Jim would have died right there if Blue Boy hadn't sidestepped at the last moment, but Jim sensed Blue Boy's muscles tense up a fraction of a second before and tightened his knee hold. He slashed downward toward the back of the Yankee cavalryman's neck just as he rode past. He felt his saber strike flesh and immediately pulled his saber up to get ready for the next blue soldier heading for him. He saw the saber heading right for his face and moved his own sword to parry and, this time, kneed Blue Boy toward the Yankee. Blue Boy slammed into the Yankee horse, stopping both of them, and Jim slashed down viciously against the right side of the Yankee's neck before he could recover his balance. He saw him fall, and he spurred Blue Boy to head for the next one.

This time he felt bullets whizzing by his ear and saw the Yankee shooting at him. He simply ducked and pointed his sword and ran the Yankee through as he rode past, gripping his sword tightly as he yanked it back out so he wouldn't lose it. To lose your sword at a time like this would be to lose your life!

He heard a bugle blowing *retreat*, and Blue Boy halted and started an about-face. Then Jim noticed the bugle was from the opposite side of the mass of fighting horsemen. He pulled Blue Boy up short and neck-reined him back and said, "No, Blue Boy, that's for them, not us" and kept Blue Boy headed for the fleeing Yankees. They reached the trees when their own bugle blew to halt their charge.

"Time to regroup!" yelled Lieutenant Hanson. "Hold your ground."

Then Jim noticed his saber was covered with blood. He wanted to wipe it off, but didn't have anything to wipe it off on. Then Lieutenant Hanson briefed the detail to hold fast and stay in the trees. "We're going to let our horses blow while we wait for further orders from the regimental commander." Blue Boy definitely needed a moment to blow. He'd been ridden a lot during the past month or so, but he hadn't done that much running since he left South Carolina. They had done a little sprinting during the mock charges they had done while drilling, but it wasn't enough to get Blue Boy into racing form.

A mounted courier rode up to the lieutenant and gave him a piece of paper. The lieutenant then gave the order to dismount. Jim saw the other troopers wiping the blood from their swords on the tall grass, so he did likewise. Then the lieutenant, as if from an after-thought, told them to sheathe their swords.

"Those of you who have carbines, get 'em out," the lieutenant then said. *So this is going to be different, huh?* Jim pulled his flintlock carbine out of his saddle boot. He hadn't checked the flashpan in days, so he got his powder flask and pouch of round balls out of his saddlebags. He put them on his belt and reprimed his flashpan. Then the sergeant came up and told them to hold on to their horses, but to form a line on the edge of the trees.

"When the Yankees start their charge, wait until they're within a hundred yards, and find a patch of blue, and shoot at it. Reload as quickly as you can, and shoot again. Keep shooting until you hear otherwise from me or the lieutenant."

CHAPTER 9

Then Jim heard the enemy bugle blowing *charge*, and Blue Boy jerked his head up as if thinking he should do something.

"Easy, Blue Boy, that's not for us," said Jim. Blue Boy acted like he understood and settled back down. Jim got down on one knee and waited until he saw a blue rider come within what looked like a hundred yards. He put his sights on the patch of blue, like Sergeant Adams said, and squeezed the trigger. The rider fell, yanking his horse's head up. The horse sat back on his haunches to get stopped and then reared up as the Union soldier fell. Jim grabbed his powder flask and started reloading again as quickly as he could, poured what seemed like the right amount of powder down the bore, followed it with a round ball, took his ramrod, and rammed the ball home, put the ramrod back in place, poured some powder in the flashpan, then put the rifle back up to his shoulder. The Union soldiers were within fifty yards now, the ones who were left. He heard the shots from the sharpshooters on both sides of him and saw Union soldiers and horses falling. He picked a target who was still mounted and riding hard toward them, put his sights on a blue spot just below the yellow bandanna, and squeezed the trigger. The soldier fell. Then he heard the Union bugle blowing *retreat*. Jim saw the lieutenant's strategy now. Most of the Union cavalrymen were armed with revolvers. You couldn't hit anything with a revolver from a galloping horse except at point-blank range, like in their first charge this morning. It seemed like a revolver, when fired from a galloping horse, wasn't any more effective than a saber. But a carbine fired from the ground was accurate up to about a hundred yards or so on targets moving directly toward you even if mounted on a galloping horse. Jim reloaded his carbine again. Just as he had finished priming his flashpan, he heard the lieutenant's loud, booming voice.

"Prepare to mount! Mount up! Sheathe your carbines. Prepare to draw sabers. Draw sabers! Prepare to charge!" Then the bugle sounded *charge*, and Blue Boy was off like a shot again. So they were chasing the retreating Yankees toward the Rappahannock River. No, they were turning northward. Did this mean they had outflanked them like he'd read about in history books? Well, they were chasing them. That was the main thing. They charged through some sparse trees over a hill, and then Jim saw a grove of trees up ahead. A staccato of gunfire then came from the trees, and he saw the men on either side of him slump in the saddle. One of them, the one on his left, fell, still gripping the reins in his hand. It made the horse swerve to the right and bump into Blue Boy. As Blue Boy recoiled toward the right, a ball whizzed by Jim's head, missing his forehead by maybe an inch, right where it would have been if the horse hadn't bumped into Blue Boy. Then Jim heard the bugle calling *retreat*, and the bugle was behind him now, so he knew it was his side retreating. Blue Boy had figured out by now that you ran toward the bugle calling *retreat* whether it was your own or not, so he turned and started sprinting back across the clearing. Blue Boy was breathing hard by now, and he was covered with sweat. The foamy, white sweat made him look more like a dappled, gray horse rather than his natural deep-blue-roan color. Jim started reining him to the right and left to make it harder for one of the Union sharpshooters to find their mark. Then they were through the trees, and he saw Lieutenant Hanson swing his arm up and down in the signal to halt. Jim reined up and swung his horse toward the lieutenant, waiting for further orders.

"Sheathe your sabers, draw carbines!" he shouted. "Dismount. Fire when they're within range." Jim held the reins in his left hand and pulled the hammer on his carbine back to full cock. He got down to one knee again at the edge of the trees. He put his sights on a Union soldier again, and when he seemed to be within range, he squeezed the trigger. Instead of hitting the soldier, it hit the horse in the neck, breaking his neck, killing him instantly. The dead horse somersaulted, spilling his rider and pinning him underneath him.

The Union soldier screamed in agony, his leg obviously broken and pinned underneath his dead horse. The Union cavalrymen behind had to swerve to avoid running into him. Jim was frantically reloading his rifle. Round balls were whizzing all around Jim's head by this time because the Union soldiers were getting so close. He had just finished priming his priming pan when he looked up and saw the Yankee within ten yards of him, his revolver pointed right at his head. Jim went to one knee and brought his rifle up to his shoulder simultaneously. Jim felt the wind of the Yankee bullet as it barely missed the top of his head. His rifle was pointed at the Yankee's brisket, and he fired as the Yankee raced past, knocking him out of the saddle. Jim fell forward to the ground. The horse leaped over him, and he hugged the ground, hoping he wouldn't get kicked in the head. The horse continued on past through a break in the trees. He then heard the Union bugle sounding *retreat*. He saw a few Union horsemen scampering back from where they had come. What he mainly saw was a sea of scattered blue bodies, horses, and an occasional gray body ahead. He didn't see how another charge could be possible without stumbling over either a dead horse or dead soldier. He reloaded again and looked around to see if he could see Sergeant Adams or Lieutenant Hanson. Whom he saw was Private Blake.

"Sam!" said Jim with relief. The fighting had been so fierce and without letup, he hadn't had time to even think of his friends, much less determine if they were okay. Sam was obviously okay. "Where's Joe?"

"He's over there," motioned Sam. "Minor flesh wound, but he's okay. He's still able to fight. The lieutenant said get ready to mount up. We have to get out of here. Artillery's fixing to open up, and we don't wanna catch it."

Jim agreed with that. He led Blue Boy back to the clearing. He mounted and sheathed his rifle. Blue Boy was covered with a white lather all over. He looked like a white horse now. He hoped he didn't founder. They formed up and followed the lieutenant, who seemed to know where they were going. He was glad somebody did. They were moving at a fast trot, which seemed to give Blue Boy a chance to catch his breath. Jim became aware now of the cannon fire in the distance and realized it had been continuous throughout all the fighting, but he just hadn't noticed. After about fifteen minutes or so, he heard cannon nearby open up in the general area he and his troop had just left. It was like all hell had broken loose. He only now began to be aware of how loud cannon were when you heard them up close. They moved back deep into the trees then, where there was lots of cover, into a small clearing.

"Prepare to dismount. Dismount. Let your horses cool off, and then give them a drink. There's a creek nearby. Let them cool off first. You'll kill 'em if you'll let them drink now." The lieutenant knew that his last remark was redundant. Every man there was a horseman and knew they had to let their lathered horses cool off before they could drink. "Loosen your cinches, and unsheathe your carbines, and have them ready. If you have rations, take time out to eat. If you have rations and your buddy doesn't, share them. There was no time to draw rations this morning."

Jim had some cold ham and hardtack in his saddlebags, so after he loosened the cinch on Blue Boy and pulled out his carbine, he got them out of his saddlebags. He was really starving by now. He found out that neither Joe nor Sam had any rations, so he divided his into three portions for the three of them. It was the last of the trail food he had brought with him on the ride up from South Carolina. They started eating. He saw the bandage on Joe's leg where a Union saber had gashed it—not enough to keep him from riding, but it obviously hurt when he moved it. Jim was just grateful both his friends were still alive. He hadn't realized just how important a friendship could be until he became aware of how it could be destroyed permanently by death!

When the horses finally stopped blowing, Sergeant Adams told them they could lead them down to the creek by twos and threes and let them drink. The roar of the cannon still sounded like a combination of an electrical storm, tornado, and hurricane all at once.

CHAPTER 10

After the horses had cooled off and drank their fill and the men all had eaten their cold rations, Jim asked Sergeant Adams what to do next. He told him the lieutenant was waiting for further orders. So Jim and his two friends went and sat down on the log again. Waiting was harder to do than fighting, all three agreed.

While they were sitting there, another soldier in their troop sat down on the log with them. They recognized him as Private Simmons. Sam and Jim both nodded acknowledgment to him, but Joe seemed to withdraw from him.

"Tough fighting this morning, wasn't it?" he said, seemingly to start a conversation, but all three of the young soldiers wondered why he would say something so redundant.

Joe just looked over at him with a glare in his eyes and said, "It didn't seem so tough on you—at least, not in that last charge. You were the last one out and the first one back." It was clear that Joe's accusation was intended to be obvious.

"I couldn't help it," Simmons almost whined. "I have a half-broke horse, and he gave me trouble."

Joe just intensified his glare. "I saw that too, and if I ever see you yanking a horse's mouth around like that again, I'll rearrange some of your teeth and see how you like receiving similar treatment."

"But I had to in order to control him. He's just half broke, I tell you!"

"You just remember what I said," replied Joe vehemently and said no more.

Simmons left then and went over to his horse and started stroking his neck as if to placate him. The horse jerked away at first as if he thought he was going to be struck and then calmed down when Simmons only continued stroking him.

"He's a straggler," explained Joe to Jim and Sam after Pete Simmons left. "He yanked his horse around to make him buck and act up so he'd be at the tail end of the charge. There's no excuse for abusing a horse, and there's no excuse for cowardice. When I got my leg cut, the sergeant made me get off my horse so another man could bandage it. It caused me to miss that last charge. That's how I came to see Simmons's scheme to avoid the fighting."

In a few minutes they saw Sergeant Adams go over and start talking to Simmons with an angry look on his face. They couldn't hear what he said, but he was obviously giving him the third degree. Then they saw Lieutenant Hanson walking over toward them. They jumped to attention quickly, but Lieutenant Hanson told them to sit back down and rest while they could.

"Private Bennett, your performance this morning warrants my highest commendation. I intended to lead each charge in person, and your gelding outran mine every time. I saw your expert swordsmanship and want to give you my personal 'well done.'"

Jim blushed because this took him totally by surprise. Come to think of it, he hadn't seen any gray uniforms ahead of him on any charge except on the first one, only blue uniformed riders heading toward him. He hadn't intended it and hadn't noticed it because he was oblivious to everything except the fighting.

"And where did you get that cavalry-trained horse?" continued Lieutenant Hanson.

"He's only been in the Army a week, sir, just like me. I broke him myself, but he's had no previous cavalry training."

"Well, he's sure a fine gelding," the lieutenant went on. "He's definitely the fastest horse in the troop. You outran me and the guidons on every charge. Are you sure you won't consider selling him?" Jim remembered his attempt to buy Blue Boy on his first day at Culpepper when he had just signed up for the cavalry.

"Oh no, I couldn't think of selling him, sir. I raised him from a colt and broke him to ride myself. I simply couldn't sell him, oh no, sir."

"I understand," replied the lieutenant with a smile, "and I don't blame you. I wouldn't sell him either if I were you." The lieutenant commended Joe and Sam too for their gallantry in their first action. Then the lieutenant moved on and started talking to someone else.

Then Jim figured out what was going on. The lieutenant was walking around, commending everyone who did a good job, and Sergeant Adams was walking around, giving holy hell to everyone who didn't carry their weight. That certainly sounded fair. Jim started thinking he was in a really fine outfit. So Lieutenant Hanson didn't like it because his horse could outrun his. He was amused at the thought. Being in the period of his life in which it was natural to be a daredevil, having never known fear, and having never been injured or had any cause for fear were the reasons for his gallantry and courage this morning. As for his excellent swordsmanship this morning, that had to have been luck. He had never touched a sword until it was issued to him a week previously. He just did what came naturally to cut and chop the enemy rider off his horse without getting himself cut or slashed in the process. As far as Blue Boy being cavalry trained, he had noticed way back when he first started breaking him that he learned exceptionally fast. He knew on several occasions this morning he would have been killed if Blue Boy hadn't seemed to just have a sixth sense that told him what to do. Maybe Blue Boy's ancestors had been cavalry horses, and maybe the ability had been bred into him. Jim's father and grandfather had both been cavalrymen. Some things probably did run in the family.

After a few more minutes Sergeant Adams walked around, telling everyone to get their horses, tighten their cinches, and lead them out of the trees toward what looked to be northwest. Lieutenant Hanson was already out there. "Prepare to mount. Mount up!" he commanded, and the troop, in unison, swung into the saddle. Funny, how Jim noticed them moving in unison now while before he had only been aware of himself and Blue Boy responding to the commands. It was as if the rest of the troop hadn't even been there. He was aware of the rest of the troop now. In fact he saw, out of the corner of his eye, another troop to their left mounting up too. It was as if his vision and awareness both had expanded to include the other men and other units present. Then came the command, "Forward. Ho!" And Jim was now in a moving sea of mounted horsemen again.

Jim also noticed that the cannon were now silent. They rode for maybe half an hour, and then they came to a wide-open field, with dead bodies, both blue and gray, scattered along the field and dead horses strewn everywhere. It was turning out to be a hot day, and you could already pick up the awful smell of corpses. The field was filled with craters where cannonballs had burst. Jim found out they were going to cross the field. Lieutenant Hanson gave them the command to draw sabers, and they started threading their way across the field, making detours around cannon craters and dead horses. Lieutenant Hanson had his revolver out. Occasionally, they'd see a horse thrashing in pain. Lieutenant Hanson would pause to shoot him to end his misery. No such mercy was shown to the wounded soldiers, and their cries and moans were very depressing to hear. Some of them were obviously in terrible pain. There would be ambulance wagons coming around to pick up the wounded when they were available, but apparently, they were employed elsewhere at present. They arrived at the other end of the field after probably a good half-hour and expected rifle fire to open up on them as soon as they were in range or, possibly, another charge from the Union cavalry, but they entered the trees at the other end without opposition.

Jim started to figure out now why they attacked initially so vigorously with cavalry. It was to give the cannon time to move up into place. Then the cavalry had been ordered to withdraw so the artillery could do this. The sight of the carnage would have made him feel a little nauseated even if the smell hadn't already done so.

After going through a wooded area with many winding, parallel trails threading through the trees, they came out on the opposite side to see two wagons crossing the river toward the opposite side, and it looked like maybe a hundred mounted Union soldiers guarding the near bank. The Confederate bugle immediately blew *charge*, and off the horses went as if shot from a cannon again. The Union cavalrymen pulled their sabers and raced to meet them. They clashed, and sabers were hacking, and for the first time Jim became aware of the screaming yell the men made during the charge. They yelled like that every charge that morning as soon as the enemy was in sight, and he hadn't even been aware of it at the time. He was aware of it now and engaged the first Union cavalryman he came to. The Union soldier aimed a slash for his throat, and he parried it. The Union soldier's saber bounced off, and he made a chop for Jim's neck, and he parried that too and, all in one motion, turned his sword edge downward and cut deep into the Union soldier's right shoulder, making him drop his sword. The Yankee immediately grabbed for his revolver with his left hand while Jim ran him through, then went on to meet the next Yankee. A rider in a gray uniform, riding from the right flank, came at the same Yankee, and while Jim was parrying a blow from the Yankee, the other Rebel ran him through with his sword. Two on one didn't sound fair to Jim, but this was war. He didn't know of any regulation against it. Then Jim noticed that the rest of the Union soldiers had dropped their weapons and were holding their hands in the air. The fighting stopped abruptly, and Jim sheathed his saber and drew his carbine to cover the prisoners. No one had given the command to sheathe swords, but that was what made sense, so he did so.

"Who told you to sheathe your sword!" hissed Sergeant Adams to his left. Jim didn't even know he was nearby.

"I did so to cover the prisoners with my—"

"None of your back talk! Now, get your sword back out!"

"Sheathe your swords!" came Lieutenant Hanson's booming voice. "Draw your carbines. Prepare to escort prisoners." Sergeant Adams scowled and moved off.

///

CHAPTER 11

The prisoners were made to dismount and herded away from the creek bank. The drivers of the two wagons were made to wade ashore.

"Sergeant Adams, pick a detail to escort the prisoners," Lieutenant Hanson ordered. "Corporal Marion, take a detail, and provide cover on the other side of the river while the wagons are being brought back."

Corporal Marion included Jim's name in his detail, so he headed Blue Boy into the stream without further ado. He forded the stream, rode up the opposite creek bank, and had a look. He saw a wagon, maybe a quarter of a mile off, disappearing in the woods. He called out what he had seen to Corporal Marion, who was about three fourths the way across by now. Corporal Marion sent Private Ashley back to notify Lieutenant Hanson of that bit of intelligence.

"Our orders are not to cross the river except to provide covering fire if needed," Lieutenant Hanson explained to Private Ashley, who forded the river again to relay this information back to Corporal Marion, who was already across. All three troopers rode up the opposite bank with their carbines and stood guard while two men waded out and climbed into the wagons and turned them around and headed back toward the west bank. After the wagons had been pulled up the bank, Corporal Marion brought Ashley and Bennett back across the stream. He had left two men on the west bank and had another two wade their horses out, one on each side of the wagons.

They heard sporadic firing off to the north, both from small arms and cannon, as they escorted the wagons back away from the river. They turned out to be ammunition wagons, which, of course, were a very valuable prize. When they approached the battlefield they had previously crossed with so many dead and wounded, Jim noticed that the wagons had taken a route to go around the worst of it to a spot where there were very few craters due to cannon fire. Jim rode near a dead Union soldier, sprawled on the ground with a revolver frozen in his fist. Jim hesitated a moment, then dismounted, holding his breath against the stench, pulled loose the revolver, undid the dead man's belt, took his holster, pouch of round balls, and primer caps, then mounted again, hurrying to catch up with the rest of the troop. He noticed other men stopping and dismounting to do likewise. He felt like a grave robber, but how else could he get a revolver to put on his belt? He undid his belt and put the revolver and primer pouch on the right side, then refastened his belt. The pouch of round balls was made to fit over his shoulder. He continued to ride in the column of mounted soldiers threading through the trees. He still heard sporadic firing and the yells of combat off to the north. They were headed north, but then headed back toward the river to the east again. They rode down to the edge of the trees and stopped where they could watch the riverbank. The lieutenant then told them they had been ordered to guard the riverbank in case the Yankees tried to cross the river again. There were three main fords for the Rappahannock River in the Brandy Station area, and this was the middle one. One regiment was guarding the one they had just left, and they had been sent up here to guard this one.

The sun had finally started getting low, and the firing had stopped all along the river. They were ordered to dismount and make camp here near the riverbank, just inside the trees. They were allowed to take their horses down to the river for them to drink and bring back buckets of camp water. Before long they had their horses picketed, campfires going, and coffee started. Corporal Marion sent someone to draw rations, and he came back with some pork and flour. The pork was divided up raw, and each man used his cavalry sword as a spit and roasted it over the open campfire. They had built three fires so it wouldn't be so crowded. Jim was completely exhausted, but mostly, he was hungry. He was accustomed to eating more than this and had not had any breakfast and had a very light, cold lunch. But the coffee finished brewing, and he poured a steaming cup. It tasted terrific. It was the first coffee he had had since yesterday at noon. So he sat on a rock with Joe and Sam sitting on a log on the other side of fire, sipping his coffee and puffing his pipe. Every muscle in his body ached from fatigue. He knew Blue Boy must feel the same way. Then the biscuits were done, and he went to get his ration—only two biscuits this time. He ate the roasted pork by holding his saber up to his mouth sidewise and taking big bites of it between munching a biscuit and taking sips of the steaming hot coffee.

After supper he rolled up in his blankets and passed out. He had been told just before he turned in that he had picket duty at midnight. The corporal of the guard came and told every man when his turn to go on watch would be. So Jim figured he'd better sleep while he could. When he was shaken awake at midnight, he could hardly believe it. He didn't think he'd been asleep more than five minutes. But he went and saddled Blue Boy and took up his patrol along the creek bank so the guard he was relieving could go get some sleep. His orders were to just patrol the creek and report anything unusual he saw. If he saw Yankees coming, he was to sound the alarm with three shots on his revolver. Every member of the troop had scrounged at least one revolver from the battlefield today. So every man now carried a revolver at his belt. Every bone in his body ached from fatigue. An exhausted young man rode his exhausted young horse in a slow walk up and down the riverbank until time for his relief to come on duty at 2:00 a.m. Then he finally saw Private Jones, sleepy eyed, who was to relieve him, ride up and assume the picket watch. He gratefully rode back to camp and unsaddled Blue Boy. He tethered him and rolled up in his blankets again. He was asleep instantly.

CHAPTER 12

Scouting Patrol

When morning reveille sounded, Jim's body was so stiff, he could hardly move. He somehow managed to push himself up out of his blankets and struggle into his boots. They formed up, and Corporal Marion took a muster. Then he sent Joe and Sam to draw rations and detailed Jim and Monday to start chopping wood for the fire. Zeke would start breakfast when the rations arrived. After that Jim, Joe, and Sam would care for the horses. Also, Sergeant Adams had scheduled a training session on small arms for the afternoon since everyone in the troop now had a revolver they had scrounged from the battlefield the day before.

Before doing anything else, Jim took the last remaining oats he had and prepared a feed bag for Blue Boy and went down to where he was tethered. He knew he'd be sore from the previous day's exertions, but as he walked down to the patch of grassy creek bank to where Blue Boy was tethered along with the other horses, he nickered at Jim. Jim put the feed bag on him and returned to get started on woodcutting detail.

Monday was already cutting wood. "Where you been?" he growled.

"I went and put a feed bag on my horse," was Jim's innocent reply.

"You went to put a feed bag on your horse! You didn't hear the corporal say you'd care for the horses after cutting wood?" Jim knew he was right and, with no further reply, took up his ax. But he also knew that keeping a horse in good shape amounted to survival if you were going to do your fighting from the back of the horse. So Jim didn't answer, but just fell to cutting wood silently.

Pretty soon Joe and Sam had returned with the rations—coffee, bacon, flour, and sugar. Zeke came and gathered up the wood that Monday and Jim had cut so far, carried it back to the place he had decided on for the fire, and got the fire going. Sam put the coffee on, and Joe started slicing bacon. Zeke started the batter for the biscuits. Zeke put the biscuits in the Dutch oven as soon as the fire was hot enough. Monday and Jim started carrying up the rest of the wood they had cut.

They all got a cup of coffee as soon as it finished brewing. They got three pieces of bacon apiece, three biscuits, and sugar for their coffee. After breakfast, Jim, Joe, and Sam—all three—went down to take the horses to water. Each took two horses at a time, riding one and leading one. They took them down to the river and let them drink their fill.

After they had cared for the horses and tethered them to their long tether rope, they were permitted to rest a couple of hours. There was enough wood chopped for dinner. They returned to their blankets and conked out again. Jim hadn't realized it was possible to be that tired.

They got up at noon and stoked the fire. Zeke started dinner. Jim and Joe chopped some more wood so there would be plenty for the supper fire that evening. Then Zeke yelled for them to come and get it—bacon and biscuits again, with coffee. Jim was starting to feel alive again. After dinner Corporal Marion mustered the detail, told them to bring along their revolvers they had scrounged from the battlefield, and took them over to a clearing where the rest of the detail had gathered. Sergeant Adams came up and told them to stand at ease.

"There's things you'd better know about handguns if you're going to use them in battle," he said. "You're not going to hit anything from a galloping horse unless he's within about five or ten feet. And by then he's close enough for you to be slashing at him with your saber. But what if your saber gets yanked out of your hand, or your horse is shot out from under you, and you lose it when you fall? You can shoot at a galloping target while standing on the ground and stand a chance of hitting him if you lead him right. You don't even have to lead him if he's charging straight toward you. So for cavalrymen, think of the handgun as a backup gun. Your saber is still your primary weapon in a cavalry charge. Also, as you well know, any gun can misfire. Since these are percussion cap revolvers, they don't misfire as often as a flintlock. And you have five or six shots, so you have a chance to try again. Make sure you always have your belt gun with you, but consider it mainly as a backup gun.

"Now check any gear you picked up when you found your gun. See if you managed to scrounge any spare cylinders." Jim hadn't even thought of such a thing. He looked in the pouch of round balls he had retrieved off the dead Yankee and found there was a spare cylinder in there, all six cylinders loaded.

"If you have more than one spare cylinder," Sergeant Adams went on, "give one to a buddy who don't have one. I want to make sure everybody has at least one spare cylinder, if possible." Checking with Joe and Sam, Jim found out that Joe didn't have a spare cylinder, but Sam had two. Sam gave one to Joe. The rest of the detail shuffled around to distribute spare cylinders to ones who didn't have them.

"Now," continued Sergeant Adams, "you only load five cylinders of the cylinder that you keep in the gun. You know how much jolting comes from a galloping horse. You don't want it to go off in your holster and shoot your foot off. So leave the cylinder empty that lines up with the barrel, but load the other five. This way, when you cock it, it automatically lines up with a loaded cylinder. But go ahead, and load all six cylinders in the spare. You'll most likely be swapping cylinders in the heat of battle and be shooting it again right away. If there's a lull in the battle and you're gun's empty, don't swap cylinders, just reload the one you've got in the gun with five rounds.

"We're going to do some practicing now. I've got the lieutenant's permission. Scouting patrols report that the Yankees are still on the run, but we've got a day of rest after yesterday's battle. In fact the brass wants three days' rest for the horses, if possible. So we don't need to worry about noise. But no target practicing on your own without permission, you hear? There might be Yankees around, and you might not want to let them know our whereabouts.

"You see that rise over there at the edge of the trees that makes sort of an embankment? We're gonna go and drive some stakes made from pieces of tree branch into the ground to shoot at. These round balls do ricochet, and I don't want anybody to git hit accidentally from a stray round. So when you practice, do it where you can shoot into a bank like that."

After a few hours used in target practice, it was noon. They went back to camp. Back at camp, Marion told them to put some water on to boil. After it was hot, he gave them some old rags he had collected from discarded bits of clothing, which he cut into small pieces to use as patches. If they didn't have a pistol ramrod, then he told them to use their carbine ramrod. If they didn't have a carbine ramrod, he told them to borrow one from their buddy. He said if they had to, they could cut a piece of tree limb about the right thickness and whittle it down to fit. Then they dipped the patches in the hot water and cleaned their guns. He said it was better to use soap, if they had it, but it took hot water, mainly, to dissolve all that black powder. He explained that burnt black powder would rust a gun quicker than anything else if you left it in the bore and cylinder long enough.

After they had cleaned their guns, he gave them some rendered pork fat to oil them with. This was nothing new to Jim. He used rendered pork fat to oil his carbine with. The thing about the hot water wasn't really new because that was also what he used for his carbine, but he didn't know how to take the revolver apart. He learned that cleaning a revolver was a lot more involved than cleaning a carbine. After cleaning and oiling his handgun, he wiped the surplus oil away, just as he was told, then loaded one cylinder with six shots and the other with five, just like Sergeant Adams had told them to do. Then he put the one loaded with five shots in his gun, holstered it, and put the other cylinder in his round-ball pouch. He learned that the revolver he now owned was a .44 caliber. His carbine was a .45 caliber, but he compared one of the round balls in his filched pouch of .44 round balls with one from the pouch he already had for his carbine and couldn't tell any difference in size. He decided he'd better ask Corporal Marion if it mattered if you used the two interchangeably. Corporal Marion told him there was a slight difference in size, but he didn't need to worry about it. Either one would work in either carbine or handgun. He explained to Jim that the infantry used paper cartridges in their rifles so they wouldn't have to use rag patches in the bore like he did with his carbine.

"They bite off the end of the paper cartridge, farthest from the bullet." Corporal Marion continued, "Pour the powder down the bore, then wad up the paper, and stuff it down the bore along with the lead ball. The paper takes the place of a patch like you have to use. Well, the .45 balls you use in your carbine allow for the use of a rag patch, so they're made smaller than an actual .45 caliber. That's why they fit in a .44 revolver chamber okay."

"Is there any reason for me to keep two pouches of round balls to keep 'em separate?" Jim asked.

"None whatsoever," answered Corporal Marion. "You can treat them like they're the same."

CHAPTER 13

After they finished cleaning and reloading their weapons, mail was brought by to each troop. Each mess sent a trooper over to get the mail for his mess. Jim found out that he had a letter from Vickie, but none from Mama and Joanne yet. He had only written them a week ago with his military address, so they wouldn't have had time to get a letter to him yet. His pictures, taken by the photographer that first day, of himself in his uniform were included in his mail. He opened the letter from Vickie first. She had heard about the terrible battle and hoped he hadn't been hurt. He was thrilled to get the letter. It was two pages, most of it about how she and her kinfolks were worrying about the men at the fighting front. Then she asked him why he didn't get a furlough just for one evening and come over to her house for dinner. She said that Papa insisted on it. She even enclosed a map showing him how to get to her house. She said they'd be expecting him any evening. "Try to be there by six if possible, but if not, come anyway," her letter read. As soon as he finished her letter, he went to his saddlebags and got out his pencil and paper and, using his saddle for a writing desk, wrote a letter to her, assuring her that he was safe and sound and doing fine. He thanked her for her invitation to supper and said that if he could get a furlough approved, he'd come over. Then he wrote to Mama and Joanne.

In his letter to Mama and Joanne, he didn't mention the Battle of Brandy Station, but wrote them each a cheerful letter describing life in camp. He wrote about Joe's harmonica and what a terrific idea he thought it was to be able to have an instrument that made such beautiful music that you could simply put in your saddlebags and even your pocket.

He opened the package with the pictures before he sealed either envelope. He found out the pictures turned out pretty good—one three-by-five inches and one five-by-seven. He decided to send Mama and Joanne the three-by-five picture and put the five-by-seven one back in the big envelope along with Vickie's letter. He then scratched out the address and return address and put her address and his own address in their respective places. They'd be mailed whenever mail was carried to headquarters, which would be daily if they weren't fighting or marching.

Jim found out from Corporal Marion that some horses had been captured from the Yankees during the battle, and he could draw a horse from the captured horses, if necessary, to make sure that Blue Boy could get his three days' rest. The Army knew the importance of getting the horses rested up after a day of hard fighting—whenever it was possible. So Jim went down to where the captured horses were kept and picked one out and led him back and tethered him with the horses for Troop C. Blue Boy saw him lead the other horse up, a bay gelding. Blue Boy nickered.

"Jealous, huh," Jim murmured, slightly amused. "It's only until you get a couple days' rest, Blue Boy." Blue Boy shook his head as if he understood and disagreed. Jim couldn't help but smile and, after he finished tethering the bay, went over and ruffled Blue Boy's mane. That seemed to settle Blue Boy down a little.

At the crack of dawn when reveille sounded the next morning, he rolled out for roll call as usual, and he learned that C Troop had been ordered to send out a scouting patrol today.

"Hustle up breakfast, and get saddled up," Corporal Marion told them. "We want to move out along about sunup."

After breakfast he went out and saddled the bay. Blue Boy nickered again, and he went over and tousled his mane again.

"You rest up those stiff muscles, Blue Boy. We'll be back later today." He then mounted up and joined the rest of the scouting detail. He found out Sergeant Adams was leading the scouting patrol. He led off in a trail through the trees and down toward the river. The detail followed him in single file down to the river ford, and they waded their horses across. Sergeant Adams reined up on the far side and waited for everyone to cross.

After the last rider in the detail pulled up on the far bank, Sergeant Adams said, "What we want to do is look and see without being seen. We know there's no Yankees within ten miles of the other side of the river from reports from other scouting patrols. Our orders are to ride out about ten miles in a wide semicircle and see if we spot any Yankees. When you ride through trees, walk your horses slowly, and stop while just inside the trees on the far side. Then hold still, and hold your horse still while you look across any cleared space, and see if you see any movement across any clearings or open space. The Yankees will be just inside the trees, just like you will be, and they'll be trying to see without being seen just like we will. Any sounds you hear or smoke you see, let me know as soon as you can. Any questions?" There were none, so they headed on eastward away from the river. After they were five miles or so east of the river, they headed southward and started their semicircle. When they reached a grove of trees, they spread out and rode through them cautiously. When they came to a fence, they rode around it if they could though most of them had jumping horses. When they came to a creek, Sergeant Adams had them hold up, and he rode across by himself to scout it out before he allowed them to cross. When he decided it was clear, he'd come back to the creek bank and silently wave them across with a hand signal. After they were ten miles or so southeast of the river ford, they swung northward and started their big, wide semicircle. They saw lots of horse tracks and wagon tracks from the retreating Yankee cavalry and supply trains. But they saw no smoke other than from the civilian farmhouses they rode near and heard no sounds except the normal sounds you'd hear in the woods of birds singing, squirrels scolding, and an occasional woodpecker pecking away at some tree. When the sun indicated that it was noontime, Sergeant Adams halted them for the noon meal and posted two lookouts, one to the north and one to the south, while they had their lunch of cold pork and hardtack, cooked this morning just before they left camp. He didn't allow them to build a fire, so they had to make do without coffee. Then Jim was ordered to take the place of one of the lookouts who came back to eat and drink from a nearby creek. It was so quiet and peaceful out here! It was hard to believe there was a war on. It was hard to fathom the fact that there were two armies killing one another en masse just two days previously.

After lunch they mounted up and finished their half circle toward the north and started easing back toward the river at about middle afternoon. They avoided towns and farmhouses. To see without being seen meant to avoid being seen by civilians too, if possible. The sun was low on the horizon when they finally reached the ford and waded their horses back across and returned along the trail, single file, toward their camp. They tethered their horses, built a campfire, and started a pot of coffee.

After Zeke left for the mess wagon to draw rations, Jim asked Corporal Marion what he had to do to get an evening's furlough to accept his girlfriend's invitation. Marion showed him how to write a request for a one-evening pass. So Jim filled one out and gave it to Marion to forward up the chain of command.

The following day C Troop remained in camp. Jim found out that Corporal Marion had a field sewing kit. Marion had told him to water the horses and then to chop some wood so they'd have a supply ready for the noon meal. So after he had finished his wood-chopping duties and watered the horses, he borrowed Marion's sewing kit to repair a rip in his uniform. He had noticed one in his left sleeve, made by a near miss from a Yankee saber. It was tending to rip worse, so he learned to thread a needle and sewed it up. It, obviously, was not a professional job, but he figured it still was better than it was before. Most important of all, he learned before it was time for supper that his request for an evening's pass to go into town had been approved!

Courtin'

After Jim got through unsaddling and picketing the bay, he saddled Blue Boy and rode by the campfire and told Corporal Marion he was heading into town. Corporal Marion nodded his assent, and Jim started riding toward town. He rode by campfire after campfire until he found a trail heading toward the south. His own regiment was, apparently, still located on the right flank of the Army because, riding to the south, he was soon away from the campfires and finally reached a road that he knew led into Culpepper. He was challenged twice by sentries and had to show them his furlough papers to prove he wasn't deserting.

When he approached the outskirts of Culpepper, he got the map Vickie had sent him out of his pocket so he could find her house. The map had the faint smell of perfume to it. He followed the map easily, and before it was dark, he rode down a street and stopped at the fifth house from the corner per instructions from the map. When he dismounted, he found that that someone inside must have heard him ride up because the door opened, showing a lighted doorway.

"Who's there?" a man's voice questioned. Jim recognized the voice as that of Vickie's father.

"Private Jim Bennet, sir," Jim replied, not thinking that he didn't really have to comply with military protocol. But Mr. Allen came out the door to welcome him.

"Glad you could come!" he exclaimed, with genuine warmth in his voice, which surprised Jim and about halfway choked him up. It was as if Mr. Allen were really glad to see him. "Bring your horse around back, and unsaddle him." Behind the house was a small stable where Mr. Allen kept his horses. There was a carriage and a tack room and a small corral. He rode Blue Boy through the gate that Mr. Allen opened for him and quickly unsaddled him.

"Your horse had any corn today yet?" he asked. As soon as Jim replied in the negative, Mr. Allen went into a shed joining the tack room and came back out with an armload of unshelled corn, went to a feed trough, and dumped it in. Blue Boy immediately started eating.

"Come on to the house. Supper's nearly ready," Mr. Allen told him. Jim already felt tingly all over again just at the thought of seeing Vickie. He followed Mr. Allen back around to the front door of the house and through the door. Jim felt his body flooded with a feeling of warmth as soon as he walked into the house. It was a feeling he wasn't accustomed to though he was vaguely aware of having felt that way before to a lesser degree—back home when Papa and Jonnie were both still alive. It was an emotional warmth. Jim figured it must be just a feeling you felt when you were around a family.

When Vickie saw them come in, she walked to the middle of the room and curtsied gracefully and said, "Hello, Jim! I'm so glad you could come. You must have received my letter." She was blushing beautifully and was apparently trying to hide it with her formal manners. Jim was kind of dumbstruck and couldn't get his vocal cords to work at first, then managed to say hi and gave her a bashful smile. Mrs. Allen then came and greeted him and told him to sit down. Vickie brought him a cup of coffee and sat down in a chair nearby. She had an exceptionally beautiful expression on her face that he had never seen on a woman's face before. He had no idea what it meant; he was just aware that he felt tingly all over to the point of being almost numb.

"We were so worried when we heard about the terrible battle. We were afraid you'd be hurt," Vickie said. Then Vickie noticed the rip in the left sleeve of Jim's uniform that he had repaired so inefficiently. "Why, you were hurt!" she exclaimed and got up and sat beside him on the couch to examine his left arm.

"No," he replied as the tingly feeling turned to a feeling of total numbness from head to foot. But he managed to say, "I just tore my uniform—is all. I sewed it back up."

"Well, take off your coat," Vickie said, with a ring of insistence in her voice. He obeyed before he thought. She stepped across the room, picked up a sewing basket from the top of a bookcase, took his jacket, and sat back down in her chair. She took her scissors and started clipping the threads to the ripped place with obvious intent of redoing his repair job.

Vickie's mother was putting supper on the table. The tableware had, apparently, already been placed on the table while he was unsaddling Blue Boy. After Mrs. Allen finished putting supper on the table, she said, "Come on to the table." Mr. Allen and Jim both got up. Since Vickie didn't get out of her chair, her mother said, "Vickie?"

"I'm not going to eat, Mama, I'm not hungry," she said. "I want to sew up Jim's jacket."

"Well, that's fine, Vickie," replied her mother, "but come sit at the table while your father asks the blessing." So with that Vickie did lay aside her sewing basket, got up, and sat in the chair across from her mother while Mr. Allen appealed to the Almighty above to bless the food, the bodies that were to consume it, the hands that prepared it, etc. After he said "Amen," she got up, returned to her chair, picked up her sewing basket, and resumed her task. She did turn her chair around so she could be included in the conversation at the table. Jim couldn't take his eyes off her beautiful face while eating. But since it had been days since he had had all he wanted to eat, as soon as he tasted his food, he became aware of how hungry he was—fried chicken, mashed potatoes and gravy, dressing, black-eyed peas, and hot biscuits. He hadn't tasted food this good since he had left his home in South Carolina. So his teenage appetite took control, and he ate with relish. He noticed that there were plenty of food prepared. It certainly looked like they had anticipated the presence at the table of someone with a big appetite. Even then, he would have been bashful about taking out seconds if Mrs. Allen hadn't been insistent. After he finished his second helping, she was just as insistent that he take out a third helping. When she tried to get him to fill up his plate a fourth time, he declined. He was filled to the brim. So he waited until Mr. Allen left the table, then followed suit. They went back to the living room, and when Mr. Allen took out his pipe and starting packing it with tobacco, he did so too.

While Vickie didn't talk much while concentrating on her work of sewing the sleeve of Jim's jacket, she still had that same beautiful expression on her face. You could say she had a certain glow about her that permeated the entire room. He figured if he had been sick, one look at her would have made him well. She finished her work and got up and returned her sewing basket to the bookcase. She brought him his jacket and showed him her handiwork. He found that he couldn't even tell it had ever been ripped unless he held it within a foot or so away. He felt tingly all over again now that she had come and sat down beside him again.

"It looks terrific!" he exclaimed. "You can't even tell it was ever ripped!" She smiled beautifully at his expression of appreciation and asked him to put it back on, which he did.

"You look so handsome in your uniform!" she told him. He blushed all over at that and couldn't think of anything to say. Since embarrassing him was not her intention, she quickly said, "Do you like music?"

"Yes," he answered. "My sister and I used to play back before I left my home in South Carolina."

"Oh, do you play too?" she asked, obviously surprised.

"Oh, a little," he answered modestly. "Joanne played the piano, and I played the mandolin."

"Father's got a mandolin!" she exclaimed. "Would you play for us? Please?" Without waiting for him to answer, she jumped up, ran out of the room, and came back within seconds with her father's mandolin. She handed it to him and went to the piano, pulled the piano bench out, and sat down.

It was just like being home! He checked the mandolin to see if it was in tune. Then he checked it against the piano to see if it was in tune with the piano. Mr. Allen, apparently, had played it recently. He struck up a tune, and Vickie immediately started up playing chords on the piano for background. Vickie could play every bit as well as Joanne could, maybe even a little bit better. In no time, Jim was back home in South Carolina, lost in the dreamworld of beautiful sounds from the mandolin and piano. Song after song and Vickie backed him up as if she'd been practicing with him daily. He figured she must really be a musical genius. Then he urged to her to play some songs. She said she preferred to back him up, but he insisted, and she relented. He played chords for her awhile. Then when she played songs he knew the words to, he started singing, and she started harmonizing. At hearing the beauty of her voice, he was flabbergasted!

They played and sang and played and sang. Mom and Pop just sat and listened to the beautiful music, awestruck. They, apparently, were seeing their offspring performing at a much higher level than they had ever seen before, and they hadn't known that her young suitor was going to be such an accomplished musician. They soon were so affected by the intense beauty being created by the youngsters that they got up and starting dancing around the floor, and Mr. Allen starting acting like a young suitor himself, flirting with Mrs. Allen and playing something of the clown while doing so. He soon had her laughing, and Jim and Vickie started to laugh too, so much that it interrupted the song they were playing.

As far as Jim was concerned, he didn't even know he was Vickie's suitor. He had no idea what she was even thinking. It didn't occur to him to even wonder. They finally regained control of their laughter and struck up another tune. When they had played until their fingers were tired, they stopped to talk awhile. Vickie got up and resumed her seat in her chair, which was a respectable distance from Jim's seat on the couch. All the ice had been thawed and had disappeared in a cloud of steam. He found himself talking to her as if he had known her all his life. She talked to him just as freely.

"Do you have your mandolin with you at your camp?" she asked at one point.

"No. I was afraid I might break it," was his answer, and then he became cautious again for a moment because he didn't want to direct the conversation back to the battle or anything the slightest bit depressing. It was too terrific of an evening to run the risk of spoiling it.

"Do any of the other soldiers have musical instruments with them at camp?" she asked, obviously reading his thoughts and wanting to come quickly to his rescue.

So he told her about Joe William's harmonica and how a harmonica could easily be stowed in saddlebags or even in a shirt pocket. He had never played a harmonica, but he explained that when he got a chance to go to a store somewhere, he intended to buy one and learn to play it.

Then Jim looked at the grandfather clock against the wall to the left of the front door and was suddenly shocked to find that it was well after midnight—almost one o'clock, in fact! Just the idea of calling it an evening was depressing, but he knew it was important to live up the rules of protocol as a gentleman and make his leave at a reasonable hour. So he bid her farewell and expressed gratitude to his host and hostesses and headed for the front door. Just walking out into the yard was depressing. But he hurried back to the stable and saddled and bridled Blue Boy. Mr. Allen accompanied him in accordance with the protocol of the times.

"Like to come by for supper again tomorrow night?" Mr. Allen suggested. He knew the Army couldn't always provide adequate rations for the troops, and while he had wisely made no reference whatsoever to Jim's age, he could tell from the beginning that he was a teenage boy and knew he must be hungry probably all the time if he depended on Army rations for sustenance. While Mr. Allen considered himself too old to join the fighting himself, he figured he could help by, at least, providing food for a hungry soldier.

"I can't tomorrow night because I have picket duty," Jim replied, "but I'd like to the night after that if my regiment is still camped near here."

"You think your regiment will be marching soon?" Mr. Allen returned.

"I don't know. It's just that if we did, I wouldn't be able to let you know if I couldn't come. If I told you I'd come and didn't, I'd be breaking my word."

"Well, you can just agree to come if your duty doesn't interfere, and if you don't show up, we'll know it was because your regiment had to march, or you had some duty preventing it. You wouldn't be breaking your word, then."

So Jim agreed with the arrangement and headed Blue Boy back to camp. When he arrived back at camp, he looked up at the Big Dipper and saw it was about 2:00 a.m. The corporal of the guard had showed him how to tell time from the Big Dipper. So Jim unsaddled Blue Boy and tethered him and went and rolled up in his blankets. Jim wasn't the slightest bit sleepy. He was still on a high from the terrific company he had enjoyed all evening. And it felt funny not to be hungry. He lay awake a long time before he went to sleep and just enjoyed the night air, the crickets singing, and the occasional frog croaking. He was just very aware that it was great to be alive.

CHAPTER 15

Guard Duty

When reveille sounded, Jim woke up from a very deep and very sound sleep. He didn't want to get up, but rolled over and forced himself to push up out of his blankets. Ooh! But it was hard to get up when you didn't want to. Joe was already up and getting a fire started by the time he had his boots on. Monday was already headed toward a patch of trees a little ways from camp with an ax in his hand to chop down a tree for more firewood. When they had time in the evening, they had started the habit of cutting additional wood to make early-morning wood chopping unnecessary, but apparently, there wasn't time to do so last night.

Joe finally got his blanket and ground cloth rolled up and pushed himself up off the ground. He went and got an ax and followed after Monday. It was getting so that his shoulder and arm muscles weren't quite so sore since chopping wood had sort of become one of his routine duties in camp. He always wore his cavalry gauntlets while handling the ax, so blisters were not something he had to worry about; in fact, he didn't even know what blisters were. After Monday had felled the tree, he went up and started helping him chop off the branches and cut them into small-enough pieces so they'd fit in the fire.

"So you went foraging last night, huh?" jibed Monday.

"What do you mean by foraging?" Jim asked, a little defensively.

"Foraging, you know, bumming a meal off the local citizenry."

Instantly, Jim was angry. "What's it to you?" His tone of voice sounded like the snarl of a wolf while attacking.

"Take it easy." Monday was instantly shocked by the intense glare in Jim's eyes. "I was only funning you. Where's your sense of humor?"

"And I'll repeat what I said. What's it to you?" The glare in Jim's eyes hadn't mellowed.

"Nothing," Monday said. "I meant no harm. Don't take it personal." Monday outweighed Jim by probably thirty pounds and was a couple of inches taller, and while he looked to be about fifty, he had the appearance of being as tough as rawhide. But something about Jim's total no-give-to-it manner mellowed him out. After all, they were here to fight Yankees, not each other. And Jim had been highly thought of by everybody after the Battle of Brandy Station. There wasn't a single soldier in the troop who didn't see him on every charge made. His fast horse kept him up front where everybody could see everything he did. They saw his brilliant sword work against what appeared to be battle-hardened Union soldiers, and they valued him as an okay man to have around. *But he sure don't have no sense of humor,* Monday thought to himself as he and Jim continued to work in silence.

As soon as Jim had cut up enough wood to make an armload, he gathered it up and headed for the fire with it. Coffee was already perking, and Zeke had arrived back from the commissary wagon with their rations.

"No meat this time," Zeke said with disdain as he laid down the box beside the fire. "Just flour and coffee and some rendered pork grease. And some molasses." And he pulled a quart can out of the box and showed it to them.

So instead of biscuits, Zeke made pancakes this morning, and the molasses was poured out for each man very carefully, into his plate, with care taken to pour the exact amount each time to make sure it was equally divided up. But there was plenty of coffee. A second pot of coffee was started when the rations had arrived. The first pot had been started with a little coffee leftover from the day before being added to the grounds left in the coffeepot from last night. They had learned that boiling the grounds more than once by just adding about half the normal amount of coffee to it again was a way to get the most out of their coffee ration. And they dreaded the day when coffee wasn't included in their ration. Private Jones had assured them it happened sometimes. He was an old soldier—probably, the only soldier in the troop besides Marion and Monday who had been in battle prior to Brandy Station. Everyone else in the troop were men who had recently been recruited at Culpepper as Jim had been. *Old soldier* didn't mean physically old. It just meant a veteran of many battles.

As soon as breakfast was over and the tobacco sack was opened, every man filled his pipe. There was a large canvas tobacco sack that was kept in the mess ration box. While tobacco wasn't included in the rations from the commissary, it had somehow been appropriated by some unknown party from another unknown party, but every man in the mess thought of it as the property of the mess. After Jim packed his pipe and lit it, he went to his saddlebags, got out his pencil and paper, and wrote out another request for a pass to go into town for tomorrow night. His picket duty started at eight this morning and went for twenty-four hours, two on and four off. That would be his only duty for the next twenty-four hours. So he requested permission to spend the evening in town the following day. He turned it in to Corporal Marion and then told him he had picket duty and went down and saddled Blue Boy. He was ready to ride down to the riverbank and take up his picket by the time the corporal of the guard came by to remind him.

Jim had guard duty from eight o'clock till ten, then from 2:00 p.m. until 4:00 p.m., then again from 8:00 p.m. until 10:00 p.m. His last watch was from 2:00 a.m. until 4:00 a.m.

But since this was his only duty, he could return to his blankets and grab some sleep or write letters or whatever he wanted between watches just so he stayed near camp. He had to be there in case the corporal of the guard needed him for anything.

After his relief came at 10:00 a.m., Jim returned to his blankets and slept until noon and partially caught up his sleep. Though when he heard wood chopping, he got up and went and helped chop wood because he felt like he should, at least, help earn his dinner. The corporal of the guard saw him and went and reprimanded him. He explained that he didn't do anything, but guard duty on the days he had the duty. *Okay,* Jim thought, *I'll play the game however they want it* and returned to the campfire.

After a lunch of biscuits and black-eyed peas, he packed his pipe and went down to the riverbank to just relax while he waited till time to go on watch again at 2:00 p.m. Then he saddled Blue Boy and went and relieved the watch again.

For the night watches, he saddled the bay and used him so Blue Boy could rest through the night. He stood his last watch from six until eight the following morning. It caused him to miss breakfast, but he had saved back some hardtack. When he got in at eight, he went to the campfire and stoked it and warmed up the coffee. If there was any left after breakfast, it had become the practice to save it for whoever came off picket duty in the morning. After a breakfast of coffee and hardtack, he felt much better.

Then Corporal Marion told him to go with Joe and Monday to the commissary wagon and pick up some corn for the horses. Upon returning to the mess camping area, he learned that his duties for the morning were going to be to grain and water the horses before starting to chop wood for the noon cook fire. This was good news to Jim because he enjoyed caring for the horses. Joe was assigned to help him, so they gathered up all the feed bags they had and carried a box of corn apiece down to the area where the horses were tethered.

After feeding the horses and taking them to water two at a time, Jim and Joe both got an empty burlap bag and rubbed each horse down. After that they went to chop some more wood to make sure they had enough for the noon meal.

Jim hadn't seen Simmons around for several days. He asked Joe if he had seen him.

"Didn't you know?" he said. "He was transferred to the infantry."

"He was?" said Jim.

"Yes. Sergeant Adams caught him abusing a horse again, so his horse was taken away from him and put in the spare-horse pool, and he was transferred to the infantry. It was figured that he wouldn't be handling horses there and so wouldn't have an opportunity to abuse them."

"Bully for Sergeant Adams," replied Jim. He was glad to be rid of Simmons anyway. He was obviously a shirker. His esteem for Sergeant Adams went up a couple of notches.

After they had enough wood, Joe got the fire started with Jim helping him. Monday was on picket duty this day, so they had to handle the wood detail without him and his special expertise with an ax though Joe and Jim were getting pretty good with all the practice they had been getting lately. Then Zeke came back with the rations.

"No beef again," he said, "but we've got some pork. And coffee and corn meal. Also some hardtack. We'll get by all right."

Zeke's cornbread was every bit as good as his biscuits. Each man was given a piece of pork, mostly fat, to broil over the fire himself. Each man just used his saber to spear the meat with and held over the fire while it cooked. After the coffee brewed, each man filled his cup and sipped coffee with one hand while holding his piece of meat over the fire on the blade of his saber with the other. Zeke would take two pairs of blacksmith tongs he kept for the purpose and lift the lid of the Dutch oven every few minutes to see how his gourmet delight was progressing.

The Dutch oven was rectangular, about a foot and a half wide and three feet long. Zeke lifted the lid, checked again, and decided it was ready and put the lid aside. Then taking both pairs of tongs again, he lifted each of the two long pans of bread out of the oven. He then took his belt knife he always carried and sliced it into large pieces. Each man lined up, holding his meat on the end of his saber with one hand and his plate in another, to get his cornbread ration.

Jim and Joe went back to the log they had been sitting on. Each would hold his saber up to his mouth to take a bite of pork, then take a bite of cornbread from their plate. Only when the piece of roast pork reached the point of nearly dropping off the sword to the ground did they then dump it in their plate. An occasional sip of coffee set the meal off just right.

After dinner they packed their pipes and had a smoke. Clouds were gathering overhead, and it was starting to look like it might rain. Jim had now wished he had brought his slicker from home. It had been fair weather so far this summer—in fact, dryer than usual. Mail call sounded, and Jim was sent to pick up the mail sack for the mess this time. He went over to the troop headquarters tent, and the troop orderly sergeant handed him the mail sack for Mess Number 9. He took it back to the mess camping area.

Since he had brought the mail, it was his job to call out the names of each man receiving mail and distribute it. He found out he did get a letter from Mama and Joanne, and there was also a letter from Vickie.

So after he had distributed the mail, he sat down and read his letters. He read Vickie's letter first as usual. It seemed funny to get mail from her since he had seen her only two nights ago and was planning to go see her again tonight (if his pass to town was approved), but when he opened it, he saw it was dated the day before his visit. She repeated her invitation to come over for supper just any-time. No advance notice was needed, she insisted. Most of the letter was small talk about things going on in town. She said Papa owned a grocery and dry-goods store in Culpepper. Business was more than usual since the Army was camped nearby.

Then he read Mama and Joanne's letter. They were still worried about him and hoped he wasn't in any danger. And how was Blue Boy doing? They missed him and hoped he could get a furlough to come home soon.

Jim got out his saddle for a writing desk and answered Mama and Joanne's letter. He asked them to send him some socks and another pair of underwear. Also would they send him his slicker? He hadn't thought to bring it when he left.

He didn't answer Vickie's letter because he would see her tonight. He put his letter to Mama and Joanne in the letter sack. After all the men had finished writing letters, Corporal Marion told him to take the mail sack back to the troop headquarters tent. When he got back, he asked Corporal Marion if his request for an evening pass had been approved. Corporal Marion told him yes. Then he wanted to know if there was any reason he couldn't leave now even though it was the middle of the afternoon. Since there wasn't much going on, Corporal

Marion told him he could. So Jim went and saddled Blue Boy and headed off toward Culpepper.

On the ride to Culpepper it started raining, and by the time he reached the outskirts of Culpepper, he was soaked. Well, that was okay, he guessed. He wasn't going to let a little rain keep him from seeing his girl. *A bath would be nice though,* he thought. Since he had joined the Army, sponge baths in the creek had been his only means of physical hygiene. He kept a small piece of soap with his outfit for this purpose.

Music

He rode up to the Allen house and dismounted. He tied Blue Boy to the fence, opened the gate, and walked up to the front door and knocked. Vickie came and opened the door.

"Jim! You're going to catch your death of cold!"

"No, I won't," grinned Jim. "If I did, one look at you would cure it instantly."

Vickie blushed and then said, "Come in, and hurry before the rain gets in."

"I have to take care of my horse first," Jim replied. "I'll be right back." So he went back out to the gate and untied Blue Boy and led him to the back of the house where the stable was and put him inside the shed. There were two empty stalls. Mr. Allen would have taken his buggy to work with him and would have taken one of the horses. That accounted for one of the stalls. So there was a spare. He unsaddled Blue Boy and took his bridle off and found an old burlap sack and rubbed him down. Then he patted him on the neck and walked back out into the rain. Blue Boy had gotten a good ration of grain that morning, so he figured he'd be all right. He was glad he had a place to keep him out of the rain though warm summer rain like this wouldn't hurt him, he knew.

Jim walked up and knocked on the door again. When Vickie let him in, he saw Mrs. Allen carrying a kettle full of steaming water to a back room.

"We heated some water for your bath. You must get out of that wet uniform," she said.

"But it's the only uniform I have," he replied.

"Pull off your boots, and I'll show you," she said.

He pulled off his boots; they were muddy enough, and he had intended to pull them off anyway, and she led him back to a back bedroom where Mrs. Allen was pouring steaming water into a big tub. He saw a shirt and pants laid out on the bed.

"You can wear some of Papa's clothes until yours dry," Vickie told him. That sounded okay to him. Mrs. Allen had just brought in another bucket of cold water this time so he could adjust the temperature of the water as he liked. She placed soap and a towel on a chair, and she and Vickie left and closed the door. He took off his wet clothes and laid them on the back of the chair, poured just enough cold water in the steaming tub so he could just barely stand it, and got in and sat down. Ooh! But it felt good to just soak in hot water again after all this time. He remembered he hadn't had a full bath in a tub since he had left Raleigh. This made him think of shaving, and he reached up and felt his face. It was still pretty smooth—not enough peach fuzz to notice yet. So after he finished his luxurious bath and toweled off, he put on the pants and shirt, without bothering with his underwear. It was soaking wet anyway. After he returned to the living room, Vickie went and got his wet clothes, wrung them out, and hung them on a clothesline that had been rigged near the stove in the kitchen so they could dry. He hoped someone wouldn't see him and think he was a deserter or a spy, but at least, he was dry.

"If someone sees me like this, they'll think I deserted," he said.

"Nonsense," said Vickie, "and besides, no one will see you. By the time you're ready to leave, your uniform will be dry. Hopefully, it'll stop raining by then.

"When is your birthday?" Vickie asked him.

"Why, it's already past," Jim answered.

"But when is it?"

"May fifth."

"When is your birthday?" he asked in turn.

"November second," she answered.

She got up and left the room and then came back in a minute or so. She brought a small package.

"Happy birthday a month and a half late," she said and handed him the package, smiling, showing her dimples.

"What is it?" he asked.

"Open it and see," she said, still showing her dimples.

He opened it and found out it was a harmonica, similar to Joe's. "Hey," he said, "just what I needed!" He put it up to his mouth and blew on it. It didn't make music, just sounds, but it had an excellent tone to it. He knew it would sound good after he learned to play it. "Thank you," he said and reached down to give her a hug. She hugged him back, still smiling big.

Vickie then went and got her father's mandolin and handed it to him. "Here, you already know how to play this." Then she sat down at the piano to see if they were in tune. Before long they were playing hoedown music. Mrs. Allen had already started supper, and she couldn't keep her feet still while tending to her cooking.

By the time supper was ready, Mr. Allen came in. He was wearing a slicker. Though his carriage had a top on it, rain still blew in from the open sides and front, so he had found the slicker a necessary accessory when it was raining.

He nodded to Jim before he reached down and took off his boots, then went back to one of the back rooms to discard his slicker. He came back to the living room and waited until Jim and Vickie finished the song they were playing, then held out his hand for Jim. Jim took his hand and shook it.

"Glad you could come out tonight," Mr. Allen said. "I saw your horse in the stall and gave him some corn."

"Why, thanks," Jim replied, "but you didn't have to do that, I grained him this morning."

"Well, I didn't know if he'd had any grain today or not, and I knew it wouldn't hurt anything to grain him twice in one day even if he had." Jim knew he was right. As much riding as he was doing on Blue Boy, the important thing was to make sure he was fed grain when it was available.

Mr. Allen sat on the couch and said, "Well, don't stop playing, you really sound good. I heard you when I first drove up even over the rain."

"Why, thanks," said Jim, and Vickie blushed a little. But they struck up another tune and resumed their playing.

Pretty soon, Mrs. Allen was putting supper on the table. After she finished, she said, "Come to supper, it's ready."

So everyone went to the dining room and sat down to a gourmet meal. They all waited for Mr. Allen to give the blessing, but he asked Jim to do so instead. It surprised Jim, but he figured it would be awkward to refuse, so he bowed his head and just repeated words he had heard his father say at the table so many times. Papa hadn't really been the religious type, but he'd say the blessing before the Sunday meal after the family had gotten back from the church service at Florence on Sundays. He took the family to church every Sunday to maintain their standing in the community.

Then they started eating pork chops, dressing, cornbread, butter, canned corn, black-eyed peas and peach cobbler for dessert—a meal fit for a king. It was too early in the season for fresh peaches, but Mr. Allen would bring canned goods from his store, so they had things like peaches and other canned fruit the year-round at his house.

After the meal, they went to the living room, and Vickie brought them coffee. Then Vickie went and got out an iron and ironing board and started ironing Jim's uniform.

"You don't have to do that," he said. "It'll just get wrinkled again."

"That's okay if it does," she said. "It's just about dry enough to iron, and I'm going to iron it."

"Why don't you and Mama play awhile, Papa?" Vickie asked.

"Oh, I don't know if I can anymore, I haven't played in so long," Mrs. Allen answered.

"Go ahead," Vickie urged. "And you too, Papa. You don't play near often enough."

So with Vickie's urging, Mrs. Allen sat down at the piano, and Mr. Allen took up the mandolin, and they struck up a tune. They hit a few wrong notes when they first started, but after a song or two, they seemed to get warmed up and started sounding pretty good.

After Vickie finished ironing his uniform, she handed it to him and said, "Now go put it on, and let's see how it looks." So he got up, and she handed it to him and went back to the back room and put it on.

When he came back, the music had stopped, and Vickie said, "Oh, you look so handsome in your uniform!" It was his turn to blush this time because she caught him totally by surprise. He was completely unaware of the effect of a uniform on the fair sex. He just knew it was Army regulation to wear it. He did feel more comfortable with it on. After being in the habit of wearing it all the time, things just felt wrong being in civilian clothes for some reason.

"I think my fingers have given out," Mr. Allen said as he handed the mandolin to Jim. "You play some more."

"Why, you sounded really great," Jim insisted.

"Well, thanks, but it's your turn again."

So with Mr. Allen's insistence he took up the mandolin again, and Mrs. Allen got up from the piano and insisted that she'd rather hear her daughter play than play herself. So Jim and Vickie resumed their concert.

Jim had never been so happy and felt depressed when it grew late and came time to make his leave again. But he made sure his new harmonica was in his pocket. He got up to go.

Mr. Allen went into a back room and came back with a dark-gray slicker. "Here's my spare slicker," he said. "Otherwise, you'll get wet again."

"But I can't do that," Jim protested.

"Take it, it's almost the color of your uniform. It'll be all right."

So Jim put on the slicker and walked out back to saddle Blue Boy. Blue Boy nickered when he saw him. Jim bridled and saddled him, and Vickie stood in the lighted door and waved to him as he rode off. The rain had nearly stopped, but it was still drizzling lightly when Jim mounted up.

As Jim rode out of town, he got his mouth organ out of his pocket and started trying to play it again. Blue Boy started and tried to turn his head around in an attempt to look at his young master as if to say, "Are you off your rocker?" But Jim continued. He started working on the song "Home Sweet Home." It seemed like an appropriate song to play, and it had been the first song he had learned on his mandolin when he had first started learning to play it when he was about ten. He just kept Blue Boy in an easy walk and took his time riding back to camp. The rain had stopped, but rain was still in the air, and he knew it might start again. In the meantime, he just kept on trying to get through the tune without mistakes.

He was starting to almost get the hang of it when he saw two riders up ahead of him. He stopped playing for a moment to see if he could recognize them. Then he heard music from a mouth organ. One of them was playing a mouth organ! Then he recognized Joe's form in the saddle. He tapped Blue Boy with his spurs and pulled up alongside them. Joe turned and looked at him and apparently recognized him in the moonlight, but he kept on playing. Joe could play his harmonica so well! It seemed like he'd never be that good on the mouth organ himself. He noticed the other rider was Sam.

After Joe finished the song he was playing, he learned that Joe and Sam had been into town and spent the evening in a saloon. You could tell by the expression on their faces that they were about half-way lit. Then Joe resumed playing his mouth organ, but he stopped when they started approaching camp. If they woke anyone up arriving at camp, they were likely to get boots or frying pans and such thrown at them.

When they arrived at camp and unsaddled and tethered their horses, it had already started to rain again. Neither Sam nor Joe had a slicker, so they placed Joe's oilcloth on the ground and put both their blankets on it. Then both of them rolled up in their blankets so they could share Sam's oilcloth to keep off the rain. Jim unrolled his bedroll and rolled up in his blankets like usual and laid his slicker over it. He still used his saddle for a pillow. If he kept his knees doubled up, it kept his blankets from getting wet. It was customary when it was raining for two men to share a bedroll in a fashion such as that of Joe and Sam to stay as dry as possible while sleeping. But after Simmons had left, there were nine men in the mess. That left an odd man. They could have slept three to a bedroll, if necessary, though it would have been a little crowded. Jim preferred sleeping alone, and Mr. Allen's gift of his spare slicker made this possible and to even stay dry in the bargain.

CHAPTER 17

//

Cooking in the Rain

The next morning after reveille, Jim learned during breakfast that he was assigned to scouting patrol that morning. Corporal Marion sent several men, including Jim, down to put feed bags on the horses and then take them to water after they fed. After a breakfast of biscuits and fat pork cooked over a fire started by Zeke by some method unknown to Jim, they drew their noon rations, which was hardtack and nothing else. Jim wrapped his hardtack in a piece of flour sack and put it in his saddlebags. Then Corporal Marion told the men to go saddle up. At that time, Lieutenant Hanson appeared. He was apparently going to lead this patrol himself. It was still drizzling rain, and Jim wore his slicker. He saw that about half the men had slickers. The other half had made a slit in the middle of the oilcloth that they slept on for their heads to fit through and wore them like ponchos, so each man had some protection against the rain.

Then with Lieutenant Hanson in the lead they rode down to the river ford and waded their horses across. It was daylight by now, but visibility was reduced because of the rain. On the far side of the river, Lieutenant Hanson dismounted and led his horse up the slippery embankment. Each man followed his example and remounted on the far bank. Jim tripped over his saber a couple of times while climbing the muddy bank. He normally never wore it except when riding. It was constantly hanging on every bush he walked close to. When each trooper gained the far bank and remounted, they spread out in a line and started riding toward the northwest. The only briefing Lieutenant Hanson had given them at camp was that they would ride out in the typical half circle and look for any sign of Yankees. They were located on the right flank of the cavalry force. That put them to the southernmost edge of the line of Confederate cavalry and made it less likely that they'd see the enemy. But the purpose of scouting patrols was to make sure. The cavalry troops were the eyes and ears of the Southern army. They could plunge deep into enemy territory, locate the enemy forces, and determine their strength and position, and if they could see without being seen, they could then withdraw back to Confederate lines and report what they learned to headquarters. This provided valuable information to General Lee in his determination of how to deploy the infantry and artillery. But Jim was only aware that it was a very wet day and a cold and chilly morning even if it was summer.

They spent the morning in misery, shivering, and rain leaking down their necks and getting inside their rain gear in spite of everything. Cap Jones's horse slipped and fell on a slippery spot, but the agile old soldier managed to leap clear, keeping hold of the reins. The horse got up, and Jones led him around a few seconds to make sure that the horse was also uninjured. Then he remounted. Jim didn't like this a bit, and it was obvious no one else did either. Even the ducks stayed home in weather this bad.

At noon Lieutenant Hanson called a halt near some trees, and Zeke took down his saddlebags. He found a spot under a tree that was relatively protected from the rain and pulled some dry tender out of one of his saddlebags. He laid it on a flat rock and sprinkled some powder out of his powder flask. Then he took a piece of flint and an old flat file and held one end of the file against the little pile of powder and struck the file with the flint. The sparks ignited the powder, and Zeke put small pieces of tender on the tiny flame, sheltered it with his hands, blew on it occasionally, added small, dry twigs from his saddlebags when needed, and shortly had a fire going. When it was hot enough, he started picking up pieces of wet deadwood off the ground and putting them on the fire. Steam would spew up from the fire, and you could hear the hissing sound as the moisture evapo rated from the drenched wood, but it didn't put the fire out. Shortly, the log would dry out enough to catch and start burning.

So that's how it's done! observed Jim. Zeke, the old mountain man from West Virginia, could start a fire even in a rainstorm like this. Jim fell to and immediately started gathering little bits of damp deadwood too and started bringing them to the fire. Lieutenant Hanson posted Sam as a lookout beyond the trees to the north. There was an open field to the south in which they could see in three directions, so he decided a second lookout wasn't needed.

Lieutenant Hanson knew that no one could see or smell the fire beyond about fifty yards or so in weather like this, so he raised no objections to Zeke's intentions.

Pretty soon Zeke had pulled a coffeepot from his gear and had a pot of coffee boiling. *Now where did he get the coffee?* Jim wondered. Zeke had just pulled a small bag of coffee out of his saddlebags that he must have saved back or scrounged or foraged from somewhere. The men had already learned to appreciate Zeke's cooking. It seemed like he could make a palatable meal out of anything. The entire patrol was impressed with his display of ingenuity on this wet and dismal day. After they had their ration of hardtack and steaming hot coffee (cavalrymen always carried their tin cups in their saddlebags when mounted), Lieutenant Hanson told Corporal Marion to send someone to the other side of the trees to relieve Sam of his watch so he could come to the fire. Corporal Marion sent Joe to relieve Sam so he could come and enjoy the refreshment of the steaming coffee to go with his hardtack. Sam had already eaten a couple of pieces of hardtack while on watch because he was so hungry, but he was very pleasantly surprised to find a pot of steaming coffee waiting for him back at the fire.

The saber was more in the way even than before. You had to grab the saber and hold it out of the way when you sat down. And it was even more awkward because of the slicker. Jim noticed that Lieutenant Hanson and several other men had taken their sabers off and just leaned them against the log or rock they sat on.

When Jim finished his coffee and while Zeke was stowing his coffeepot in his saddlebags, Lieutenant Hanson said, "It's okay to take your sabers off and tie them to your saddle, men. It would be impossible to get at them in a hurry from under a slicker anyway. I know regulation says to wear your sabers, but I don't think the regulations were written during a rainstorm like this." So Jim gratefully pulled up his slicker, undid his belt, pulled his saber off, and then refastened his belt. He left his revolver where it would be protected from the rain. The metal would rust, and the rain would warp the leather worse than it already was. But the sheath for the saber was made of metal. The sheath would probably rust, but the blade was protected. And it would be where he could get at it in a hurry if need be. So he took the chain that connected the saber sheath to the belt loop and tied it through the hole in the fork of his saddle and then mounted up. The patrol resumed their scouting mission, looking to see any sign of Yankees on this dreary wet, cold day. It was impossible to tell the time of day since there was no sun visible, and Jim wondered what kept them from getting lost, but Lieutenant Hanson seemed to know the way.

Finally, Lieutenant Hanson pulled his horse up and raised his hand and lowered it in the cavalry signal for the patrol to halt. "This is the river, boys," he said, "better dismount and lead your horses down the bank carefully."

It wasn't until Jim was leading Blue Boy down the embankment that he recognized the spot as the river ford opposite from where their troop was camped. He led Blue Boy down to the water's edge, remounted, and waded Blue Boy across. Soon they were at their camp, and Zeke was demonstrating his genius at starting a fire again. Each man unsaddled his own horse, but Joe, Sam, and Jim were detailed to stretch out the long tethering rope over a place where there was grass left and fasten each horse's picket rope to it. When they walked back to the campfire, Corporal Marion told them to go get the corn ration for the horses and feed them. By the time they had finally finished their chores with the horses, supper was ready—corn bread and roast pork and plenty of hot coffee again. Jim had already learned to appreciate the soldier's priority of coffee as the most important staple of any meal. Coffee and tobacco—if they had those two things, they could get by.

CHAPTER 18

Giving Chase

At dawn the next morning, it was still raining. Jim, Joe, and Sam had decided to, all three, sleep on Jim's oilcloth since they had converted theirs both to ponchos the day before. They laid their oilcloth-converted ponchos on top of the blankets in such a fashion as to have the slits they cut to convert them into ponchos not lined up so they would keep the rain out as much as possible. Each of the three rolled up in their blankets and pressed their bodies together in an attempt to stay warm. How could it be so cold in the middle of the summer?

Then reveille sounded as usual, and Jim hated to leave the warmth of his blanket and rise and shine. Maybe you could rise on a morning like this, but you couldn't shine. It took considerable effort just to force himself to a sitting position and pull his boots on. Since Joe and Sam were also trying to pull their boots on without rolling into the mud beside the oilcloth, the necessity to dodge elbows complicated the matter further. Jim wound up getting an elbow in the eye before he finished pulling his boots on. But he finally succeeded. They were hip boots that came up over his knees and halfway up the thigh. He then went looking for his slicker, down near his feet, and put it on. Then as soon as he stood up, he slipped and fell, getting his slicker and boots muddy. Joe and Sam both laughed, and he resisted the impulse to punch both of them.

They finished rolling up their blankets, attempting to keep them as dry as possible. Then Corporal Marion came and told them to hustle with breakfast and saddle up. They had marching orders. The reports from scouting patrols of various units of cavalry had established that the enemy was, indeed, retreating, and the Confederate Army was going to give chase.

Zeke demonstrated his ingenuity again as usual and got a fire going in spite of the rain. Joe and Sam started cutting wet wood to feed the infant fire that Zeke was nourishing and babying. As soon as the fire was far enough along to dry wet wood and start it burning, Zeke started adding the wet logs to the fire cautiously. Monday Mane and John Ashley had gone to the mess wagon to collect their rations. Anyone not busy doing something else were getting their gear together, packing saddlebags, filling canteens, tying gear to their saddles, and getting ready to head out.

Monday and John returned with the boxes of rations, each carrying one large box, and Zeke had the Dutch oven ready and took some of the flour and spread it out on a piece of oilcloth to start kneading the dough for biscuits. While he was starting the biscuits, Cap Jones and Sam started slicing bacon into the skillet. Zeke had put the coffeepot on as soon as he got the fire to going good.

So after a breakfast of bacon and biscuits and coffee, they got ready to start their march. They had hardtack stuffed in their saddlebags for the noon meal and, possibly, the evening meal too and maybe the following morning, for that matter. The ration of hardtack was larger than usual. Jim learned from Zeke that it was a three-day supply. On a march, the cavalry didn't always have time to wait for the mess wagons to catch up every time they stopped for the night, so they packed extra rations just in case.

After breakfast everyone finished packing. All the canteens, sabers, tin cups, and other gear, customarily hanging on the lower tree limbs, were either fastened to their saddles or tossed aside to be left behind. Then they carried their saddles and bridles down to the horses and saddled up. The long picket rope was rolled up and handed to Joe to tie behind his saddle. Jim tied his saber to his saddle on the left side. He decided he wouldn't try to wear it anymore. He wouldn't be likely to draw it unless mounted on his horse anyway. Along with the bulging bedroll tied behind the saddle, canteen tied on the right, and the saber tied on the left, the added burden of the picket rope made Blue Boy look more like a packhorse than a saddle horse, but he was a big horse, weighing around twelve hundred pounds. Jim knew he could handle the extra burden.

Lieutenant Hanson and Sergeant Adams came and formed them up and led them down to the river. When they got clear of the trees and neared the creek bank, it became apparent how much shelter from the rain was afforded by the trees. It was raining right down. It was just starting to get daylight as they forded the river and dismounted to lead their horses up the muddy embankment. Then they remounted and followed Lieutenant Hanson and Sergeant Adams through the trees and fields. They kept to the grassy meadows whenever possible to avoid the slippery and boggy mudholes and headed north—north toward the Potomac and Maryland. They were going to catch the Yankees before they could get away if possible.

Visibility was still greatly reduced by the rain, and in spite of the slicker, Jim got wet. His cavalry cap was wet, and rain ran down his neck. His leather gauntlets were wet. He was grateful for the warmth offered by his cavalry hip boots. They spread out as they rode across the wet meadows, but they'd tend to join up into columns when finding trails through wooded areas. When they came to a fence, if it was of wood, the troopers in the lead would halt, dismount, and dismantle a section of the fence by removing the rails and laying them on the ground. If they came to a stone fence, they had to ride around it.

They kept their horses at a rapid walk and avoided the muddy spots and kept to the solid turf of the grassy places when possible. When it came time for their noon halt, Lieutenant Hanson picked a spot in some trees for their noon camp, as usual, and posted two lookouts to the north of the troop.

Zeke got a fire going in his customary fashion, with the other men helping out by gathering wood, striving to find wood that was as dry as possible. The rain was a light drizzle by this time. After the fire was going, Zeke told everyone to turn in to him their ration of hardtack, and he put a skillet on the fire and some bacon grease that he had saved over from breakfast. Then he soaked the hardtack in some water from his canteen for a few minutes then fried it in the bacon grease. The end result was an excellent-tasting meal. At least it tasted excellent to Jim. But he was hungry enough by then that cooked tree limbs would have tasted good.

Two men were posted to relieve the lookouts so they could grab a bite to eat. After they had eaten, they broke camp and mounted up again to resume their march north.

About middle afternoon, the rain stopped, and the sun came out. After an hour or so it started to get warm. Jim took off his slicker and rolled it up and tied it on the front of his saddle, tucking it behind his canteen and saber. His cavalry cap and the neck and shoulders of his uniform started to dry, and everyone's spirits lifted. The ground was still muddy and slick anyplace there wasn't grass, but it felt great to be dry and warm again for a change.

They continued their march until it was nearly sundown, and they came to a town. Jim learned it was the town of Warrenton. They had made a good twenty miles this day in spite of the rain. They made camp in a wooded area. Soon there was a roaring campfire. Lieutenant Hanson posted the picket watches, and he doubled the watch this night, so Jim was included in the picket set up along the northern edge of town. This meant he had to ride back and forth across a cornfield for an additional two hours before he could go back and enjoy the fire.

But when Private Ashley came and relieved Jim of his watch, he went back to the fire and had a meal of fried hardtack and hot coffee. Greatly refreshed he unrolled his ground cloth and blankets to grab a couple of hours' sleep before having his next turn on watch at 6:00 a.m.

The corporal of the guard came and woke him up a 5:45 a.m., and Jim went to saddle Blue Boy again. He wished he still had a spare horse. But Blue Boy was his only mount, and picket duty didn't require any hard riding. The mess wagon hadn't caught up yet, and there was no corn for the horses. They had to make do on grass and water. Cap Jones was the man he was relieving—Cap, the old soldier. He wasn't really that old—probably, thirty or so—but he seemed old to Jim. Having been through many battles, he seemed even older.

Cap had been in the Army since the start of the war in 1861. When he saw Jim ride down to relieve him, he touched his cap and rode off toward camp and breakfast. Jim had just left the fire and had the usual breakfast of coffee and fried hardtack.

It took three days to reach the Potomac. They stopped on the near side of the river, and picket riders were set up along the river-bank in a fashion similar to what they had done at Brandy Station. Jim was assigned to picket duty starting at eight in the morning following their arrival at the river.

After a night's rest and a skimpy breakfast, Jim assumed his picket watch. He had been riding up and down the riverbank for about thirty minutes or so and looked across the river. He saw a rider in a blue uniform, riding a similar post on the opposite riverbank—a Yankee! He started to spur Blue Boy and then thought better of it and simply rode over to the next picket rider to the east of him, which was actually southeast. The river ran in a southeasterly direction at this point. The other picket rider turned out to be Monday Mane.

"There's a Yankee picket rider on the opposite bank," said Jim, trying to be calm.

"So?" replied Monday.

"Shouldn't we report it?" insisted Jim.

"It's been reported," answered Monday. "No need to worry about it. It's good you're keeping your eyes peeled, though, because there are Yankees on the opposite side of the river."

CHAPTER 19

///

So Jim resumed his picket post and continued to look across the river occasionally. He spotted several Yankees riding along the opposite bank, which was about a quarter of a mile away at that point. So they had caught up with the Yankees already. *Why didn't we cross the river and attack them?* he wondered.

By the time his picket watch was over at 10:00 a.m., he had his answer. The men were breaking camp and were to ride southeast along the riverbank and find a place to cross the river. Lieutenant Hanson told them that if they saw Yankees, to try not to be seen and not to fire unless fired upon. They were essentially on a scouting patrol to look and see if they could find where the main force of the Yankee Army was.

So the men formed up and moved far enough away from the riverbank so that their movements couldn't be spotted from the opposite side. They started riding southeast. At about 2:00 p.m. they came to a place where the river became fairly narrow. It seemed only a hundred yards or so across. Lieutenant Hanson spurred his horse into the water and started swimming him across. The rest of the troop followed. On the opposite bank they spread out, looking for cover from the trees whenever possible and started the "see without being seen" technique of riding up to a grove of trees, riding the horses just to the far side of the trees, and halting to look across any meadows or fields to see if they could detect any movement while still in the cover of the trees themselves.

They made a semicircle on the far side of the river and saw no sign of the enemy by nightfall. They camped near a creek, and since they had scouted the area for miles around with no sign of the enemy, Lieutenant Hanson gave Zeke permission to start a fire.

But first, Zeke and Monday cut some small tree limbs, about a half inch in diameter, and fashioned a couple of fish traps by tying them together into a conically shaped cagelike affair with a second conical cage inserted and lashed just inside the mouth of it. The inside cone had a hole in the middle big enough for a fish to swim through. They set their fish traps in the creek and tied them to a nearby sapling along the shore.

Then they built the fire and brewed coffee, and Zeke cooked the last of their hardtack. Lieutenant Hanson told Sergeant Adams to post three men on watch that night. Jim's first watch was from 10:00 p.m. until midnight.

The following morning there was no reveille. There was to be no unnecessary noise in case the Yankees were nearby. The fish traps did yield a few fish during the night. One trap had five fish, and the other had four—one fish per man, and they were small. It never occurred to them to share with the other messes in the troop. It was assumed they'd do their own foraging. They were permitted a small fire since they were well hidden in the woods. So each man had a breakfast of fried fish and creek water. They had used the last of the coffee the night before. Then they mounted up and resumed their patrol—still no sign of Yankees. They were deep into Maryland by then; in fact, Jim figured they weren't very far from Pennsylvania, because he knew the neck of the state of Maryland wasn't very wide at this point.

After a while Jim paused at the edge of some trees and saw a blue-coated rider on the opposite side of the clearing! He kept perfectly still and waited until he rode out of sight in the trees. He scanned the border of the trees everywhere his eyes could see, very carefully, then reined Blue Boy around and looked for Corporal Marion. He saw him about fifty yards away. He rode up to him.

"I saw a Yankee," he whispered.

"Where?" Corporal Marion whispered back.

"Over there, on the opposite side of the meadow, riding that way," he pointed to the north first, then to the west when he indicated the direction he was riding.

"Go tell Lieutenant Hanson."

"Where is he?" queried Jim.

"About a quarter of a mile that way," answered Marion.

Jim reined Blue Boy around and spurred him in the indicated direction. He rode through several groves of trees and saw several riders he knew were from the troop, then he saw the guidon bearer, Private Jack O'Henry, holding the Confederate flag above his horse's head. He knew that Lieutenant Hanson would be somewhere near the guidon bearer. Then he saw Lieutenant Hanson. He rode up to him.

"I just saw a Yankee, sir," Jim still whispered.

"Where?" asked Lieutenant Hanson, not in a whisper, but in a normal tone of voice.

"Over there, sir," Jim answered.

"Take me to where you saw him."

"Yes, sir," he replied and reined his horse around and galloped away. Lieutenant Hanson spurred his horse to keep up, and the guidon bearer did likewise. Jim led Lieutenant Hanson to the place where he saw the Yankee cavalryman. He answered the lieutenant's questions pertaining to exactly where he was when he saw him, which direction he was riding, and how fast. He was simply walking his horse in a westerly direction, Jim explained.

Corporal Marion had ridden up when he saw Lieutenant Hanson arrive.

"Corporal Marion, take Bennett and another man, and scout that area, and determine what's over there. Report back to me here. Take a count of men, horses, wagons, anything you see. Be back here in two hours or less with your report. We'll wait here for two hours. Don't be seen. Don't fire unless fired upon. If you're not back in two hours, I'll assume you're not coming and take whatever action seems necessary. Any questions?"

"No, sir," answered Corporal Marion and yanked his head to Joe to follow him and Jim.

"You take the lead, Bennett," Marion ordered, "you're the only one who saw him."

"Okay," replied Jim. He was finally learning not to call non-commissioned officers *sir*, but it still didn't seem natural to him.

He first scanned the open area beyond the thin row of trees where their horses were standing. Then he led them into the open area. He spurred Blue Boy into a gallop to get across the open area as fast as possible. The horses' hooves made very little sound on the damp turf. They reached the place where Jim saw the Yankee cavalryman, and then Jim reined up. He looked at the ground. Sure enough, there were the tracks of a horse on places near the row of trees where there was no grass. Jim followed the tracks through the next line of trees and halted at the westerly edge to scan the next meadow before crossing it. When he was sure he saw nothing moving, he galloped Blue Boy across that meadow too, with Marion and Joe following close behind him. He halted at the next row of trees and looked for tracks the same way. It was like following deer tracks when he was a boy on deer-hunting trips with his father.

But he knew you never got into shooting position following deer tracks. If you were following deer tracks in snow or after a rain so you could tell if they were fresh, but before you got close enough to see him, he would have heard you and would start looking for the next county. And a deer could run faster through the brush than a man. He could run faster through the brush than a man on horseback too.

So the reason he was following tracks was just to determine the actual direction the Yankee cavalryman was following. After riding cautiously through several clumps of trees and galloping quickly over several open fields, he decided the direction was actually westerly. He didn't want to surprise the Yankees; he just wanted to find out how many they were, and were they all cavalry? Did they have any infantry with them or any artillery?

Then while pausing to scan an open meadow on the edge of one of the groves of trees, Jim spotted him again. He pointed silently and looked at Marion. Marion looked in the direction Jim pointed and nodded. Jim made the word *wait* with his lips, but did so silently, and Marion understood. Jim scanned the clearing again to make sure the one Yankee was the only rider in the clearing. Then when the Yankee rider disappeared in the trees, Jim whispered to Marion to wait a little longer to make sure they weren't heard. Then after a few minutes, Jim pulled Blue Boy back toward the easterly edge of the trees and started skirting the line of trees to the north. Since he seemed to know what he was doing, Marion and Joe followed him. After riding northward, maybe a hundred and fifty yards, Jim pointed down to the ground at a horse track heading west into the trees—So a second cavalryman and heading the same direction too! In fact, further investigation showed that more than one horse had traveled west along this route. There had been either several horses traveling together or maybe just traveling the approximate same route at intervals. Then Jim yanked his head in a northward direction as if to say, "Come on, and I'll show you more."

Then they came to a road with fresh wagon wheel ruts and many, many mule tracks—uh-huh, a wagon train—most likely, a supply train. So the cavalrymen were just a screen for the supply train! Jim led them a hundred yards or so farther north beyond the road, and they found another set of horse tracks heading westerly. It also appeared that more than one horse had traveled along that path. They rode on another half mile or so and saw no more tracks. That meant no horses had traveled by there since the recent rain.

So just by reading the sign, they had figured out that it was a wagon train, escorted by cavalry and heading westerly. It appeared to be a supply train intended for the Union Army!

But Lieutenant Hanson's orders were to get a count of men, horses, wagons, equipment, etc. So Jim led them westerly, galloping quickly across each open meadow and walking cautiously through each grove of trees they came to. He knew the enemy cavalrymen would match the speed of the wagons, so they could outdistance them easily. When Jim thought they had time to get slightly ahead of the wagon train, he headed southward, staying as hidden as possible along the edge of a wooded spot.

When they got within about fifty yards or so to the road, they hid in a clump of trees and held perfectly still. Shortly, they heard the cursing and yelling and whip popping of the mule skinners. Then after a few more minutes they rolled into sight. The drivers were cursing the mules and cursing the mud, the war, and everything else in general. It was a train of covered wagons, each manned by a driver and a guard, the guard holding a musket and sitting on the left side. The three men in gray barely dared to breathe while the wagon train rolled past. They knew they were hidden from the road and also from the path the northern cavalry rider would probably travel. Jim had made sure they rode across a meadow with solid-enough turf not to show their tracks when they intersected the intended path of the northern edge of the cavalry screen.

So the three scouts counted the wagons as they drove by. They'd have to estimate the number of the cavalry escort since they were keeping just out of sight in the woods on either side of the road. But they'd have an accurate count of the wagons. After the last wagon had passed, Jim thought, *Twelve wagons*. But now they still had to evade the rear guard of the cavalry screen. Jim motioned to Marion and Joe to head back northward, the direction in which they came. They rode back north along the same row of trees on the same solid turf they had used coming down near the road. When they were out beyond the picket line, they found another clump of trees to hide in to wait for the cavalry picket to ride by. Sure enough, in a few minutes a blue-coated rider rode cautiously by, looking all around as he rode. Then a hundred yards or so behind him came another horseman. They waited a little longer, and as Jim expected, there was another one. Shortly thereafter another bluecoat was seen riding just on the other side of the road. So this was probably the rear guard of the screen. They waited a few more minutes to make sure they weren't detected and reined their horses around toward the east.

Now the main project was to get back to their own troop without being detected. It would be much better if the men in the wagon train didn't know that there were Confederate forces in the area and especially important that they not know they had been seen by these same Rebel forces.

The three gray-coated riders used the same tactic, riding back from whence they came as they had while looking for the Union force. They still paused while still in the trees to scan each meadow carefully before running the risk of being seen. And once they started across an area, they went at a swift gallop to minimize the amount of time exposed while in the open. Then they saw a gray-coated rider and recognized him as a picket guard.

He challenged them, and Marion gave them the countersign and asked him where Lieutenant Hanson was. The picket guard pointed back toward a clump of trees. They rode up and found Lieutenant Hanson and gave him their report.

CHAPTER 20

Advancing

After they gave their report to Lieutenant Hanson, Corporal Marion was sent back to the troop. Lieutenant Hanson decided to take Jim and Joe with him to report to Captain Wilson, the troop commander. Lieutenant Hanson tightened the cinch on his horse, which was tethered nearby. He had removed the bit from his mouth so he could graze. He put the bit back in his mouth and mounted up. Jim and Joe climbed back on their horses and followed Lieutenant Hanson to Captain Wilson's tent. All three dismounted when they arrived, and Lieutenant Hanson saluted when he saw Captain Wilson. Jim and Joe did likewise. Captain Wilson returned their salutes. Jim had never met Captain Wilson face-to-face before. He had only seen him while drilling the troop or when they were marching as a troop, so he, at least, recognized him.

"Your scouts have returned?" Captain Wilson said to Lieutenant Hanson expectantly.

"Yes, sir," answered Lieutenant Hanson. "I brought them to give you the account of what they saw firsthand in case you have any questions to ask them."

"Good," said Captain Wilson. "And?" He looked at both Jim and Joe as if to let them know either of them could speak as they wished. Jim immediately started explaining everything they saw.

"Show me where they were on the map." Captain Wilson pointed to a map he had set up on a tripod just outside his tent. Jim looked at it and saw an *X* drawn in pencil just north of the Potomac River.

"Is this where we are?" he asked, pointing at the *X*.

"That's where we are," Captain Wilson answered. Then Jim looked at the legend to determine the scale of the map. After estimating the distance they traveled that morning to be about ten miles and after locating the road on the map in the general area, he located the approximate position of the wagon train at the time they saw them.

"Here," he said while placing his finger on the map.

"And about how fast were they traveling?" queried the captain.

"Because of the mud and all, I'd estimate they weren't doing more than about two miles an hour."

"Any other sign of enemy forces in the area?" Captain Wilson asked.

"No," replied Jim. "And we'd have seen their tracks because of the recent rain if there had been."

Reports from other scouts had affirmed that there was no sign of any other enemy forces within ten miles of the riverbank in a direction almost parallel to that the wagon train had been traveling.

Captain Wilson turned to his orderly sergeant nearby. "Pass the word that we march in two hours. Fires are allowed to cook rations, but tell everyone to hurry." He then turned to Lieutenant Hanson. "I'm going to borrow these two men from you to use as scouts on this mission, Lieutenant." A look of chagrin came upon Lieutenant Hanson's face. "Oh, you'll get them back later. But I might take them from you again another time." Then he turned to Jim and Joe and said, "Report back to your troop for rations, and be back here in two hours." Then after a pause he added, "Dismissed."

Lieutenant Hanson saluted again, and Jim and Joe followed his example. Then they mounted their horses and rode back to where their troop had camped. They already saw the smoke of campfires spaced out along the line of trees ahead of them. The men apparently had their campfires ready and were just waiting for the word to start them. But Jim wondered what they needed fires for. There was no food. Or had the mess wagons caught up with them by now? He didn't see how that was possible as fast as they had been traveling.

As they rode closer, they caught the smell of meat cooking. Well, they obviously had gotten some rations from somewhere. As they rode by several of the campfires, they saw the men rigging what looked like skinned squirrels and rabbits and other small game over spits to broil. So the other men had been out hunting while he and Joe had been out scouting. He learned later the squirrels and rabbits had been captured in snares to avoid noise. As they arrived at C Troop, they smelled pork roasting. Then they saw quarters of a good-sized pig broiling over the fire! As hungry as they were, this was really good news. Jim had become a very firm believer of the adage that "an army marches on its stomach." He didn't like being hungry. And right now he was starving, especially after he started smelling the meat cooking.

After they loosened their cinches and tethered the horses so they could graze during the noontime, they learned the story behind the pig. It appeared that Monday had been put in charge of the mess detail in Corporal Marion's absence and had decided to go out foraging with a couple other men. They had come upon this stray pig. Now Monday could tell that the pig had lost its way. He obviously couldn't find his way home. Now a pig without a home had no one to feed it. This would result in a slow death by starvation for the poor pig. So Monday decided, the humane thing to do was put the pig out of its misery. Since they were under orders not to fire a shot, he decided he'd best do it with his saber, so he rode his horse up to the pig and stabbed it in the neck just to the side of its neck bone where he knew the sword would cut through the jugular vein. The pig squealed when first struck and starting trying to run away, but the other two riders appeared then to turn the pig and herd it back in the direction of camp. The pig bled to death quietly on the walk back. Since they had no means of scalding the pig, scraping it was out of the question, so they just field dressed him and skinned him out. Then they quartered the carcass and got it ready to cook just in case they got permission to start a fire.

Fresh pork was all they had for lunch, but it tasted like a gourmet meal to the starving men. Each man got a portion of meat bigger than he could eat. They ate all they could, and each man wrapped what he had left in a piece of flour sack or something and stowed it in his saddlebags. They all anticipated a camp without campfires that night with a resulting cold supper. But at least they'd *have* supper.

After eating, Joe and Jim tightened their cinches and explained their orders to report back to troop headquarters to Corporal Marion, who merely nodded. They could tell he was a little jealous that he wasn't to come too.

When Jim and Joe showed up at the spot where Captain Wilson's tent had been, they found the tent had been already struck, and all preparations had been made to start their march. Captain Wilson gave them their briefing. He explained that Lieutenant Barry would lead a detail to be the advance screen and introduced them to Lieutenant Barry. Lieutenant Barry was blue-eyed, about 5'8" in height, with medium build and dark-brown hair. Captain Wilson told them they were to ride ahead as far as necessary to locate the enemy wagon train and ride back and report to Lieutenant Barry any changes in the train's speed or direction or anything else pertinent.

So Jim and Joe rode off toward the west, riding rapidly across meadows and open fields and going cautiously through trees as usual, keeping their eyes peeled at all times. They looked for tracks along each grove they came to and, in general, were alert for any sign of anyone having been in the area before the rain.

They headed in a northwesterly direction at the point where Jim thought the wagon train would probably be by the time they reached it. Jim figured the wagons could probably make about another ten miles or so by nightfall in spite of the mud the way they were going. It was about 4:00 p.m. when they spotted fresh horse tracks a couple of hundred yards from the road. Jim was pretty sure it was one of the enemy cavalry riders in the screen around the wagon train. A half an hour of careful stalking verified this fact. The two young Rebels cautiously withdrew, and when they knew there was no danger of discovery, they rode as fast as they could back to where they expected Lieutenant Barry to be. It only took about an hour and a half to locate the advance screen of the advancing cavalry troop. Joe spotted Lieutenant Barry and rode up to him.

He reported to Lieutenant Barry what he saw, and Lieutenant Barry sent a mounted courier back to relay this information to Captain Wilson. Jim and Joe both rode alongside Lieutenant Barry until the courier returned with Captain Wilson's reply. Lieutenant Barry read the message the courier handed him silently and told Jim to ride ahead again with Joe and see where the wagon train would stop for the night and to report this intelligence back to him as soon as possible.

Since Joe and Jim knew where the wagon train was by now, it and their own cavalry troop were obviously traveling enough faster to gain on them. It only took about an hour to locate the train again. They shadowed the train, being careful not to be spotted, until they stopped and made camp for the night. It was almost sundown when they rode back and found Lieutenant Barry again to notify him of this information. He and Joe found Captain Wilson riding with the advance screen when they arrived, so they were able to give their report directly to him. Captain Wilson thanked them and told them they were dismissed.

So they fell back with their almost-exhausted horses, glad it was nearly time to stop and camp. When they arrived back to the troop, everyone was full of questions. Where was the wagon train? Would they attack? When? Jim was noncommittal as was Joe. They tried to pacify everyone that they'd have to do what the troop commander decided, whatever that was. But everyone knew the wagon train was nearby, and it was obvious to everyone that they were maneuvering into position to attack.

They continued their march for a while after dark, the hunger pangs steadily growing worse, and the fatigue they felt was probably more from lack of nourishment than the rigors of the march though Joe and Jim had done quite a bit of hard riding this day. Jim hoped Blue Boy could keep going till time to stop. It was possible to literally ride a horse to death, and Blue Boy deserved better than that.

They finally halted, and the captain's orderly sergeant came around and told everyone to pitch a camp with no fires. They'd roust out at dawn without bugles or any excessive noise. So the men gratefully dismounted, tethered their horses where they could graze, and rolled up in their blankets. They had managed to water the horses at one of the last creeks they crossed, so they only needed a chance to graze and rest up. The men ate the cold leftovers from lunch. Then they unrolled their bedrolls and were instantly asleep except the ones posted on watch. By some stroke of luck, neither Jim nor Joe were chosen for a watch this night, and they were able to sleep the night through. They slept like children—honest, deep sleep that could only come as the result of prolonged vigorous activity.

CHAPTER 21

Attack!

Jim woke up when someone shook him. It was still dark—must have been his imagination. He readjusted his head on the saddle he used for a pillow and started to drop off to sleep again. Then someone shook him again. It was Corporal Marion. "Get up, and get your horse saddled. It's time to move out."

"In the middle of the night?"

"Troop commander's orders. We saddle up and move out now."

So Jim pulled on his boots and fastened his belt and gun about his waist. Then he put on his cavalry cap, rolled up his blankets, and went and saddled Blue Boy. Jim was in the advance screen of riders as they rode to find the wagon train. Lieutenant Hanson briefed the patrol before they started out and gave them detailed instructions about what to do once the attack started. So they were going to attack the wagon train now! Jim felt a surge of excitement. Then Lieutenant Hanson told Jim to take the lead and head for the spot where the enemy wagons had camped the night before.

Shortly after daylight, Jim saw Joe, who was a couple of hundred yards to his right, pull up and raise his arm, then point. He was pointing at a spot hidden from Jim's view by some trees, but Jim knew that Joe had spotted one of the enemy pickets. So Jim cautiously threaded his way through a dense grove of trees to have a look himself. He saw a blue-coated rider, not fifty yards ahead of him—obviously, not the same one whom Joe saw. He waited until the Yankee rider rode out of sight beyond some trees then he withdrew back south of the grove and gave Joe a signal similar to the one he had received from him a few minutes before. Joe waved in acknowledgment. Jim and Joe both cautiously moved their horses back away from the road and from the direction they knew was toward their own approaching cavalry troop. Jim found Lieutenant Hanson and gave him his report.

Lieutenant Hanson sent a mounted courier to relay Jim's report back to the troop commander, and in the meantime, the patrol moved west, paralleling the road. Jim pulled the carbine from his saddle boot and reprimed the flashpan. As they rode, they came to a place where the road turned toward the north with dense brush on both sides of the muddy ruts. The patrol crossed the road at this point, out of sight of the wagon train pickets. The plan was for the patrol to attack from north of the road while other elements from the troop attacked from the southwest and southeast. But first each man was to get his carbine sights on one of the picket riders. A whiff of morning air brought with it the smell of coffee and bacon frying. It made Jim feel half crazed with hunger. *But for now, just keep your attention on the task at hand,* he told himself.

Jim rode down to what looked like the picket rider who was farthest east on the north side of the road. Then from the cover of some trees, he held his carbine on the man's blue coat, waiting for the signal to fire. It didn't come right away, and Jim's arms tired after a couple of minutes. He leaned his gun down against the pommel of his saddle for a moment. The Yankee rider was riding slowly west-ward, gradually coming closer to Jim as he rode. He was maybe fifty yards away by now.

Then Jim heard the signal to fire—three quick shots from across the road! The picket rider immediately reached for the carbine in his saddle boot, but he never finished pulling it out. Jim's bullet caught him with his carbine half out of the boot. The soldier fell from his saddle to the ground. Jim immediately sheathed his carbine and undid the flap on his revolver. *Damn,* he thought, *I should have already done that.* But he got his revolver out. He didn't intend to try to take the time to reload the carbine every time he fired, not when he had a repeat-action arm right on his hip. And a six-gun was all you needed for close quarters like this. So six-gun in hand, Jim charged the train. Men were running from the campfires in all directions, grabbing up their rifles where they were stacked, some of them pulling handguns out of their belt. Jim pulled Blue Boy to a halt and found a target for his Colt .45 and fired. It misfired! He pulled the hammer back and squeezed the trigger again. It fired this time. The rider in blue fell. Then he saw a Yankee rider riding toward him from the west, firing at a full gallop as he rode. Two bullets whizzed by Jim's ear. He pulled up his gun and held the sights just above the horse's neck at the center of the blue body and fired. He couldn't miss. The Yankee was within twenty yards. But you couldn't hit the broad side of the barn from a galloping horse. Apparently, no one had told the Yankee that. Jim then saw a man standing on the ground, pointing a musket at him. He reined Blue Boy to the side to distract the Yankee's aim and put the front sight of the revolver in the middle of the blue target and fired just as he felt a bullet whiz by his ear. He saw the Yankee flinch and fall when Jim's bullet struck him. There were plenty of targets for several minutes, and he kept firing. Then his gun clicked empty. He reined Blue Boy into the nearby trees and hid in the thick brush while he pulled his spare cylinder out of his bullet pouch. Then he changed out the cylinders as quickly as he could and rode back toward the shooting and yelling. He saw a blue-coated soldier holding a rifle to his shoulder, aiming at one of the other Rebel cavalrymen. Jim immediately brought up his gun and fired. It hit the Union soldier in the shoulder and spun him around. Jim quickly moved Blue Boy to another spot while looking for another target. Then he saw a Yankee throw down his gun and raise his hands in the air.

Within seconds the firing stopped, and all the Yankee soldiers still surviving were standing with their arms high above their heads. But there were bodies lying everywhere, blue intermixed with gray.

The prisoners were all disarmed and marched off south of the road a ways where they were held under guard. The wounded were cared for as well as was possible. It was discovered that one of the prisoners was an Army surgeon and that he had medical supplies in one of the wagons. He was quickly removed from the other prisoners and put to work caring for the wounded.

As for the breakfast the Union soldiers were cooking, well, what wasn't kicked over or otherwise spilled during the fighting was immediately consumed by the first hand that grabbed hold of it. Within minutes after the last shot was fired, the bacon and biscuits had all disappeared from the Dutch ovens and skillets.

Then the men started going through the wagons. They found cured hams, canned sardines, and peaches as well as an abundance of flour, cornmeal, coffee, sugar, tea, and several barrels of white Army beans!

Captain Wilson and all three lieutenants arrived very quickly to restore order, but not until each man had filled his pockets and any spare room he had in his saddlebags with various foodstuffs.

Since the men hadn't eaten since the night before, they were permitted to prepare breakfast, now that adequate rations were available. They had orders to also feed the prisoners and provide them with the same rations as that of the Confederate soldiers. Since the attack was initiated while the Union soldiers were still cooking breakfast, it was assumed that none of the Federal soldiers had managed to have breakfast yet. So cooking utensils, the tools needed to cut wood to start a fire, and rations were carried down to the prisoners, so they cooked breakfast for themselves for the second time that morning.

The tally for the raid was twelve wagons, mostly hauling food supplies intended for the Union Army, but including two wagons hauling ammunition only. Also captured were seventy-two mules and twenty horses. There were ten Union soldiers killed and fifteen wounded, the remaining seventeen taken prisoner. Confederate losses were three men killed and eight wounded.

When Corporal Marion took roll, it was learned that Private Ashley was killed outright with a round ball in the head and that Monday Mane and Sam Blake were both wounded. Monday had a round ball in the side of the chest that broke one rib, but missed the heart and lungs. He'd be evacuated, but was expected to pull through. Sam had a minor flesh wound on his left bicep. He refused to let the surgeon look at it. He was afraid he'd want to amputate his arm. But Joe bandaged it for him well enough. He sat with a cup of coffee in his hand and a plate of bacon and biscuits in his lap and worked on figuring out how to eat with one hand.

But bacon and biscuits were intended just for appetizers. Cured hams were being broiled over every campfire. Cans of peaches were opened and devoured. They found one wagon was full of corn for the horses. So soldiers that had feed bags were feeding a generous helping of corn to their horses so they could join in the banquet too.

Somebody found several cases of cigars in one of the wagons, so after the men had stuffed themselves till their bellies hurt with the delicious food, they each lit up a Havana cigar to smoke with their after-dinner coffee. Well, it was actually after-breakfast coffee.

Then Jim thought of his weapons. He hadn't reloaded yet! This could be fatal if there were other Yankees in the area! Then he thought about how they hadn't been cleaned in several days as well. So he put a pot of water on the fire to heat and remembered the one misfire he had with his six-gun. He got the cylinder out of his ball pouch and checked the primer cap. The primer cap had fired okay, so that wasn't the problem. Corporal Marion saw what he was doing and remembered to tell the rest of the men to look to their weapons too. So everyone set out to clean and reload their carbines and six-guns.

Jim got up from the fire and laid his cigar on a rock and moved away from it to troubleshoot the problem with the misfired chamber in the revolver cylinder. He borrowed a nipple wrench from Corporal Marion and removed the nipple for that chamber. He found out it was clogged. He took the ramrod from his carbine and put it in the cylinder and poked the powder and ball through, and Corporal Marion, as if he knew what would be his next problem, handed him a piece of thin wire to clear the obstruction in the nipple with. The water was hot by this time, so Jim went over to the fire and dipped his tin cup full of the hot water and, using some of the soap he got from his saddlebags, washed the cylinder clean, taking care to clean each chamber and each of the other nipple holes. He took the other cylinder out of his revolver and found only one chamber that wasn't fired. For the sake of thoroughness he took the nipple out of it, poked the powder and ball through, and cleaned it in the same way. Then he cleaned the bore of the revolver with his ramrod and a piece of old rag, which Marion kept a supply of for this purpose. He wiped it dry and greased it good with pork grease. Then he reloaded one cylinder with six shots and put it in his round-ball pouch. He loaded five chambers of the other cylinder and placed it in the gun. Then he holstered his six-gun, finished cleaning and oiling his carbine, reloaded it, and put it back in his saddle boot. Only then did he return to the tree stump where he'd left the cigar. It had gone out. He lit it again and resumed puffing on it. *Excellent tobacco!* he thought. *Excellent!*

The next order of the day was to evacuate the wounded since the surgeon had done all he could for them for the moment, and they had all been fed—at least, the ones who were able to eat.

There were eighteen men, including both Union and Confederates, wounded severely enough that it was decided to evacuate them south to the Potomac to a spot where a field hospital could be established. One of the wagons included medical supplies in its cargo. Three of the wagons were converted into ambulance wagons, and the wounded loaded and prepared for travel. The walking wounded were permitted to ride their horses since each soldier owned his mount, or if his horse had been killed, he would ride in one of the wagons in front, next to the driver. There had been three horses killed by stray bullets during the fray. Private Sam Blake was one of the men who, with his arm in a sling, mounted his horse and waved goodbye and started off with the wagons. He would serve as part of the cavalry screen for the ambulance wagons while traveling back toward the river.

The next task at hand was to bury the dead. It was decided to assign this task to the prisoners. Jim found himself appointed to guard duty during the supervision of this project. Graves were dug individually for each of the thirteen men slain, with a headboard made from a slab of pine with the man's name, rank, and unit engraved on it with a knife. Jim stood on the perimeter of the men in blue, his carbine at the ready, along with about a dozen other Confederate guards, until the graves were dug. Four of the prisoners were assigned the task of preparing the headboards.

After the graves were dug and the headboards ready, the troop chaplain read the funeral service from an old, worn Bible, then said a prayer for the brave men whose careers had ended so abruptly and violently. Then the slain soldiers were lowered into the graves. A nine-gun salute would have been customary, but since the presence of the enemy in the area was unknown, the deceased were lowered into the graves silently.

Then the prisoners were marched south, under guard, toward the river, and Captain Wilson ordered D Troop to prepare to march. Three of the wagons loaded with food were brought along to serve as mess wagons for the troop, and another wagon loaded with guns, ammunition, and other supplies was included as D Troop resumed their march north. Jim found himself on the right flank, a little toward the rear of the point. It was apparent that the troop commander wanted to give some of the other men in the troop a chance to get their share of glory. Jim didn't mind. His belly was full, Blue Boy had a good bait of corn at noon, and his guns were cleaned, oiled, and loaded. And the sun was shining—a little hot, but Jim decided he could stand the heat better than the wet, cold, and mucky rain.

Jim would frequently see gray-coated riders behind him on either side. They'd be men he didn't recognize. But he knew the entire cavalry corps was on the march. So he concluded that they were other troops from the squadron that had crossed the river and, apparently, caught up with them during the delay caused by their raid on the Yankee wagon train.

Gettysburg!

They continued their march north. Jim found out they were in Pennsylvania when he learned they had passed by the town of Hanover. They were briefed to be very polite to the civilian population and to refrain from stealing any crops or livestock. The purpose of the war was not to spread terrorism among the civilian population, but to demonstrate to a tyrannical government that state's rights still reigned supreme. The sovereignty of the states was the basis of the original constitution of the United States when independence was won from Great Britain. In fact every Rebel soldier looked upon the war as just a fight for their independence all over again, just like in the previous century. The federal government had gotten so very like the British government that the colonies had rebelled against eighty-six years previously that it was normal for history to repeat itself.

But where was the main force of the Union Army? Several wagon trains had been captured by other regiments of the cavalry corps, Jim had heard, but their purpose for being so deep in enemy territory was to find the Yankee Army and whip them once and for all so they'd be receptive to terms of peace, which would recognize the independence of the seceding states. But so far supply trains escorted by cavalry were the only enemy forces they had seen.

On July 1, they reached the town of Carlisle, which Jim knew was deep into Pennsylvania, and had camped outside town for the night. Jim had heard that instead of going farther north, there was talk that they'd camp there for a while and send out scouting patrols in all directions to see if the Yankee Army could be found. Jim was on the midnight-to-2:00 a.m. picket watch that night when the corporal of the guard rode out and told him that they were going to march. A courier had arrived and notified General Stuart that the enemy was at Gettysburg. This intelligence had actually arrived before nightfall, but General Stuart knew they'd kill the horses if they didn't stop for at least a brief rest after the day's march. And it was a black night. The moon would rise at about 2:00 a.m. and would give them enough light to resume their march.

So when Jim got the word from the corporal of the guard, he hurried Blue Boy back to camp and helped with the preparations to move out. There weren't many preparations to make since they had just made camp a few hours earlier. They mainly just drew some hardtack for marching rations, filled their canteens at the creek, and formed up.

Blue Boy had been in excellent shape when they had first left Brandy Station. But he was starting to look rather gaunt now. While the daily ration of corn he had received had helped somewhat since they had captured the wagon train, the long daily marches would kill any horse eventually, and Jim knew it. But while Blue Boy had obviously lost a considerable amount of weight, he had had a good feed of corn the night before and was still full of spirit and vigor. But Jim was tired—tired and sleepy. He had expected to grab two or three hours' sleep when he got off watch, and now it was obvious that he'd be marching all night.

As soon as the moon rose, they started out. Since they had a known destination, they were now marching as a regiment, and there was a stretch of nothing but open fields when they left Carlisle and headed south. So Jim had the feeling of marching in a sea of mounted riders again. In any direction he could see nothing but horses, the reflection of the gray uniforms and cavalry caps moving in rhythm with their horses. And since horses usually didn't learn to keep in step, the movement of the caps up and down had a random kind of rippling effect to it. Jim had the feeling again he remembered so well from Brandy Station of being a single cell in a huge organism. And a surge of pride and excitement went through him as this feeling swept over him. He kept his saber tied to his saddle, but he'd reach over and feel of the haft occasionally to make sure where it was. He didn't want to fumble for it when the order came to draw sabers.

At sunup they continued their march, walking their horses rapidly. They kept their horses at a walk to save their energy. They knew they'd need it when they arrived at their destination. Jim wondered if they'd be going up against cavalry again or infantry. He had been briefed that if they went against infantry, their tactics would be different. A cavalry charge against infantry wasn't that effective because the infantrymen weren't going to stand still while you rode up to them, brandishing a saber. They'd simply fire, volley after volley, into the charging cavalrymen, from a position of cover if possible. While Jim had never fought infantrymen from horseback, he had been instructed by Lieutenant Hanson in one of their briefings on how to do it. You could still use your horse to enjoy the advantage of rapid movement. You moved into position to fire, halted your horse, picked out a target, fired, reloaded as rapidly as possible, moved to a new location if it seemed tactically beneficial to do so, and fired again. If you were within six-gun range, you used your revolver instead so you could have the added benefit of repeat action against the muzzle-loading muskets the infantrymen used. But the whole thing seemed like an awkward way to fight a battle to Jim. He thought it would be better to just swoop down on them with revolvers and shoot as many of them as you could and then withdraw quickly to change cylinders and/or reload as necessary and then charge them again. When he suggested that to Lieutenant Hanson, the lieutenant explained that such a tactic would be feasible only if you were charging from cover such as a grove of trees. If you had to attack in the open, you'd just have to reload while under fire from the enemy. But the enemy had to reload too. Whoever got there "fustis with the mostis" and fought the hardest was the side that would win.

They continued their march until nearly noon. When they crossed a creek that had enough water in it, they'd stop long enough to water their horses and fill their canteens. At noon a halt was called to give the horses an hour's rest. The men were allowed to build fires to boil coffee, but they had only the rations that each man carried along with him, which was mostly hardtack.

Jim took some corn he had tied in a burlap bag behind his saddle and put his feed bag on Blue Boy during their halt. He figured his mount needed all the energy he could get.

Then after an hour's rest they resumed their march south. At about 2:00 p.m. they approached the town of Biglerville. At 4:00 p.m. they started seeing units of Confederate soldiers. Then Jim saw the smoke and could hear the gunfire from the distance over toward where he imagined the town of Gettysburg to be. Would they be in battle by nightfall? He wondered. A thrill of excitement surged through him, and he felt for his saber again. Then he reached down and felt for his carbine and touched his revolver at his side probably for the fifteenth time that day. Then the order came to make camp. It was about 5:00 p.m. They made camp toward the west and a little of south of Gettysburg. It appeared that most of the fighting for the day was over, and a temporary cease-fire had been tacitly agreed on, and ambulance wagons were busy trying to clear as many of the wounded from the field as possible before nightfall.

CHAPTER 23

The mess wagons caught up with them in time to draw rations for supper. Zeke was at his best as usual, but in spite of having had skimpy rations all day long, no one had an appetite. They still filled up their plates, but most of the men just picked at their food. Jim was no exception. He had a jittery feeling in his belly that he couldn't understand. Always before he had only felt excitement at the brink of battle. At Brandy Station Jim had had no advanced warning of the battle. The Yankees launched a surprise attack at dawn. The capture of the Yankee wagon train had only been planned the night before, and since the Confederates had the Yankee escort so badly outnumbered, it would actually be classified more as a raid than even a skirmish. But he had known now for two weeks that they were seeking out the enemy. He had known all day that the whereabouts of the enemy had been located and that they were marching to battle. Jim was just in the process of learning that going into battle had a different effect on a soldier if he had a day or two to think about it.

Jim rolled up in his blankets and couldn't sleep. He was actually glad when time for his picket watch arrived at 2:00 a.m. and gave him an excuse to get up and do something other than lie in his blankets and try not to think.

The moon was up when the corporal of the guard came by and told him it was time for him to go on watch. He went and saddled Blue Boy and assumed his picket post. He was relieving Joe Williams. When he assumed his watch, in the moonlight he could see a blue-coated soldier not two hundred yards' distance to the northeast! He was not mounted, so he was obviously infantry instead of cavalry. Since he had other mounted pickets on either side of him not fifty yards away, he didn't walk Blue Boy, but mainly allowed him to stand

and rest his weary bones. Jim still had the jittery feeling, but he also had part of the feeling of excitement return, which offset the jittery feeling to a degree and strangely had a calming effect.

When he was relieved at 4:00 a.m., he returned to his blankets and actually went to sleep, but only to be awakened again at 6:00 a.m. Still, two hours of sleep refreshed him a noticeable amount, and he found himself craving a cup of coffee. His appetite still had not returned completely, but he made himself eat two of Zeke's hot biscuits and a couple of pieces of bacon.

Then the order came to check their weapons and saddle up. The bugle wasn't used because they didn't want to give the enemy any advanced warning of their intentions. Then they mounted and formed up. They started riding to the northwest and obviously skirting the enemy lines along Culp's Hill. So they were going to attack on the flank. Then they were hidden from the enemy by the trees, obviously maneuvering to the enemy's right flank. But then they kept riding. Why, they were moving around to the enemy's rear! Jim could see the rise of Culp's Hill over to his right, and they were apparently moving around to the north side of the hill. So they were going to attack the right flank from the enemy's rear while the infantry attacked the enemy's front line. The tactics appeared sound to Jim. He didn't see how the enemy could avoid being crushed by being hit from front, rear, and on the flank at the same time.

Then they were in position to attack. The disadvantage was, they had to cross an open field at the beginning of the charge, and the enemy had the advantage of cover from the trees that dotted Culp's Hill. And Jim didn't even know if they were going against cavalry or infantry. But the order came to draw sabers, so he drew out his saber and held it at the ready. The Confederate Calvary had cover of some trees at the moment, but the open field they had to cross was at least a quarter of a mile. *Why sabers?* Jim thought. *Why not start with carbines?* Orders were orders, but he couldn't see how sabers were going to help unless they had a cavalry charge from the enemy to repulse.

Then they were just waiting. He wondered what they were waiting for. Why didn't someone give the order to attack? There was just waiting and more waiting. Then he heard Lieutenant Hanson's voice off to his left.

"When you hear the cannon barrage start, hold your ground. We start our attack when the infantry starts up Cemetery Ridge, which is just to the east and a little south of here. Just wait for the bugle to sound *charge*."

Well, at least we got a last-minute briefing, thought Jim. *At least we know what to do.* But Jim didn't like this—not one little bit. It seemed to him to be stupid to charge the enemy from a direction in which there was such a long open area to give the enemy time to concentrate their fire and decimate your ranks before you could even get close enough to them to hit them. He wondered why they didn't attack from the enemy's flank instead of the rear. There was plenty of cover there. But, of course, there was plenty of cover there for the enemy too; that must be the reason.[1] Okay, so they could close with the enemy much faster by charging through open ground rather than trying to maneuver through the brush. All right, he felt better about it now. But he wished it would start! This waiting was what was terrible!

Then he heard the cannon barrage start. Before long he could see the black smoke rising from the trees. That was obviously from the Union cannon. Then he noticed that a line of smoke was also rising from a little distance to the south and a little west of the Union cannon. That would be the Confederate artillery. So there was only a little longer to wait. Blue Boy's head had yanked up when he heard the cannon fire begin. It was as if he knew there was some significance behind it.

Then the cannon finally ceased their artillery duel, and you could hear the piercing Rebel yell from a distance as fifty thousand Rebel infantrymen started the famous Pickett's Charge. In fact General Pickett only commanded one flank of the charge up Cemetery Ridge though the charge was later named after him.

---

[1]   In fact, the Confederate infantry did charge up Little Round Top on the Union left flank the previous day repeatedly, but were beaten back each time. Jim was just unaware of this.

Then Jim heard the bugle call, and he and Blue Boy both recognized the sound of *charge*, and Blue Boy started like a racehorse out of the starting gate. Blue Boy easily outdistanced the other horses in the cavalry line as usual. There was no movement from the line of trees at the foot of Culp's Hill as yet. When Jim guessed there were two hundred yards of open terrain left, he saw puffs of smoke come from the line of trees, probably from enemy infantry. Then he saw enemy cavalrymen emerge from the trees and come to meet them. So they were going against cavalry after all! Jim was now glad of the saber that he was holding at the ready. Blue Boy swerved a little on his own without any movement of the reins from Jim to meet the foremost blue-coated rider, also brandishing a saber. As they came close to each other, Jim reined in Blue Boy and got ready to parry and slash, and the Yankee rider did the same. Then the Yankee spurred his horse again and charged him with his saber extending to run him through. Jim parried it by coming up into an overhand parry hitting the Yank's blade from Jim's right and then following through with a thrust of his own, which the Yank just as quickly parried with a similar technique. Then Jim slashed from right to left, and the Yank parried again, but Jim's sword bounced over to the left this time. The swords clanked loudly, but Jim's sword was now in a position to slash at the right side of the Yankee's neck, and the Yank did not have time to bring his sword back to parry again. The cutting edge of Jim's sword sank deep into the Yank soldier's neck with an ugly sound of metal cutting flesh. Jim didn't wait to see him fall, but went on to the next charging enemy rider. He reined Blue Boy to the left and cut across the Yankee's horse, just barely avoiding a collision of horse against horse, and guided his sword just over the Yankee horse's head and ran the Yank soldier through. The Yank wasn't in position to parry without hitting his own horse on the head. Jim gripped his saber tightly, and he rode past to yank it out of the falling body of the dying Yankee. From the corner of his eye he could see similar sword duels going on all around him.

Off to his right Jim saw a mounted Yankee charging him with a six-gun blazing. Bullets were whizzing all around him, but it would be mere chance if he hit him while riding at a full gallop as he was doing. The Yankee must have come to the same conclusion because he reined his horse to a halt to get braced for an accurate shot, but too late. Jim merely spurred his horse and slashed the Yankee in the neck as he rode past. When you were holding a six-gun in your hand, you had nothing to parry with. It was stupid to go up against a saber with a six-gun in a cavalry charge, and that Yankee didn't even know that.

Then Jim was almost to the line of trees at the western edge of the clearing at the foot of Culp's Hill and saw a puff of smoke, and Blue Boy's head immediately dropped. Jim quickly kicked loose from his stirrups as Blue Boy fell and jumped clear. One glance at the glazed eyes of Blue Boy as he sprawled on the ground made it obvious he had been killed instantly by a shot in the neck. Jim saw an infantryman rushing out from the trees with his bayonet at the ready.

He was obviously the one who had killed Blue Boy! "You god-damned son of a bitch," Jim caught himself saying through clenched teeth as he ran to meet the infantryman's charge. Jim had never cursed before. He had heard other men curse, but having been raised a good Presbyterian, he had been taught not to swear. But he had never felt such rage before! This cur had killed his horse! This goddamned ass-hole had killed Blue Boy! *And he is gonna pay,* thought Jim as he halted and drew his saber back to swing at the Yank's neck. He saw the bayonet aimed directly at his belly and sidestepped to the right as he started his swing at the left side of the Yankee soldier's neck.

But the Yankee soldier apparently was prepared to anticipate his side step and adjust his thrust accordingly. Jim felt the twenty inches of steel go into his left side, even with the navel, just as he felt his saber hit the side of the Yankee's neck. Both men fell backward. The bayonet had gone all the way through Jim's abdomen, and a foot of it was sticking out his back as he fell backward, the bare steel of the bayonet sticking into the soft, sandy earth, pinning Jim to the ground. The rifle, high in the air, swung back and forth several times from the spring action of being jammed into the ground. For Jim everything went black. His last thought was, *I guess this is what it's like to be dead.*

CHAPTER 24

Water, Water!

Jim felt a vague return of consciousness long enough to hear a bugle calling retreat—then nothing but blackness again. After what seemed like years later, he vaguely heard someone say, "He's done for, let him lie. They'll pick up the dead ones later. Looks like he took a draw with that Yankee infantryman there."

"I'm not done for!" Jim tried to say, but he couldn't make his vocal cords work.

"Just a minute," he heard the voice say again. "I saw his lips move. Also his eyes are closed. He's alive." Then Jim felt something heavy fall down on his stomach as if someone stepped on him. Then he felt a ripping pain in his abdomen. It felt like his insides were being blown up with dynamite or something! He managed to open his eyes. He saw a man in a gray uniform, tossing a musket with a bloody bayonet away from him. Then the man in the gray uniform reached down and took hold of his legs; he felt someone else lifting him from under the arms. He felt himself being laid in what looked like the hard wooden bed of a wagon. His throat was parched. He wanted to ask one of the men if they had a canteen, but he couldn't make the words form. Then everything went black again.

He woke up again to the rumbling of the wagon over the bumps in the road. The ground had dried now, so the bumps made by the ruts during the recent rain made the road even rougher than usual. But the only pain he felt was in his throat. His throat felt so dry that

127

it felt like it was swelled shut. It seemed like he wouldn't be able to swallow even if he had a drink of water. As for his abdomen, his whole left side felt numb, from his left shoulder all the way down to his hip. He then lapsed into a state of semiconsciousness in which he was only aware of the parched, tight feeling in his throat. The wagon then came to a halt. Someone came and poured a trickle of water into his open mouth. He tried to raise his arms to grasp the canteen, but his arms wouldn't move.

"Easy," he heard a voice say from off in the distance somewhere. "Doc said only enough to wet your throat. You have an abdominal wound. If you swallow any of the water, it'll kill you."

Jim wanted to ask him how it would be possible for him to swallow any water with his throat swelled shut like it was, but he still couldn't make the words form. But he did hold his mouth open, and the man did splash another trickle of water into it. The blissful, cool feeling was wonderful, but it had kind of a funny taste to it. It seemed like the swelling in his throat went down a little. Then he heard someone curse and crack a whip and felt the wagon in motion again. Then he heard water sloshing against the sides of the wagon. So they were fording a stream. Jim had no idea how long he had been riding in the wagon, but he noticed it was sultry hot. *It must be the heat of the day,* he thought. Then he felt groggy and went to sleep. A dose of laudanum had been dissolved in the second trickle of water, which had resulted in the blissful sleep.

Jim woke again when the wagon stopped again. Men were being removed from the wagon. He couldn't tell for sure, but the way light was reflecting into the wagon, he thought the sun was probably low.

"This one too," he heard someone say. Then he felt someone touch him on the forehead. "Not this one though. He's still alive. He won't make it till morning, but he's still alive so far."

Jim wanted to yell, "I will, too, make it till morning," but he still couldn't make his swollen vocal cords function. He figured out what was going on. The wounded in the wagon who had died during the afternoon were being unloaded. A burial detail must be disposing of corpses. They'd decompose rapidly in this heat, and a slight smell of death was already present in the wagon.

In a few minutes the wagon started again, but only to halt, and a man came around with a canteen again. Jim still only got enough to wet his throat. Then he noticed someone inside the wagon, doing something to his right side. He opened his eyes and looked up at a man in a gray uniform and gray beard, removing a bloody bandage from around his waist. He had a pan of water and a rag and washed his wound, then lifted up his side a little to wash the wound in the back as well.

"Ouch," Jim managed to say to his own surprise as well as to that of the Army surgeon.

"Feelings returned, huh?" he heard the Army surgeon mutter. "Well, that's a good sign. Maybe you'll make it after all."

"I'll make it," Jim managed to say, his voice barely audible. "But how about some water?"

"You can rinse your mouth, but don't swallow any of it," the Army surgeon replied. "With the kind of wound you have, you mustn't have any water for at least two days so the healing process can seal up the punctured intestines." He finished putting a fresh bandage around Jim's waist, then took a canteen, and poured another trickle of water into Jim's eager mouth. "Now don't swallow it," he admonished. "Roll it around your mouth, and wet your mouth as much as you can."

Jim tried to do as he was told, and his mouth and throat felt a little better. The doc gave him another trickle of water laced with laudanum, again to relieve the pain and make him go back to sleep. His mouth was still so dry that it absorbed the moisture and the laudanum without his having to swallow any of it. The doc then laid a blanket over him and went on to tend to the other wounded. The ones who couldn't be moved were left to sleep in the wagons. The others were taken out of the wagons and allowed to sleep on the ground, which wasn't as hard as the wooden wagon beds.

Jim slept soundly until the laudanum wore off. Then he woke up feeling his parched throat again. It was morning. He wanted to call out for water again, but thought if other wounded men were sleeping, maybe he should remain silent. Before long, however, he heard other men moaning and the word *water* repeated over and over again—so much for a bright idea. When he heard the tinkle of canteens from someone apparently moving among the wounded on the ground, he joined in the chorus. Pretty soon someone came over to the wagon he was lying in and gave him what was probably a tablespoonful of water, laced with laudanum again, so he managed to get back to sleep.

The following morning he smelled bacon frying and also coffee boiling. He wasn't the slightest bit interested in eating, but the coffee smelled delicious. What he mainly wanted was a drink of water. Before long someone came by with a canteen and gave him another stingy trickle of water to wet his throat. Then he noticed they were loading men back into the wagon. Before long they were moving again. The feeling had returned by now to the trunk of his body, and each jolt of the wagon over a bump felt like somebody stabbed him with a knife. And the moans from the other men in the wagon made him want to get up and strangle them to shut them up. Between the groans, there alternated cries for water and someone asking someone to please kill him to end his suffering. He would gladly have obliged both requests if he had had some water to give them and the strength to get up and strangle the guy. So he tried not to cry out from the pain each time the wagon hit a bump and got angrier and angrier at the depressing noises from the wagon. He noticed when he felt the anger, the pain in his side lessened, and he wondered about that.

Finally, the wagon stopped, and they started unloading men again. Two men lifted his head and shoulders carefully and placed a blanket under him. Then they lifted his lower body just as carefully and slid the blanket the rest of the way under him. Then wrapping each side of the blanket around a musket, a makeshift stretcher resulted, and they gently lifted him and passed him down to two men on the ground, who carried him over and laid him in a row of wounded men. Jim could see the sun and could tell that it was nearly noon.

Jim felt his throat swell up again and wished he had some water. The sun got hot. He wished he could move. It seemed like forever before he heard the clink of canteens. Then he saw a woman with a dress reaching to the ground. A woman's dress always reached the ground, of course, but the skirt was what he saw first. Then she knelt down beside him and held a canteen to his lips. He reached for the canteen and was surprised to find that his arms actually moved!

"Easy," she warned. "With that wound you mustn't drink. Just rinse your mouth out." But he cheated and actually swallowed a mouthful of water. She immediately found out he had tricked her and withdrew the canteen. She was a matronly-looking woman who looked about forty. She was slightly on the heavy side though not overly fat. *Probably the local doctor's wife,* he thought. She looked like a doctor's wife anyway. She moved on to give a drink of life-giving water to someone else. In no time Jim regretted the swallow of water he had taken. He felt a burning pain in his side that felt like someone had inserted a knife blade in his abdomen and started twisting it slowly, over and over and over. He groaned in agony for probably thirty minutes before the pain finally eased up. So they weren't kidding when they told him he couldn't have water. The pain in his side even hurt worse than the pain in his parched throat.

They were just outside the town of Hagerstown, and thousands and thousands of wounded men had been unloaded and bedded down on the ground until more permanent quarters could be arranged for them. When the surgeon made his rounds that afternoon, he was amazed that Jim was still alive. Men with a bad bayonet wound in the lower intestinal tract like that seldom lived more than a day or two. Well, a day and a half had passed in Jim's case, and he was still obviously alive and trying to persuade someone to give him a drink of water. If he lasted another day, maybe he had a chance after all. The doc gave him another dose of laudanum, and Jim gratefully drifted off to sleep again. It turned out to be a clear, starry night. They were near Hagerstown, Maryland.

Bad News

Vickie was worried. She had been helping her father at the store except for the days that Mama needed her to help out around the house, like on washday or if they were cleaning house. She hadn't heard from Jim in almost three weeks. She had learned that the reason Jim didn't come over for supper the last time she expected him was because the Army had marched north. The last time she had seen him was on the evening of the fourteenth when he had come over for supper in spite of the rain—bless him. It had made her feel so flattered that he wouldn't let the rain stop him from his plan to come and see her. But he should have written to her.

When she had expressed her concerns to her father, he explained to her that when soldiers were on the march, they usually didn't have the time to write. Abe Allen was a veteran of the Mexican-American War. So he was knowledgeable about such things. He assured her that she'd probably get a letter from him any day now, explaining that he hadn't the time to write sooner because of long marches day after day. But that was a week ago. Another week had gone by, and she still hadn't heard from him. Oh, but she wished she had gotten the address of Jim's mother. Any official word from the Army always went to the next of kin. No one would ever tell her a thing. Was there maybe a way she could find out the address of Jim's home in South Carolina? She wondered.

People who came into the store would bring news with them sometime. And Vickie read the newspaper every day. But so far all she had read was that the Confederate Army was still marching north and was in Pennsylvania.

This morning she rode with her father to the store as usual. He stopped and unhitched the horse and put him in the stable behind the store like always. Then while he was unlocking the store, she ran two doors down to the newsstand. The headlines filled her with an overwhelming sense of dread: "Major Battle at Gettysburg." She put the newspaper under her arm and hurried back to the store. Mr. Allen was getting the store ready for business. She didn't want to read any further. But she forced herself. She went and sat in a chair in the back of the room. She read the account of the battle—tens of thousands killed or wounded! She read on to see if she could get a clue about Jim. She knew he was in the cavalry. It seemed like the heavy losses described applied mainly to infantry and artillerymen.

Mr. Allen could tell something was wrong. He walked over and glanced at the newspaper over her shoulder. He saw the headline and understood what his daughter was thinking. He understood the tragic feeling of not knowing.

"There'll be a list of the killed and wounded at Town Hall," he said. "Maybe not this soon after the battle, but within a few days."

She wanted to go right then to Town Hall and check. Mr. Allen told her to go ahead. It wasn't a long walk. Nowhere in Culpepper was a long walk. So she took her parasol and set out. When she arrived there and asked someone if there was a list of killed and wounded, she was told the casualty list wouldn't be out until the following morning. So she had to wait another full day!

The mail was normally sorted and up about 11:00 a.m., so when she got back to the store, she told her papa she wanted to go get the mail whenever it was ready. He looked at the clock and merely told her it would be a couple of hours yet. She wished time would pass faster!

She was at the post office before the mail had all been sorted. The postmaster gave her the mail for the Allen family. She flipped through it and still no letter from Jim. She had to find out!

But time didn't pass faster just because you wished it to. In fact, Father Time seemed to be contrary enough to make it pass slower instead—spiteful fellow, that Father Time. But Vickie had no other choice, but to wait another day. She tried to busy herself as well as she could with duties in the store, but she couldn't add up figures without making a mistake. She couldn't take goods out of boxes and put them on shelves without dropping every third one. For the most part it was just a very trying day. Mr. Allen tried to be as patient as he could. He considered sending her home, but he figured if she had nothing to do, that would only make it worse. So Vickie endured one more day.

The next morning after the store was opened, she walked down to Town Hall again. The casualty lists were there! She was afraid to look at the sheaf of papers the clerk handed her. They were in alphabetical order. She found his name finally after going through about a dozen pages: Private James Bennett, abdominal wound. Private James Bennett! That would be Jim! So he was alive at least. *An abdominal wound! Isn't that a bad kind of wound to get?* But he was alive! Now she needed to know where he was. The people at Town Hall couldn't tell her. But then she thought again, *A newspaper—maybe it will tell.* So she went to a newsstand and got a newspaper and carried it back to the store. Mr. Allen was waiting on a customer. She went to the back of the store and sat down to read. And she learned what she wanted to know. Most of the wounded were in a temporary hospital at Hagerstown, Maryland.

When Mr. Allen finished taking care of his customers, he walked back to Vickie to find out what she'd learned. She filled him in on what she had found out and said, "I have to find a way to get up to Hagerstown. I know that's where he's at."

"But what will you do if you find him?" Mr. Allen asked.

"Why, care for him. Change his bandages. Make sure he has enough to eat." Mr. Allen was sorry he asked, since her answer was so obvious.

"Do you think Mama would mind the store while you take me up there?" Mr. Allen knew what the answer would be and knew there was no point in contesting her intentions. Vickie had been his pride and joy ever since the day she was born, and his main priority in life since then was to give her whatever she wanted. He strived to be a conscientious father and not spoil her, but he just couldn't seem to be able to refuse her anything. So he told her to go home and tell her mother everything she had learned and start to pack. They'd leave the following morning, provided her mother agreed to watch the store while they were gone.

Vickie packed food, blankets, and pillow, and when her father came in from work that night, she asked him to load a cotton mattress in the back of the buckboard. That was to bring Jim home in, she explained, as soon as he could travel.

The following morning they left for Hagerstown. They stopped the first night in Warrenton. Mr. Allen let Vickie out with their luggage and then went on to the stable to put up the horse and rig. Then he walked back to the hotel. They got two adjoining rooms, and then after taking their luggage up, they came back down to the restaurant to eat. They were tired from traveling all day and didn't tarry long after they had finished eating. They didn't talk much either. They went back upstairs and turned in, with plans to get an early start the following morning.

The second night they stopped for the night at Leesburg, then crossed the river at White's Ferry the next morning. The third night of their trip they were in Maryland at the town of Brunswick. One more day should get them to Hagerstown.

CHAPTER 26

Field Hospital

The morning of the fifth of July, Jim awoke, the thirst worse than ever. He also felt hot, especially his head. He was aware of the hard ground he was lying on. The woman came by with the canteens shortly after sunup. He heard a man's voice telling her, "Give him a fourth of a dipper, then come back, and check on him in thirty minutes. If he's still alive, give him another fourth of a dipper." The doctor knew that Jim would not survive another day without water. The only way he had survived this long was because the bayonet had remained inside him, sealing off the wound, thereby preventing loss of blood until it had time to coagulate. It bled a little when the bayonet was removed, but the loss of blood was much less than it normally would have been with this kind of wound. And there was no sign of internal bleeding yet though there must have been some small amount.

The woman reached under his head to hold it up while holding the dipper to his mouth. Jim started to reach up and help hold the dipper, but a stab of pain in his side caused him to change his mind and just leave his arm where it lay. The fourth of a dipper of water felt like heaven sent from above. The swelling in his throat went down, and the feeling of thirst was appeased for at least five minutes. Then he had a stomachache. He gritted his teeth and tried not to let anyone notice, because he was afraid they'd change their mind about giving him more water. After about thirty minutes or so the pain in his abdomen had ceased. The thirst was as strong as ever. It was probably another fifteen minutes before the nurse came back to give him another drink.

"How's your tummy?" she asked.

"It's stopped hurting," he said.

"About how long did it hurt?" she queried next.

"About half an hour," he answered.

"Okay, Doc says you get another quarter of a dipper." By pouring it into a dipper, he couldn't cheat and drink more than the allotted amount like she knew he'd do if she just handed him the canteen. By instinct he reached for the dipper again and instantly regretted it again and allowed the nurse to hold his head up and the dipper to his mouth. He found that moving his arms the slightest bit made his left side hurt. The cold, wet liquid felt wonderful, running down his throat. Then the nurse left, and a wagon drawn by mules drove up. Jim was able to turn his head enough to see what they were doing. They'd cover a man's face with a blanket, then move him to a stretcher, and put him into the wagon. So it was a burial team picking up the wounded who had died during the night.

After that wagon moved on, another wagon drove up, and two men started moving men onto stretchers and loading them up, but this time they were loading up live patients. "Glad I missed the other wagon," Jim muttered to himself, "and hope I make this one." When they came even with Jim, sure enough, they moved him onto a stretcher and loaded him into the wagon. He stifled a groan while they were loading him onto the stretcher. The wagon had the capacity to hold six prone men. When it was loaded, the driver popped his whip, and Jim winced with each bump in the road. He wondered where they were going. Before long he found out. They drove up to this mansion. One of the wealthier citizens of Hagerstown, apparently, was allowing the use of their home for a hospital. The wagon stopped, and medics walked up with their stretchers and carried the men in one at a time. Jim was taken up some stairs to a back room and placed on a cot in a corner. Another man was placed on a cot against the other wall, and two men were placed on the floor.

Then a nurse came in with blankets, a kettle of hot water, and some clean rags. She carried the kettle of hot water by a bail in one hand, and in the other, she had four pans that she poured the hot water into, one for each man. The ones who were able to bath themselves were allowed to do so. Since Jim couldn't raise up or roll over, he didn't try. She removed his clothing underneath the blanket or what was left of them. They were mostly rags by now. He wanted his gun belt, but she put it in a canvas bag along with his boots and what was left of his uniform and attached a tag to it with his name on it. She put the bag in the closet in one corner of the room. Then she took one of the rags and, wetting it in the pan of water, held up the blanket while she bathed his body, legs first, then arms, and shoulders.

"We'll wait until the doc comes by before we change your bandage. He wants to look at your wound."

"Can I have a drink of water?" he asked.

"Yes," she said, "I'll bring you a canteen as soon as I can." She then checked on the other men who apparently were able to bathe themselves. She then left, and in a few minutes she brought back four canteens, one for each man, and handed them out. When she handed Jim his, she said, "Now go easy on this at first. Doc says you can have all you want, but take it easy till your stomach gets so it can handle it better, okay?"

Jim nodded. He remembered his bellyache that morning. He decided he'd try to move his arms again. He found if he moved them very slowly, his left side only hurt a little. So he took a small swig of water and put the cap back on the canteen. The dryness in his throat went away, but the pain in his belly came back—kind of a crampy feeling. It looked like he had a choice between a bellyache and a throat ache, but he couldn't stand the thirst any longer. He waited until the bellyache finally eased up and then took another swig of water. The bellyache came back again.

Shortly before noon the doctor came around. He was a slightly obese man with gray hair. His face was weathered. He looked about sixty or so. He unwrapped Jim's bandage and looked at his wound. Then he pulled up on Jim's side to inspect the place where the bayonet had made its exit. It looked almost like an incision about two inches wide just above the hip bone at a right angle to the backbone.

The doctor decided they appeared to be healing okay. He rubbed some salve on both sides of the wound and bandaged it up again. He checked the other patients in the room and changed bandages for them too.

At noon the nurse came back again. She brought with her a tray with four bowls of beef broth. Jim hadn't really noticed her until now. She was medium height and brunette—a really pretty girl. She looked to be about twenty-two or so.

She handed Jim his bowl of soup, and he explained he wasn't hungry.

"Doctor said for you to have a bowl of soup!" she insisted.

"I'd like a cup of coffee instead," he replied. He had been about three days without food. The glands that secreted the gastric fluids into his bloodstream that induced appetite no longer functioned, so he felt no hunger. In fact the idea of food repulsed him, but a cup of coffee? Yes. And his pipe—he wanted his pipe.

"If you'll drink your broth, I'll ask the doctor if you can have coffee," she offered, thinking a bribe might work.

"Promise he'll say yes?" he suggested.

"I promise no such thing," she said, "and I have other things to do than to try to get a spoiled baby to eat!"

Jim simply sulked at the insult and laid his head over to the side away from her. He didn't touch his soup. The idea of drinking the soup repulsed him.

In a few minutes the nurse came back with coffee cups and a pot of coffee, one cup for each of the four men. Jim sipped his coffee and wished he could get up and go retrieve his pipe from the pockets of his clothes in the nearby closet. But he couldn't even wiggle without his side hurting, much less roll over or try to get up. But the coffee really tasted good. He enjoyed the warm feeling in his stomach. And his belly didn't hurt this time. That was good news. After drinking it, he shortly went to sleep. He slept until suppertime.

At supper the nurse brought him another bowl of meat broth. He drank it this time. He knew he needed the nourishment, and so he dutifully sipped it alternately with the cup of coffee that the nurse also brought.

That night the nurse noticed he was burning up with fever, so she brought a pan of water and a rag and bathed his forehead and face and upper body. She encouraged him to drink some more water. Finally, he drifted off to sleep again, so she checked to see if the other men needed anything. They were already asleep, so she left.

Shortly after the nurse left, Jim reached for his canteen, making no sudden movements. When he found it, he hugged it to him. He was able to unscrew the lid and drink with very little pain now. He replaced the cap to the canteen and then held it to him. He hugged the canteen like a teddy bear while he went off to sleep.

The nurse came in to check on Jim again at about 2:00 a.m. and felt of his head. It felt hot. He apparently still had a fever, so she brought a pan of cold water and started bathing his forehead. The other three men in the room were sound asleep, but she had left a candle burning in the room so she could check on the men periodically during the night.

When Jim felt something cold on his forehead, his eyes opened, and he said, "Vickie, is that you?" He saw a blurred figure of a girl's face. *It must be Vickie,* he thought. The nurse didn't answer at first. She just kept bathing his forehead and the sides of his face. Then Jim's vision cleared, and he saw that the woman before him wasn't blonde; she was a brunette. And Vickie was blonde. "You're not Vickie," he muttered.

"No, I'm not Vickie," she answered. "I'm Sarah. Who's Vickie?"

When he didn't answer, she asked her question again, "Who's Vickie?"

"She's someone I know," was all he said. He pulled up the canteen he was clutching, uncapped it, and took a swig of it. "I feel much better now. I'm not near as hot as I was." He closed his eyes as if to go back to sleep. Sarah took the hint and took her rag and pan of water and got up and left.

The next morning Jim refused to eat again, but he wanted a cup of coffee, and he wanted the nurse to refill his water jug as he had started calling it. She did so and felt of his forehead again. He still had a fever. She gave the other men their breakfast of corn mush and coffee, then she bathed Jim's forehead again. He asked her to get his pipe and tobacco out of the haversack in which she had stored his personal effects. She went to the closet and got the canvas bag with his name tag tied to it. She rummaged through it and found his pipe and tobacco. She brought it back, packed it, and lighted it for him. Then she put it in his mouth.

"Thanks, Sarah," he said when he looked up at her gratefully. She actually blushed a little. He had used her name this time. But she had other patients to look in on, so she smiled at him and left.

CHAPTER 27

Wounded in Action

At noon Jim drank the broth she brought without argument. He reached for the coffee eagerly when she offered it, but then he winced at the sudden movement. He had hidden his pipe under his blankets after he had finished smoking it that morning and asked her for his tobacco and some matches. Then he wanted paper and pencil.

"My mother and sister don't know if I'm alive or dead," he explained. "I need to write to them and tell them I'm all right." Sarah finished administering to the needs of the other men and left. She came back in a few minutes with pencil, paper, and an envelope.

"I need two envelopes," he explained. She said okay and left and came back later with the other envelope. He was trying to hold the tablet over to his right side and get in position to write and not having very much luck at it. Sarah finally offered to write it for him. So he dictated a letter to Mama and Joanne, explaining that he had been wounded at Gettysburg, but was recovering from his wounds nicely. He was at a hospital at Hagerstown, Maryland, and would they please send him some underwear and socks. He explained that he also needed a new uniform and suggested that they might maybe give a tailor in Florence his size and have one made for him since his uniform was mostly rags by now. Then assuring them he was going to be all right, he asked Sarah to hand it to him to sign. He managed to sign it without wincing. He only gritted his teeth.

Then he dictated a letter to Vickie. It was similar except he left out the part about needing underwear and socks or a new uniform. She handed it to him to sign also and waited, stoic faced, while he signed it and handed it back to her.

Then he dictated the address for each envelope to her, and she sealed each letter and left.

When Sarah went downstairs to put Jim's two letters in the mail sack, she grimaced when the letter to Ms. Vickie Allen went into the sack. But she stifled the thought of taking the letter and throwing it in the trash can or taking it out somewhere and burying it or burning it. But Sarah felt a sense of anger and jealousy for the first time since the war had started.

Sarah's decision to become a nurse wasn't really because of any desire to achieve career goals. She had no intention to pursue a career as an Army nurse or a civilian nurse either. Sarah was a widow. Her young husband had been killed in the First Battle of Bull Run, the first major action in the war. He had died from a bullet wound in the abdomen. Her home was at Manassas, so when she had heard of the battle, she immediately had gone to the battlefield and searched for him and found out he was among the wounded. She had gone to where he had lain on the battlefield, waiting for the ambulance wagons. When the ambulance wagons came by to pick up the wounded, she followed them to the temporary hospital that was set up in Manassas, very like this one. She cleansed his wound, changed the bandage, and mopped his brow with a damp cloth to alleviate his fever, but for all she could do, he died within two days. At first she was overcome with grief and unaware of the wounded and dying around her. But the cries of the wounded finally reached her, and she came out of her trance and started carrying canteens to the men crying for water. Then she recovered herself enough to go back to Manassas and find her father so arrangements could be made for her husband's burial.

After the funeral she went and sought the nearest Army surgeon and asked him what to do. Without hesitation he gave her instructions and put her immediately to work. She found solace partly not only in staying busy, but also in hoping she could save the life of some other young man and, hopefully, save someone else the overwhelming grief that had been her lot to bear. She wasn't really in the Army, but had been playing the role of an Army nurse ever since.

When she saw Jim lying there with an abdominal wound, very similar to that of her husband, his forehead burning with fever, it was like she was fighting to save the life of young Chester again. Jim even appeared to be the same age as Chester. She assumed Jim to be about twenty-five or so.

So her discovery that Jim had a girlfriend was a shock and disappointment to her. And it had made her feel angry. During the time she had served as a nurse, she had recovered from the grief of the loss of her husband and felt mostly pity for the wounded men she strived to care for. Some of them were so badly mangled that amputations were necessary. But this was the first time she had felt angry since the beginning of the war.

She immediately busied herself preparing to serve supper to her patients. The amputee victims were able to eat regular food—beef or pork, biscuits, and gravy. The men with abdominal wounds would be on a bland diet, mostly just soup, until their injured intestines had healed enough to handle solid food.

After serving supper to the patients, she went back up to Jim's room, but this time to check on one of the other men, the one on the cot on the opposite side of the room. He had taken a turn for the worse. She noticed that Jim was sleeping peacefully when she entered the room. She was glad of that at least. She turned to the man groaning in agony at the wall opposite from Jim and sat down with a pan of water and a rag to bathe his face and forehead in an attempt to ease his fever.

The two men on the floor were sleeping peacefully. They were considered to be out of danger by now. Their wounds weren't as severe as that of Jim or Sid. That was the reason they were placed on the floor instead of one of the cots. Sarah was up most of the night trying to reduce Sid's fever, but in spite of all her best efforts, he was dead by morning. She went and woke up two medics to come and carry his body out before the other men in the room awoke.

When Jim woke up, he looked over and noticed the empty cot. The two men on the floor noticed it too. No one said anything about it, but they knew the reason for the vacancy. And neither of the men on the floor wanted the cot. They preferred the floor, they said. When Sarah came in, she felt of Jim's forehead to discover that his fever was gone. She then changed the bandage to discover that the swelling in his abdomen was still getting less. She felt relief. *At least we'll save this one,* she thought. Then she went downstairs to get breakfast to bring up to them.

Jim ate a big bowl of corn mush and wanted a second cup of coffee. Another patient was brought in and put in the spare cot. They didn't have enough beds to allow one to remain unoccupied. By now Jim was feeling well enough to feel the urge to get acquainted with his roommates. It was funny how he discovered them all at once this way. He had been barely aware of their presence in the room until now. The men on the floor were Jeff and Johnny. Both had been shot in the abdomen, but vital organs had not been injured. There had been the concern about blood poisoning and gangrene, but the danger was past for them as it was for Jim. Young Sid had caught a musket ball in his lower intestinal tract, and blood poison had set in. It was more than his weakened system could handle.

Privates Jeff Woodley and Johnny Jordon were both infantry-men who had participated in Pickett's Charge. They regarded them-selves fortunate, first of all, because they survived. Second of all they survived without losing an arm or leg. The big .54-caliber musket balls tore up so much flesh that when it struck an arm or leg, the stricken limb was normally so badly mangled that amputation was the only possible means of saving the life of the victim.

A new man was brought in to the empty bed. He was recovering from a head wound. He was in a coma most of the time or least in a deep sleep. He was kept doped up on laudanum most of the time to alleviate the splitting headaches he had when awake. He had appar-ently had a brain concussion. The surgeons hadn't yet arrived at a prognosis as to whether or not he would make it. It wasn't possible, of course, to ask him his name, since he wasn't conscious.

But Jim's conversation with Jeff and Johnny didn't awaken him at least. Jim learned that Jeff and Johnny had both grown up on small cotton farms in Southern Virginia. They had both joined the Confederate Army as soon as they were old enough in the fall of 1862. They were experienced veterans when they had marched to Gettysburg.

By Jim's fourth day in the hospital, he was able to roll over onto his right side without it hurting too much, if he did it slowly and cautiously enough. This made it easier for him to sleep, since he normally slept on his side. He usually slept on his left side, though, so having to either lie on his back or his right side still felt a little strange.

On the fifth day of his incarceration in the small room he asked Sarah if he could have some solid food. She told him she'd have to check with the doctor. At noon she brought him a bowl of stew, so the doc obviously gave his consent. He did feel a little cramping in his lower abdomen later that afternoon, but it passed after a little while. Sarah and the doctor both were obviously pleased with his progress. That afternoon he managed to sit up on the edge of his bed for a few seconds. But then he felt dizzy and decided to lie back down.

The news of Jim's misfortune didn't reach South Carolina and Mrs. Bennett and Joanne until July 9. The letter they received in the mail simply said "wounded in action" with no details. It gave no clue to the severity of his wounds or his whereabouts. The last letter they had gotten from him was from Brandy Station. They had read the news about the Army marching north in the newspaper and had read about the Battle at Gettysburg. They were greatly relieved to find out that he was, at least, alive. But where was he? And how badly was he wounded? Joanne had been asking Jamie to go harness the carriage and drive her into town to check the mail every day.

Jim's letter finally arrived on the eleventh. Joanne opened it immediately and read it. It wasn't his handwriting, which immediately made her almost panic. But she read the letter and saw it was his signature. So he was so badly hurt, he couldn't write, but was, at least, able to sign his name. Hagerstown, Maryland—where was that? She went back out to the carriage, climbed in the back, and told Jamie to drive back to the plantation. As soon as they arrived, she ran into the house and showed Mama the letter.

"So he needs socks and underwear and a new uniform!" Mama exclaimed. "The battle must have been really terrible if his clothes were all in rags! We must get the things he needs and mail them to him right away," Mama said.

"I wish we could go up there!" Joanne suggested.

"I don't see how we can. It would take too long," Mama replied. "But we'll need to get him a new uniform and the things he needs."

Joanne hugged her mother and said, "Yes, we do. I'll go tell Jamie to have the rig ready right after dinner, and I'll go shopping this afternoon. And we'll mail a package to him tomorrow. His new uniform won't be ready by then, but we can mail it to him later."

Emma then came into the room. "Has you got word from Mars Jim?" she asked expectedly.

"Yes," Joanne explained, "he was wounded at Gettysburg."

"Wounded. My Jim! Lord have mercy! Can't nothing happen to my Mars Jim!"

"His letter said he's going to be all right," Joanne assured her.

"Whew! Then he ain't wounded bad, then?"

"No," Joanne assured her. She didn't mention that the letter had obviously been written by someone else—a detail that her mother apparently hadn't noticed either.

That afternoon Joanne had Jamie drive her into town to buy the things they needed for Jim. She bought him some long-handled underwear and several pairs of new socks, and remembering his earlier letter about hearing someone play a mouth organ at his Army camp, she went into a music store and bought a harmonica and an instruction book. She knew he must miss his mandolin something fierce. Then she carried her packages out to the carriage. As soon as Jamie saw her carrying the packages herself, he hurried to help her.

"I'd a carried the packages for you Ms. J'an," he said as he relieved her of three fourths of her burden.

"I didn't mind," she said. "They're for Jim."

"For Jim?" he said. "Then he needs stuff, huh?" Then it occurred to her that no one had filled Jamie in on Jim's condition or where he was. So she explained everything to him.

"Well, I hopes that Mars Jim will be okay—is all I can say. And I's glad you's sending him all that stuff, cause I's sure he needs it." Then Joanne went to a tailor's shop and ordered Jim a new uniform. She gave him Jim's size statistics that she always kept in her private files for use at birthdays, Christmas, and such. After that she had Jamie drive her to the railroad depot so she could check the train schedules. She found that a train was leaving for Richmond the following morning at 10:00 a.m. Then she went back out to the carriage and told Jamie to take her back home.

The next morning Joanne baked cookies and put them in a sack. Then she started packing all the things she had bought for him in the box. Then she wrote him a letter and included it, explaining that it would be another week before she could send him the new uniform. She then had Jamie harness the team so he could take her to the post office to mail her package to Jim. She didn't know what address to put on it. The postmaster just told her to mail it to the Army Hospital, Confederate Army, Hagerstown, Maryland. He assured her that he'd get it.

CHAPTER 28

Recovering

Vickie and Mr. Allen arrived in Hagerstown on the evening of the tenth of July. When they neared the town, a Confederate sentry stopped them and wanted to see their papers. Mr. Allen wanted to know what kind of papers he was supposed to have. The sentry was very polite, but explained that he had to have some identification. Hagerstown was in Confederate hands, but they had to take security measures to keep Yankees or contraband out. Mr. Allen found an invoice from one of his suppliers in his coat pocket that satisfied the sentry's request for an ID. Then he asked Mr. Allen's permission to search the buckboard. Mr. Allen gave his consent.

After the sentry was satisfied that Mr. Allen and his daughter weren't Yankee spies or saboteurs, he told them they could go on. Mr. Allen asked him where the hospital was. The sentry explained that there were several private homes that had been converted to temporary hospitals. Further questioning determined that a big mansion donated to the Army by a Confederate general's wife temporarily for use as a hospital was probably the right one. So he gave Mr. Allen directions. He and Vickie arrived at the front of the mansion just before dark.

Mr. Allen tied the horses to a hitching rail out front and escorted Vickie up the steps of the mansion. There was a desk just inside the door with a slightly obese, matronly-looking woman sitting at it, doing some kind of paperwork. When they asked if she had a patient listed as Private Jim Bennett, she pulled out a folder and drew a sheet of paper from it.

"Yes, there's a Private Bennett upstairs in the north wing. That's Sarah's wing. She's taking supper to them now. She'll be down in a minute and can show you his room."

The hospital had a variety of smells including the smell of medication and a very rank smell that seemed to come from a room off to the right. There was also the smell of many human bodies that hadn't bathed recently. The sponge baths administered to them didn't really take the place of a real bath in a tub of water with soap. There were men lying on blankets on the floor in what apparently was the foyer of the mansion.

Then they saw a dark-headed woman come down the stairs. She had a gaunt, tired look, but her hair was well combed, and she looked well-groomed. It was hard to tell if she was pretty or not in the dim light.

"There are guests here to see Private Bennett," the woman at the desk said to Sarah after she had descended the stairs. Sarah glanced at the two guests and thought, *Father and sister probably.*

"Good. Follow me," was all Sarah said and started retracing her steps up the stairs.

When they walked into the room and Vickie saw Jim on the bed, she ran to him. Then she saw his face in the light of the candle that Sarah had lit in the room. She was shocked by the gaunt, hollow-cheeked man she saw lying on the bed.

"Oh, Jim!" she said, her breath coming out all at once, and knelt by his bedside.

"Vickie!" he answered and brightened up instantly. He couldn't roll over that quickly, so hugging her wasn't practical, but he did lean his head up slowly and kiss her lightly.

Vickie tried to hide her shock at the change in his appearance. He looked ten years older and twenty pounds lighter. And he was slender to begin with. He now looked like a scarecrow.

Mr. Allen walked up and reached down to shake hands. He was careful to take his hand gently and barely squeeze it. He didn't know if it would hurt him or not.

"This is a wonderful surprise!" Jim explained. "I had no idea you were coming up here!"

"It had been so long since you had written!" exclaimed Vickie in return. "And I got so worried!"

"But I wrote you four days ago," Jim returned.

"Papa and I left Culpepper four days ago. So, of course, I didn't have time to receive it." Then after a short pause, she added, "How are you?"

"I'm fine," Jim told her. "I figure I'll be up and around in a few days."

Then Vickie explained to him about the cotton mattress in the back of the buckboard and how they intended to take him back to Culpepper with them if he was able to travel.

"Do you think you could travel?" she asked.

"I don't know. You'll have to ask the doc," he answered.

Sarah waited and watched the first part of Vickie's reunion with Jim and felt a sinking feeling go over her. Vickie didn't behave like a sister. And when he moved his head up and kissed her on the mouth, he wasn't exactly acting like a brother. Besides, she had learned, their names were Mr. and Ms. Allen, and she knew Jim's last name was Bennett. Then Sarah felt like she was intruding and left. She'd come back after the patients had had time to finish supper to pick up their dishes.

Then Vickie noticed that they had interrupted Jim's supper. He had a piece of boiled beef and biscuits and gravy and black-eyed peas. Jim looked drawn and haggard and emaciated, but he seemed to be eating with an appetite.

Mr. Allen explained that he needed to go find lodging for them and a place to put the horses. He told Vickie he'd come and pick her up in an hour or two.

Vickie had so many questions. She wanted to know how Blue Boy was. Then she wished she hadn't brought up the subject when she found out that the gelding was dead. But she wanted to know mainly how badly was he hurt. He explained that he had sat up in bed a few seconds that afternoon for the first time since his injury.

Then Mr. Allen came for Vickie, and they left so Jim could get his rest. Sarah had told them not to keep him up past 9:00 p.m. or so. She explained that injuries would heal faster if patients were allowed to get all the rest they could.

After they left, Sarah came back to the room and said, somewhat accusingly, "Kind of robbing the cradle, aren't you? She must be at least fifteen years younger than you."

"She's two years younger than me," Jim answered.

"Why, that child! She couldn't be more than thirteen! You're not that young." Then she noticed for the first time that Jim was clean-shaven while the other men in the room wore beards. And he had not asked for a razor during the time he had been here. "When's the last time you've shaved?" she asked, giving attention to the smoothness of his tanned, gaunt face.

"A couple of months ago," he answered without thinking.

"And how many times have you shaved?" she challenged.

Still a little slow in the thinking department, Jim honestly replied, "Once."

"And you're old enough to be in the Army?" Suddenly, Jim realized that he had said too much.

"I'm eighteen, and she's sixteen," he lied.

"She's sixteen, is she?"

"Yes, she's older than she looks," he tried to be as convincing and sincere as possible.

"Prove it!" Sarah said, still a little angry at having been fooled.

"My enlistment papers prove that I'm eighteen, wherever they are," was his only answer.

So he had lied about his age to get in the Army, Sarah thought to herself. She still couldn't believe the age showing in his face for someone that young. But she decided not to pursue the argument. Apparently, she was the one with a secret wish to rob the cradle, not Jim. So her manner mellowed, and she asked him if he needed anything before going to sleep for the night. He told her he didn't.

The following morning Vickie and Mr. Allen were back to visit Jim again. Vickie insisted that someone ask the doctor if Jim could go back to Culpepper with them. The doctor said if Jim could walk down the stairs under his own power, then it would be safe for him to undertake such a trip in a buckboard. When Jim heard this, he resolved to accept the challenge and asked Mr. Allen to help him up to see if he could stand. With Mr. Allen supporting the right side of his body, he managed to get to his feet, but he winced with pain and felt a wave of dizziness come over him and decided he'd better lie back down.

"Guess I'll need a couple more days," said Jim.

Mr. Allen knew he had left the store with Mrs. Allen longer than he should have already. Mrs. Allen had helped out with the store before, but she didn't always get along with the customers as well as she should. Some of them got on her nerves. So he was thinking he'd better be getting back to Culpepper. After discussing Jim's attempt to stand up with the doctor, they learned that the doc actually expected it to be two more weeks before Jim could travel. The jolts in the rough roads might reopen the internal injury and bring about internal bleeding. It would be better if it had more time to heal first.

So Vickie persuaded her father to allow her to stay at the hospital and help out with the nursing for two weeks so she could be near Jim. The hospital was obviously very shorthanded and needed all the help they could get. Mr. Allen didn't want to let his daughter stay, but he agreed partly out of a sense of patriotism and partly because Vickie had a way of persuading him to give her her way. So Mr. Allen headed his buckboard back to Culpepper alone.

CHAPTER 29

Deserters

When Sarah found out Vickie was going to stay on and help out at the hospital, she felt mixed feelings. She was grateful for the prospect of extra help because they were so shorthanded. But she felt jealous and a little bitter to find out she had such a formidable rival and that Jim was so much younger than he looked. Still, she sat out to train her new assistant.

Vickie learned very quickly that there was nothing glamorous or romantic about being a nurse. She had to transform her face into a mask to hide the grimace when she had to change a bloody bandage. And she felt especially appalled at this task with the amputee cases—so many young men, in their prime, who were maimed for life just because of this cruel war. Administering medicine to the men didn't bother her, and she enjoyed taking them their meals. While she'd look in on Jim anytime she had an excuse, she didn't shirk her work. In the Confederate Army the men fought without pay, and the nurses worked without pay. They were provided food insofar as it was obtainable from the Army supply system, and she wasn't accustomed to the poor quality of food.

But most of all what Vickie hated was having to go into the room set aside for the men who had developed gangrene. Gangrene in an arm or leg could be remedied with amputation, but was fatal for wounds in the chest, shoulder, abdomen, etc. In such cases there was nothing to do, but keep them as comfortable as possible and wait for them to die. But the stench in the room was what was so appalling. Vickie knew for sure she did not want to make a career as a nurse. She decided that the first day. But in one sense she did get satisfaction from her activities. She felt for the first time that she was actually contributing to the war effort. So she felt a sense of utility she had never felt before.

Sarah had seemed to resent her when she first arrived, and Vickie couldn't imagine why. But after a few days when Sarah found out that she was a good worker and never shirked her duties no matter how unpleasant, she seemed to accept her.

One week after Vickie's arrival, Jim was able to walk across the room and back on his own. Mr. Allen had said he'd be back in two weeks, so Jim figured he had one more week to get his strength up enough to try the stairs.

Jim hadn't heard from Mama or Joanne, but he figured it would take time for his letter to reach them and some additional time for them to respond. On July 18 he got a response in the form of a large package. It had the underwear, socks, and a big box of cookies, but no uniform. He found the letter from Joanne and read the explanation about the uniform—that they'd mail it when they could. Then he saw the small package. He had already taken out the cookies to share with the other men in the room before he noticed the small package, about seven or eight inches long, oblong shaped. He opened it and found the mouth organ that Joanne had bought for him. Vickie was watching while he opened it, and she smiled a knowing smile and immediately wanted to see it. She looked it over good and decided it wasn't more expensive than the one she had bought for him, and then she noticed one more item in the box. In the bottom was an instruction book for learning to play the harmonica—looked like Joanne was one up on her after all. Vickie hadn't thought of the idea of an instruction book. Jim had apparently written home about his wish for a mouth organ for use in Army camp, and his sister apparently didn't know he already had one.

"It'll be good to have a spare," Jim told Vickie, and she just reached over and hugged him, trying to be careful not to put pressure against his left side.

So now Jim had something to read to occupy his time and had Vickie find his haversack in the closet and get the harmonica she had given him out so he could practice the things he was learning in the instruction book. It seemed to take very little practice to draw dry comments from his roommates, so his practice sessions turned out to be necessarily short for that reason. Besides, he found out he couldn't play without discomfort in his side.

After another three days, Jim made it to the head of the stairs and chickened out at the last minute because of a dizziness and slight nausea. At the end of the two weeks he managed to walk down the stairs with Vickie to hold on to. Heading back up the stairs was much harder and took longer, but by sitting down to rest several times, he made it.

Mr. Allen was as good as his word and arrived the following day. He had hired a clerk to handle the store temporarily so his absence wouldn't be quite as big a hardship on Mrs. Allen this time. He also had brought the buckboard loaded with food supplies to donate to the hospital that he had loaded up while in Culpepper. He was able to take advantage of wholesale prices that he was entitled to since he was one of the local merchants. So the patients at the hospital enjoyed better food for several days because of Mr. Allen's generosity.

Vickie explained to her father that Jim still hadn't made it down the stairs under his own power yet, but she gave him an update on their adventure the day before, and Jim assured them he'd succeed the next time he tried.

And Jim's prediction proved true. Shortly after dinner, he had Vickie walk on one side and Mr. Allen on the other to catch him should he stumble, but he made it all the way down the steps of the staircase without help. He refused to walk back up the stairs because he insisted that was not in the deal. The doctor smiled at him and wrote out leave papers granting him thirty days convalescent leave. Vickie had taken a sewing kit and done a good-enough repair job on his uniform that it looked almost presentable. He wrote a letter to Mama and Joanne before he left to tell them he was leaving the hospital and gave them the Allen address. He also left his forwarding address at the hospital. Then he walked out of the hospital and climbed into the buckboard, and they rode off. He started out sitting in front with Vickie in the middle, but it was only a few minutes before he decided to take advantage of the cotton mattress and blankets Mr. Allen had brought along and placed in the back of the buckboard. He now had his six-gun, and he pulled it out and checked it. It hadn't been reloaded since Gettysburg. But the spare cylinder was still loaded, so he changed out the cylinder. It was simply the soldier's instinct to keep his gun ready whether on leave or not.

At about sundown, Mr. Allen pulled his rig over to the side of the road and found a place to camp. He unhitched the team and took the horses to a nearby creek and watered them. Then he tethered them in some lush grass and came back and built a fire for Vickie to use while cooking supper. Jim was already exhausted in spite of the fact they had only been traveling for a few hours, so he just stayed on his bed in the back of the buckboard. Vickie brought him his plate of food and flashed her beautiful dimples for him. He accepted the plate of food and smiled back. Vickie looked different after her two weeks at the Army hospital. She had seen the grim, horrible aftermath of the war firsthand for the first time. The biggest change was that she just didn't smile as much as she had, and when she did smile, it was usually a forced grimace rather than a real smile. The natural smile she flashed him tonight was especially refreshing to see. Maybe it was camping in the fresh night air that had perked up her spirits and knowing that she was taking her man home.

After supper it was completely dark, so Papa got two ground cloths and two blankets out of the buckboard, and he and Vickie each made themselves a bed on the ground. They turned in and went to sleep, happy and exhausted.

Jim remained in his bed in the buckboard. He didn't know how long he'd been asleep when he woke up to the sound of hoofbeats. He immediately reached over to his side and pulled the six-gun out of his holster. Two men rode up. They halted when they saw the buckboard in the moonlight. Jim could just barely make out the outline of a soldier's cap. The man reached for something on the other side of his saddle. Jim knew what that movement meant. By the time he saw the rifle drawn from the soldier's saddle boot and before he had drawn aim on the mound of blankets where Mr. Allen was sleeping, he pulled up his revolver and fired, knocking him out of the saddle. The other rider wheeled his horse around and ran. Jim eared back the hammer on his revolver and snapped a shot at him, but he had already disappeared behind some trees.

Mr. Allen was on his feet instantly. "Are you okay, Jim?" he called.

Jim answered, "Yes, I'm fine. Do you have a light?" Mr. Allen got a candle out of the buckboard, lit it, and held it up to the still body—a Yankee soldier.

Jim managed to get out of the buckboard, moving very carefully. "A Yankee deserter. He was drawing a bead on you with his musket. Must have been aiming to murder you and steal your buckboard and horses."

"You shot a second time," Mr. Allen said. "Was there more than one?"

"Two of 'em," answered Jim. "I got a shot at the other, but I know I didn't hit him."

Vickie had gotten up by this time and had walked up to listen in on the conversation. She saw the dead man on the ground and sucked in her breath in horror.

"Guess we'd better mount a guard for the rest of the night," Mr. Allen stated in a grim voice. He bent down and picked up the musket that the dead soldier had dropped.

"I guess I should take the first watch," Jim replied.

"No, you're going to get back in the buckboard and get back to sleep. The doctor's orders were very explicit. I've got a musket now, I'll stand guard."

Jim already felt weak enough from the few minutes he had been on his feet that he didn't argue. Jim climbed back in the buckboard and pulled his blanket around himself again, but he didn't holster the revolver. He kept it in his hand underneath the blanket where he could pull it out and get it into action in a hurry if he needed to.

Vickie returned to her blankets, and Mr. Allen pulled the dead bandit out of the road and went to check on the horses. He found a place where he could watch the camp and horses both from a place shadowed from the moonlight so that he wouldn't readily be seen. It brought back memories of when he had been a soldier himself during the Mexican-American War. He knew how to stand guard duty.

When morning came, Mr. Allen built the fire again so Vickie could cook breakfast while he took two feed bags and some corn and went and grained the horses. Mr. Allen kept the musket handy during breakfast. After Jim finished his breakfast of biscuits and bacon and was drinking his second cup of coffee, he wanted some tobacco for his pipe. Mr. Allen handed him his tobacco pouch, and after Jim returned it, he packed his own pipe. He had no shovel to bury the Yankee deserter with.

"We'll report it to the authorities of the first town we come to. They'll send someone out to bury the corpse," Mr. Allen decided.

Jim agreed, so Mr. Allen hitched up the team, and they resumed their journey. They stopped for the night at Brunswick, Maryland, and Mr. Allen got two hotel rooms—one with two beds for himself and Jim and a single room for Vickie. He decided camping out wasn't safe with so many deserters roaming around and didn't want to expose his daughter and Jim to any danger unnecessarily.

Jim tried practicing on his mouth organ while traveling, and while it didn't draw any critical remarks from his audience, he found that it required exertion from his stomach muscles, so he had to quit after a few minutes. But every few hours he'd get out his harmonica and practice some more until his belly started hurting. He figured the right amount of exercise to his belly muscles would be good as long as he didn't overdo it.

The trip to Culpepper took six days this time because they had to stop frequently so Jim could rest. He could stand so many bumps, it seemed like, and then his side would start hurting. The doctor had told them this would happen and to make sure they stopped until the pain went away. They finally pulled into Culpepper on the thirtieth of July.

Jim was exhausted as usual, so when they went in to greet Mrs. Allen, he asked Vickie to show him a place where he could lie down. She did so, and he was sound asleep in minutes. She didn't wake him for supper, but just saved a plate back instead. She figured he'd wake up in a little while, and she'd warm it up for him, but he didn't wake up until the following morning.

Convalescing

While in Culpepper, Jim started recovering more rapidly. Three square meals a day and all the attention he could possibly want from the most beautiful girl in the world were better than any healing potion ever invented. It wasn't long before he was able to get up and walk around the house and down the steps to the yard with no problem. He started the habit of sitting in the backyard and practicing his harmonica. At first, his side would start hurting after a few minutes, and he'd have to quit. But his practice sessions gradually got longer and longer. He found out that a mouth organ did require some wind. So it was probably the ideal exercise to restore the strength in the abdominal muscles and diaphragm. He'd still play Mr. Allen's mandolin to Vickie's piano accompaniment whenever she asked him to. But this was mainly in the evenings. It was too hot to hang around inside the house during the afternoons. His thirty days' convalescent leave would be up the twenty-fifth of August. He would then report to the nearest Army post to the surgeon for physical examination. If pronounced fit for duty, he was sure that he could get an additional furlough to return to South Carolina for another horse. It was the customary procedure for a dismounted cavalryman. The alternative would be to join the walking cavalry, which was just a fancy word for infantry, except you wouldn't have had any infantry training. And he didn't want to go to the infantry or the walking cavalry.

Vickie still went to work with her father at the store, but if business was slow, she'd walk home to spend time with Jim. She'd sit in the backyard with him and listen to him play his harmonica. His expertise with his new instrument had improved dramatically. He had been practicing the same songs he knew on the mandolin, so he wasn't really learning new songs. It was so hot in the house that in the afternoons Mrs. Allen would come out and sit in the backyard also and enjoy Jim's concerts.

Jim had fashioned a hammock between two trees where there was plenty of shade. It was fairly cool even in the heat of the day if there was any breeze. A swing had been rigged also under a big shade tree, and Vickie and Mrs. Allen would sit and listen to him play by the hour. Mrs. Allen had already concluded that this was her future son-in-law. Vickie had secretly made the same assumption. As for Jim? He had simply never thought about it.

The new uniform that Joanne mailed him finally arrived in the mail. It had gone to Hagerstown first and was then forwarded to Culpepper. So Jim now had a nice brand-new uniform. Joanne had also enclosed some money in an envelope in the package in case there was anything else he needed. He decided he did need some new boots. He didn't like wearing his hip-length cavalry boots except when riding. They didn't really fit his feet that well, which was not that big a deal when on the back of a horse. And the boots he had worn when he joined the Army, while he still wore them, were very down-at-the-heels and worn. He'd had them a year or more. So he went down town and bought some knee-length riding boots. They fit good and were comfortable enough for the amount of walking he intended to do. He had grown up a horseman and didn't really intend to do any extensive walking. He preferred travel on the back of a horse.

As it grew near the end of the month, Vickie wanted to schedule a going-away party for Jim. She invited many of her friends and any of the young soldiers whom she knew of who were on furlough. At the party Jim and Vickie were the main source of entertainment. They had practiced many of their songs together for the past several weeks. This time, however, Jim would play several songs on the mandolin, then change to the harmonica and play a few. Vickie mainly just played background for him on the piano, but they also sang several duets with Jim singing melody and Vickie doing the harmony. They sounded beautiful! Everyone enjoyed the party.

Then the day for his departure arrived at last. There was still an Army post at Brandy Station, so Jim reported in to the medical officer for physical examination. The doctor determined he was fit for duty. So Jim turned in a request for a furlough to go to South Carolina to get some horses. His request for leave was approved as he expected. He went to the train depot to check the railroad schedules. He bought a ticket to Florence, South Carolina. He stopped by the telegraph office and sent Mama and Joanne a telegram notifying them of his expected arrival in Florence.

Vickie had gone with him and had gone shopping while he was getting his medical examination. He had borrowed Mr. Allen's rig to make the trip. His train was scheduled to leave the following day. Culpepper had a train depot, but the particular train he wanted to catch left Brandy Station the following morning at 9:30 a.m.

So the following morning, Mr. Allen gave him a ride to the train depot at Brandy Station before going to work in his store. Vickie came along, carrying a cardboard box. Jim wondered what the cardboard box was.

"It's your lunch," Vickie told him. "They don't serve food on trains, you know." Jim didn't know that. He'd never ridden on a train before.

Jim wore his six-gun at his belt and his loaded spare cylinder in his coat pocket. He carried his powder flask and pouch of primer caps in a duffel bag with the rest of his luggage. He had left the musket that he had taken from the Union deserter they encountered on the road from Hagerstown with Mr. Allen. He had no ammunition for it anyway. He wanted a cavalry carbine, but he wanted one with a rifled barrel. He didn't want a smoothbore musket. He did carry a regulation cavalry saddle along with his luggage, however. He had managed to get one issued to him at Brandy Station after explaining that his own saddle had been lost in battle.

Then Jim thought of the horses at the plantation that he would choose from. He knew he wasn't going to bring Blue Bonnet. He figured she'd get killed. She was good breeding stock and a good jumper, but didn't really have the endurance that was needed in a cavalry horse anyway. He thought about Foxy, one of Papa's old horses that Joanne liked to ride. He was a good jumper and sprinter and had quite a bit of endurance. Foxy was about ten years old, but there weren't that many horses left to pick from. There were still maybe half a dozen saddle horses back at the plantation that would be suitable for cavalry work. He wanted to bring back two horses at least—one good horse with plenty of speed for cavalry charges and a spare horse. He had learned the value of a spare horse for cavalry work. He could see now how it would be entirely possible to run a horse to death just because of the urgency of the missions. The lives of both horses and men were secondary to defeating the enemy.

When the train whistled on the loading platform and the conductor yelled, "All aboard," Vickie gave him one last hug and turned her face up for a kiss. She made him promise to write to her often. Mr. Allen gave him one last handshake, and he climbed on the train. He found a seat near a window. Just before the train started into motion, another Confederate soldier sat down by him.

He introduced himself as Private Andy Kirkpatrick, from the Fifth Calvary Regiment. Jim was grateful for someone to talk to. Andy was about Jim's height and lanky, but not especially well-built. His shoulders were a little too narrow in proportion to the rest of his body, and his facial features weren't especially handsome. He had light-brown hair and was clean-shaven. He explained he'd been in the walking cavalry since his horse had broken his leg, sliding down a creek bank when crossing a creek two weeks ago. He'd had to shoot him to end his misery. Instantly, Jim decided he didn't like Private Kirkpatrick. He didn't ask any details, but he felt sure that Andy was not a true horseman. He probably was trying to ride him up a steep bank when he should have gotten off and led him up. Private Kirkpatrick was a talker, and he talked incessantly. He'd been through Gettysburg, he explained. He'd participated in the cavalry charge up Cemetery Ridge. So he was a liar, Jim concluded to himself. The cavalry didn't charge up Cemetery Ridge. The charge up Cemetery Ridge was an infantry charge.

At noon, Jim got out the lunch box that Vickie had prepared for him. He found out that Andy had nothing to eat, so he shared his food with him. The train made a noon stop for anyone who wanted to get off and eat at a nearby restaurant. Jim wished they'd keep going.

When evening came and the train stopped for supper, Jim left the train to find a place to eat. Andy came along. They found a hotel with a restaurant about two blocks from the train station. They had to eat quickly to get back to the train before it left. It turned out that Andy had no money, so Jim had to pay for his own meal and that of Andy's. It was obvious to Jim by this time that Andy was a deadbeat. What he mainly wanted was to find a way to get rid of him. He was following him around like a dog and reminded him of Private Simmons, the shirker and abuser of horses who had been transferred from his troop to the infantry shortly after Brandy Station.

That night they had to try to sleep on the hard wooden seats because there were no sleeping facilities on trains. When Jim heard Andy snoring, he got up and walked down the length of the car, heading forward. He went through the door. Candles had been lit in the car, so there was enough light; you could see the aisle between seats. But he had to wait a few minutes and let his eyes adjust to the dark before attempting to step from one car to the other. When he could see the ramp on the adjoining car and the handhold by the door, he jumped and grabbed for the handhold. He opened the door and walked through that car. He looked on both sides of the aisle for an empty seat. He saw none. In the next car he found a seat with no one in it and sat down and tried to find a comfortable position to sleep. He finally got into a position, leaning against the far side of the seat next to the window with his legs doubled up and his feet in the seat, and managed to get to sleep. The train whistle would blow every time they came to a crossing and would wake him up. Then he'd drift off to sleep again. They pulled into the station at Wilmington, North Carolina, at about sunup. He knew it was time to change trains.

He got off and waited by the baggage car while the luggage was unloaded. He retrieved his luggage and carried it into the station and checked the schedule for his next train. It left at eight o'clock. He left his saddle and bags in the baggage room and went to find a place for breakfast. The nearest hotel was three blocks away. He ordered breakfast and was grateful to be eating alone. After he paid and started walking back toward the station, he met Andy heading for the café.

"I've been looking for you!" Andy exclaimed. "I wondered what happened to you!"

"Feel free to keep wondering," Jim replied in a firm voice.

"Is that a way to talk to a friend?" asked Andy in a shocked tone of voice.

"Don't call yourself my friend," replied Jim with a glare in his eyes. "I don't make friends with deadbeats!"

"So I'm a deadbeat, am I?" replied Andy, trying to look offended and angry.

"You've got it right," replied Jim with the glare still in his eyes.

Andy's eyes fell, and he said, "I'm hungry and hoped you'd loan me the money for breakfast."

Jim understood hunger and felt a surge of sympathy. He took twenty-five cents out of his pocket and gave it to him. "That should be enough to pay for your breakfast," he said.

"But I was also hoping you'd loan me the money to buy a horse to take back to Virginia with me," Andy said.

"What! You came all the way down here to get horses, and you don't even have horses to bring back with you?"

Jim's voice was cold as steel by now, and he no longer tried to hide his anger.

"You take that quarter, and beat it! Unless you want me to remove some of your teeth! And maybe some other rearrangements to your face."

"No need to get sore!" whined Andy.

Jim raised his arm back to hit him, and Andy backpedaled away quickly. "I'm going! I'm going!"

As Jim walked back to the railroad station, he wondered if Andy was really on leave or a deserter. He figured if he ever saw him again, he'd ask him for his leave papers.

It was still about an hour before time for his train to leave, so Jim packed his pipe and lit it. He decided he'd just walk for a while and stretch his legs. His new boots squeaked with every step. *Well, walking in them should break them in,* he thought.

When Jim climbed on the train again, he saw nothing of Andy. He was glad. While Southerners were known for their hospitality and generosity, it was not against Jim's upbringing to be a social snob. He felt no tinge of conscience whatsoever at his rejection of Andy's companionship.

CHAPTER 31

Home

When Jim got off the train at Florence, he looked for Mama and Joanne in the crowd. He didn't see them. He wondered why they didn't meet him like he requested. It was about noon, and his money was gone. He'd have had enough money to go to a café for dinner, but feeding Andy for a day caused his eating money to disappear twice as fast as it otherwise would have.

He reclaimed his luggage and placed it in the baggage room inside the station. He told them he'd be back for it later. He decided to walk the seven miles to the plantation. By the time he was halfway there, he regretted it. He had never done that much walking. He had always preferred riding. While his boots fit, they were designed for riding, not walking, and they were brand-new. After walking three miles, his side hurt, and his feet hurt. And the hunger was getting worse. He stopped at a creek and got a drink of water and rested awhile. The doc had told him to always stop and rest if his side started hurting. He had thought his side was completely healed by now. *But there must still be some weakness to the belly muscles,* he thought, *or my side wouldn't hurt just from walking like this.*

After his side stopped hurting, he got up and resumed his hike. His feet started hurting again. The last mile was especially exhausting, but he finally walked up to the plantation grounds. He came up to the door and opened it and walked in. Joanne was sitting on the couch, reading a book. She jumped up and squealed and ran to him to hug him. Mama laid down her knitting and got up to come and get her hug.

"Jim! It's so good to see you! Why didn't you write that you were coming?" Joanne said while hugging him tightly.

"I sent you a telegram day before yesterday," he answered.

"You did? We didn't get it." Then after a moment's reflection she added, "We haven't picked up the mail yet today. They don't deliver telegrams to us way out here. If you don't come in to pick it up the same day it's delivered, they just drop it in the mail." *So it was my goof-up after all,* Jim thought. He should've planned ahead sooner and wrote to them, telling them his plans sooner.

"Mars Jim! Mars Jim!" Emma had come into the room from the kitchen. "I's so glad to see you, Mars Jim! Are you okay now? Do you hurt anymore?" Her face was beaming with pleasure.

He returned her greeting and assured her he was okay and then turned back to Joanne and Mama.

"Well, I need to hitch up a team to the buckboard and drive in to Florence and get my luggage. But I'm going to change to some shoes first. My feet are killing me. Then I'm going to eat something. I haven't had dinner yet."

Emma went to the kitchen to find something she could fix for him to eat, and he went upstairs to his old room and pulled off his boots. He pulled off his socks and surveyed the blisters on both feet. He'd live, he guessed. He got some clean socks from his dresser drawer and put them on. Then he put on some low-top shoes that he used to wear when lounging around the house or in the garden.

Joanne had gone out and told Jamie to harness the team to the buckboard. Jim wanted the buckboard so he could haul his gear in the back. Emma had some cold chicken and biscuits on the table when he came back downstairs also some warmed-over beans and a piece of cold apple pie. He devoured the food with enthusiasm.

Jamie had the team harnessed by the time that Jim had finished eating. Joanne wanted to go along, so Jim decided not to have Jamie drive them this time, but to drive the team himself. After they climbed in, with Joanne on the left side, Jim popped the whip over the horses and headed them down the driveway toward the road. He kept the horses at a trot all the way to Florence. He figured the exercise would do them good.

After Jim picked up his luggage at the railroad depot, Joanne wanted to stop by the post office and get the mail. Sure enough, among the envelopes was Jim's telegram telling when he was to arrive. Jim popped the whip over the team and headed them back to the plantation again.

When they came back inside the mansion, Jim sat down and pulled off his shoes. His feet still hurt. He pulled off his socks and looked at his blisters again. A couple of them had burst, leaving some spots of blood on his socks. Joanne saw his feet and went and got some liniment to put on them. He decided to lounge around barefooted the rest of the evening. Joanne wanted to know if he got the harmonica she sent. He got it out of his pocket and showed it to her, being careful not to get out the wrong one. Then he played a few tunes on it for her. She was amazed at how quickly he had learned to play it!

"You're really a natural with music!" she proclaimed. He didn't think it was so very unusual since he had done almost nothing else but practice for the past month. Then it occurred to him that he never had told them about Vickie. They thought he'd been in the Army hospital all this time.

After playing the mouth organ awhile, Emma announced that supper was ready, so they went to the dining room to eat. Emma was at her best, and the food was delicious. She remarked about how much thinner her Mars Jim was and that the Army must not a'been feeding him right. The food was excellent, and Jim dove in.

After supper Jim got out his mandolin, and Joanne sat down at the piano, and they had a concert, just like old times.

The next morning Jim put some pieces of adhesive tape over each blister on his feet and put on his socks and his new boots. He managed to get them on without too much problem. He came down to breakfast and ate like he was starved again. Joanne saw his new riding boots and figured out he was going out to look at the horses.

"Can I go with you?" she asked. She knew her question was redundant. He never objected to her going riding with him. They walked out to the horse pasture. They mounted a rise to the north of the house and saw a herd of horses grazing. A blue roan looked up and whinnied. He recognized her. It was Blue Bonnet. She started running toward him. Apparently, she recognized him too. She got up to where Jim and Joanne were standing and ran around them twice before she managed to get herself stopped and nickered again. Jim reached out and rubbed her on the nose and patted her neck.

"I've missed you too," he told her. He started walking back to the stables, and Blue Bonnet followed him, like the pet she was. He put a saddle on her and bridled her.

Jim rode down to the horse herd and rode around Lady, Joanne's horse. He separated her from the herd and drove her back to the stable, then dismounted to saddle her for Joanne. Joanne had gone back to the house to change into her riding skirt and boots when she found out they were going riding. Jim was waiting out in front of the mansion with both horses when Joanne came out, and he helped her mount her horse. Then he swung up on Blue Bonnet, and they started their ride around the plantation. They rode down to the cotton fields and reviewed the field hands, who were hard at work, chopping cotton.

They rode up to Mose, who had held the job of supervisor of field hands ever since Papa and Jonnie had left. Jim was still thought of as a boy back then though he'd ride out and oversee their work each day during the summer when the farmwork was going on.

"Well, hello, Mars Jim!" Mose exclaimed as he rode up. There were about two dozen Negroes chopping cotton and hoeing weeds. "I heard you was wounded in action. I's sure glad you weren't hurt too bad."

"You can see I'm fine now," Jim replied with a smile. It was good to see old Mose's shiny face and shiny, white teeth. He had a broad, toothy smile and smiled often. He just naturally liked kids and had petted and pampered himself and Joanne every chance he got ever since Jim could remember.

The rest of the cotton choppers paused and gawked at Jim with awe for a moment. They had never seen him in his Confederate uniform before.

"Is he home from the wah?" one of the women paused in her work long enough to ask Mose, then turned to Jim and said, "Is you home from the wah, Mars Jim? Is de wah over?" Her name was Janine.

Mose barked at them, and they immediately resumed hoeing. But Jim figured Janine's question deserved an answer. "Just home on furlough," he replied. "And no, the war isn't over. I have to leave to go back to Virginia in a few days."

Mose loved farming and prided himself with his profound knowledge of how to make things grow from the soil. "I's a gonna raise you the best cotton crop you ever see this year. Just look at that cotton!" he said as he gestured toward the straight, even rows of green cotton stalks with abundant leaves. It was already nearly knee-high. "We had lots of rain this year, and dis cotton is really growing."

Jim did gaze out over the cotton field and was awed by the beauty of the growing plants as he had always been. Mose could sure raise a good crop if he got enough rain on it.

"Let me show you my garden," Mose suggested. He turned back to the other workers and said, "Now you folks keep bendin' them elbows. Don't let me catch no one loafing when I come back." He then led Jim back toward the house and off a trail down past a few trees. Jim and Joanne both followed on their horses. After about fifty yards or so, they came to the vegetable garden with the peas and beans, potatoes, pumpkins, and squash. Mose showed them off proudly. "And here's the watermelon patch," he said and pointed toward the light-green vines already starting to spread along the ground.

"Looks like you're doing a mighty fine job," Jim told him after he'd taken a minute to look everything over. Mose was beaming.

"I'd better go and check on my field hands," Mose said after he'd showed Jim the fruits of his efforts for the summer. "They might slough off if I leave 'em alone too long." Mose was a regular slave driver. But he normally did as much work as any two of them in spite of the time he had to devote to his supervisory duties. Jim knew they had a very valuable hand in Mose.

Jim and Joanne then left the garden and cotton field and rode to the northern end of the plantation and rode along the creek, which had been a favorite picnic spot for Joanne and himself in times past. The scenery was as beautiful as ever, and the cool shade of the trees presented an atmosphere of total serenity and peacefulness. They dismounted at the creek and watched the water running downstream for a while. Not only was it a beautiful picture to behold, but also the sound of the creek was something Jim had always thought was tranquilizing.

"How's Blue Boy?" Joanne asked.

"He's dead," Jim replied.

"What!" Joanne sucked in her breath. "Was he shot?"

"He was shot by a Yankee infantryman at Gettysburg and killed instantly. He never knew what hit him. I killed the Yankee."

"What? You killed someone?" She was horrified.

"Why, you'd expect me to kill the Yankee who killed Blue Boy, wouldn't you? Besides, he was trying to kill me. That's how I got my wound."

"Oh, you killed him in self-defense." She sounded relieved.

It was apparent to Jim that Joanne had no concept whatsoever about what war was all about. He decided to change the subject, but he couldn't think of a new subject.

CHAPTER 32

"How long will you be home?" Joanne asked, apparently thinking the same thing.

"Only for a few days," answered Jim. "I was authorized to come home to get a couple of horses. A cavalryman has to have a horse, you know."

"You mean, that was the only reason you came home?"

"I said that was why I was authorized to come home," he corrected her.

"Which horses do you intend to take back with you?" she ventured further.

"I'm taking Foxy and Brownie," Jim answered.

"But I like to ride Foxy," Joanne protested.

"I know, but there aren't that many horses we have left that are suited for cavalry use." Then after a pause he added, "I don't want to take Blue Bonnet because she's too good a brood mare, and besides, she lacks endurance and is too high-strung. I think she'd go to pieces at the sound of cannon fire." Joanne winced at the mention of cannon fire, so Jim knew he'd goofed again.

They watched the water meandering down the creek and heard the pleasant sound of the water rippling against the small rocks of the creek bed. The trees on both sides of the creek were tall enough to keep the entire creek in shade at this point. They decided to mount their horses and ride the rest of the length of the creek. This put them at the west boundary of the plantation. Then they headed back toward the house. The sun was almost straight overhead. It would be dinnertime by the time they got there. When they reached the house, Jim rode Blue Bonnet down into the horse pasture and ran several horses up to the corral, Foxy and Brownie being in the bunch. Then he let all of them go except Foxy and Brownie. He unsaddled Blue Bonnet and turned her out to graze. When he unsaddled Lady, he put her in the corral in case Joanne wanted to ride her again that afternoon. Jamie didn't understand why Jim was doing all this saddling and unsaddling himself. That was Jamie's job. Jim just explained that he had gotten in the habit of saddling his own horses in the Army.

Jim walked toward the mansion. When he walked in, Emma was still beaming at her Mars Jim being home from "de wah," and she had cooked all his favorite dishes—pork chops and dressing, black-eyed peas fresh shelled from the garden, new potatoes, and corn bread with plenty of fresh butter. He ate with an appetite as usual. Apple pie was for dessert again, made from apples freshly picked from the apple trees out near the garden. Joanne was silent for the most part during the meal. Jim sensed there was something on her mind that she had intended to bring up during their ride this morning and somehow didn't. But he wasn't going to probe. He figured if she had thoughts she wanted to keep secret, she could just keep on keeping them secret.

After dinner, Jim asked Joanne if she wanted to go riding with him again, and she explained that the morning's ride had tired her out. He knew she was not accustomed to riding all day like he was, so he assured her that he understood. He explained that he just wanted to ride Foxy and Brownie a little since he figured they hadn't been ridden in a while. He wanted to get the kinks out of them.

Jim went out to the stables to saddle Foxy, and Jamie was there to help him. When he walked up to Foxy, he shied away from him like he had halfway expected him to. But Jamie opened the gate to an empty stall in the stable, and Jim ran Foxy into the waiting stall. In the close confines of the stall he was able to overcome Foxy's objections to being saddled. He slipped the bridle on him first, and he tossed his head by way of objecting. Jim just talked to him soothingly and didn't rush him. When he laid the saddle blanket on his back, he perked his head up. When he felt the weight of the saddle, he humped his back. Jim continued to talk to him soothingly and waited a minute, stroking his neck to let him get used to the weight on his back before he reached down and tightened the cinch. Jim had always remembered Foxy as a gentle horse, but Joanne must not have ridden him in a long while for him to be this standoffish about being saddled.

Jim led the saddled Foxy out of the stall and up and down the corral several times and continued to talk soothingly to him. After he had settled down enough, he put his left foot in the stirrup and swung up quickly. Foxy pranced around and stomped a few times, then resigned himself to the fact that he was going to be ridden. Jamie was grinning big when he opened the corral gate for him to ride Foxy out of the corral. The way Jim had handled Foxy was something Jim had watched Jamie do many times back when he was small. Jamie loved horses, and the reason he was chosen as the stable hand was mostly because he could keep the horses settled down and "regentle" them very easily if they hadn't been ridden in a long time. So Jamie mainly just felt a sense of pride in young Mars Jim being able to handle his own horse so well. He figured Jim's knowledge of horses must have just kept on getting better while in the cavalry.

Jim rode Foxy down into the meadow by the creek along the same basic path he and Joanne had taken that morning. He reined Foxy to the right and left a few times, then he touched him with his spurs, and ran him a little bit. He figured if he was going to ride him up north, he should exercise him a little every day to start getting him in shape. When Foxy broke a sweat, Jim rode him back to the stable through the corral gate that Jamie swung open for him. Jim dismounted and led him back into the vacant stall and removed the saddle and bridle. Jamie would wait until he had time to cool off before he'd let him out to get a drink of water from the watering trough. Jamie already had Brownie in the adjoining stall, ready to be saddled. Jim just handed the bridle to Jamie across the stall fence and hung the saddle on the fence between the stalls. Jamie had him bridled and was just putting the blanket in place when Jim climbed over the fence himself. Jim then took the saddle and placed it on Brownie's back. Brownie was more docile than Foxy even if he hadn't been ridden in a while.

Jim led Brownie out of the corral before he swung up into the saddle. He rode down by the creek again and gave Brownie a workout similar to what he had done for Foxy. Jim wondered why Joanne preferred Foxy to Brownie since Brownie was actually easier to handle. Maybe it was because Foxy was a better jumper. He also had a beautiful sorrel coat while Brownie was a dark chestnut. And Jamie always got the kinks out of him for her before turning him over to her to ride. As soon as Brownie broke a sweat, Jim decided he'd had enough for the day and rode back to the stables and turned him over to Jamie to unsaddle and rub down. He told Jamie to leave both horses in the corral and that he'd ride them both again the following morning. He knew Jamie would rub them down and feed them some grain and plenty of hay without being told.

Jim went back into the mansion and sat down on the couch. He got out his tobacco and packed his pipe. Joanne seemed to be in a better mood than she had been at noon. She wanted to play music. He told her he agreed. He took several puffs from his pipe, then laid it on the coffee table, and took his seat near the piano. He took up his mandolin, and she assumed her seat at the piano. It seemed like if they quarreled or disagreed, playing music made them forget their differences. They both felt in high spirits by the time Emma called them to supper.

After supper they went into the living room where they normally played music. Joanne asked Jim, "Aren't you planning to try to call on Phyllis while you're home? She'll be very disappointed if you don't. In fact, she'll be hurt."

"I have a lady friend in Culpepper," Jim explained.

"What?" Joanne asked. "Why didn't you tell us?"

"I never thought about it. Her parents insisted that I stay with them while my wound was healing well enough so I could travel," Jim explained further.

"So you went to her house first? Before coming home?" Joanne was flabbergasted.

"I recovered enough to leave the hospital. But the only reason the doctor released me was because Vickie and her father were taking me to their house until I got well enough to travel. I could barely walk when I first got out of the field hospital. No way I could have stood up under a train ride all the way down here at that time."

"What does her father do for a living?" Joanne asked.

"He owns a dry-goods store," Jim explained.

"What?" Joanne came back. "Phyllis Ballard is a Southern planter's daughter. And you're going to marry the daughter of a storekeeper?"

Now marriage was something Jim hadn't even thought of. He hadn't thought that far ahead. But now that Joanne had brought up the idea, why not? He certainly had never thought of any girl but Vickie since he'd met her.

"I don't see anything wrong with that," Jim said.

"But think of your family! What it will do to us if you marry below your station," Joanne insisted.

"It's my life. My decision," was all Jim said and got up and walked out. He just took a walk out in the evening air. It was sundown. He walked around the plantation so he could look to the west and see the sunset. He did not know that his sister was going to turn into a social snob. But then he knew he had that same tendency himself at times. It just showed itself differently. But he had a right to pick his own sweetheart.

Joanne didn't follow him out. She just sat there and watched him walk out. She had gotten the telegram telling about him being wounded in action almost two months ago. So he hadn't spent all that time in the Army hospital. He'd spent a month or more with his sweetheart before he even came home! She was stunned. And why hadn't he told them about her? Was he ashamed of her? No. He probably just hadn't thought about it as he said.

The next morning Joanne had recovered somewhat from the night before. She decided she wanted to go riding with Jim, but she didn't want to ride Lady. She wanted to ride Foxy. Jim said that would be fine. Jamie saddled Foxy for Joanne, and Jim put his cavalry saddle on Brownie. Jamie told Jim he had given them both a good feed of oats that morning. He knew Jim wanted to get them both in good shape for the ride north.

Before they left the stables, Blue Bonnet was looking over at them from the fence to the horse pasture and nickered. Jim turned and waved at her as if she were human.

"I think she's jealous," Joanne muttered with a smile. Jim just smiled back.

CHAPTER 33

They rode down into the meadow along the creek again and gave both horses a good workout. Joanne wanted to run the jumping course, so Jim agreed. Foxy took each obstacle with ease as Jim knew he would. So did Brownie. Both horses had done plenty of jumping. When they paused to let the horses blow, Jim mentioned that he wanted the money to go into town to buy a carbine since his other one had been lost at Gettysburg.

"There's something I must tell you," she explained. "We had to mortgage the plantation to pay bills this summer. The price of cotton has been at rock bottom ever since the war started."

Jim was dumbfounded. It caught him totally by surprise. He had no idea. He thanked Joanne for filling him in and asked why she hadn't told him sooner.

"Mama didn't want you to worry. She thought you had enough to think about with the war."

Jim knew he had to have a carbine, and he had to have one for the trip up to Virginia. He didn't want to make the trip with only a six-gun. A carbine was necessary for any long-range shooting you needed. And who could know what or who you'd meet on the road between here and Virginia? He'd heard that deserters from both the north and south roamed the roads and highways, looking for someone to rob.

After dinner Jim took Papa's dueling pistols off the wall and got out the individual boxes for each. He first cleaned and oiled each gun then packed them in their boxes. Then he told Mama and Joanne he was driving into Florence.

"You're going to sell Papa's dueling pistols?" Joanne had figured out what he intended to do.

"Yes. No one in the family's likely to do any dueling."

"But they're a keepsake—a family heirloom!" Joanne protested.

"They're useless against modern firearms. But I figure they'll bring enough to pay for a good carbine," Jim answered.

Jim went out and whistled at Blue Bonnet. She came running. He let her into the corral and saddled and bridled her. He told Jamie he was heading into Florence and would be back in a few hours. He tied the saddlebags behind the saddle and put one boxed dueling pistol in each saddlebag.

He rode into Florence to a gun store. He walked in and showed the two pistols to the storekeeper. They were in excellent shape and had collector's value to boot. When the shopkeeper asked him how much he wanted for them, Jim pointed to a Sharps .58-caliber carbine in the gun rack behind the counter.

"And a saddle boot and fifty .58-caliber round balls thrown in," Jim said. "Also I want a box of primer caps."

"You'd have to come up with twenty dollars to boot," the storekeeper replied. "That's a breech-loading, automatic-priming rifle you're talking about."

"That's what I intended to talk about," Jim told him. "We trade even or no trade."

"Then it's no trade," the storekeeper told Jim.

"All right," Jim answered back and put both dueling pistols back into their respective boxes and picked them up and headed for the door.

"Oh no! Surely, we can make a deal. But the dueling pistols are so old. And that carbine is brand-new."

Jim just turned back his head and said, "Good day." Then he continued toward the door without pause.

"Wait!" the storekeeper insisted. "At least allow me five dollars for the saddle boot. It is made out of the finest leather."

"Two dueling pistols for the carbine, saddle boot, primer caps, and fifty round balls. Either yes or no." He paused for a moment to give him time to think about it. The storekeeper reached for the carbine and laid it on the counter. Then he went against the far wall and took down a saddle boot from a nail on the wall.

Jim walked back to counter, laid down the dueling pistols again, tried the carbine in the saddle boot, and made sure it fit. "Now the fifty round balls."

The shopkeeper grudgingly laid a sack of round balls on the counter. Jim looked inside to make sure of the caliber. He didn't count them. It looked like enough to be fifty of them.

"Now the primer caps," Jim told him. The storekeeper laid a drum on the counter.

"This carbine doesn't use caps. It uses a primer disk. You load the disks into the drum," he said and showed Jim how to mount the primer drum and how to load the disks into it. "You can also load the primer disks individually, if you want," the storekeeper explained. Jim knew the storekeeper was getting a good deal. The collector's value of the dueling pistols made them worth every bit of what Jim insisted on getting in trade and more.

Jim thanked the storekeeper and walked out with his new carbine and gear. He went out and fastened the saddle boot to the saddle underneath the right stirrup and took a powder flask out of one of his saddlebags. He knew they had paper cartridges that would fit this carbine in the Army, but he had only loose ammunition with him. So he held the carbine muzzle down and pushed a round ball down into the chamber with his little finger. When it wouldn't go any farther, he figured it must have engaged the rifling. Then he poured some powder into the breech until the chamber was full. Then he took one of the percussion disks from the box and primed it. The drum for the automatic primer feed would have protruded up above the breech and would make it difficult to make it fit into the saddle boot. And he wanted it so he could get it out in a hurry if he needed to. He placed the carbine back in the boot and mounted Blue Bonnet. He headed for home.

Jim saddled up Foxy and put a packsaddle and halter on Brownie and left for Virginia on the thirtieth of August. He had his bedroll, rations, and mess kit in the packsaddle carried by Brownie, but he kept his six-gun at his belt and his carbine in his hand. He didn't know if he'd have any trouble or not. It just seemed like the natural way to travel after the lifestyle he had been living during the past four months. But he remembered that on the ride with Mr. Allen and Vickie back from Hagerstown, they hadn't expected trouble either. So he decided he'd better be ready for anything. He needed a new cavalry saber, however. It still hadn't been replaced.

Mama had given him some traveling money before he left the plantation—five dollars. So he wasn't completely broke. But it wasn't enough to stay in a hotel every night. That was what Mr. Allen had decided to do on the way down from Hagerstown when he determined that camping out along the roadside wasn't safe.

When the sun started reaching low on the western horizon, Jim rode up to a farmhouse and hailed the house from the yard. A dog started barking. An old man came out carrying a rifle. He saw Jim's carbine in his hand and the gray uniform.

He held his rifle in Jim's general direction and said, "If you've got leave papers on you, show 'em to me. Otherwise, you'd better hope you can shoot straighter and faster than me," pointing his rifle directly at Jim as he finished the sentence.

"Sounds fine to me," answered Jim nonchalantly. "Take it easy with that rifle while I holster my carbine." And he put the carbine in his saddle boot. "My leave papers are in my pocket." And he slowly unbuttoned the pocket of his waistcoat and pulled out his leave papers and held them out to the old man. The old man carefully and slowly walked up and took them in his hand. It was just still light enough for him to be able to read them.

"All right," he said. "Get down. Supper's nearly ready." The dog was still barking. "Shut up, Rover! Lie down!" he said, at which the dog lay down on the porch. "You can unsaddle your horses over in the corral there with mine."

Jim put his horses in the corral and unsaddled them. He pulled his carbine out of his saddle boot and put his round-ball pouch and primer pouch on his belt. He put a dozen or so .58-caliber round balls in the pouch. Then carrying his carbine with him, he walked to the house.

He walked in, and a woman, who was a little bit obese and appeared to be about fifty, was putting supper on the table. When Jim came in, the old man stuck his head out the door and said,

"Rover! Go guard the horses!" The dog immediately got up and ran out toward the corral.

"Ole Rover'll warn us if anyone tries to bother the horses. I've heard there's a few deserters prowling around, stealing what they can. But don't go to the barn without letting me know first. Old Rover don't know you, and he'll think you're out there to steal something."

Jim leaned his carbine against the wall near his chair during supper. The old man didn't seem to object to that. His own rifle was leaned against the corner next to the door. Jim could tell he didn't trust him completely, but he obviously was loyal to the Southern cause and wanted to extend his hospitality to a Confederate soldier who was headed back to the front. Jim explained he had gone home on leave to get horses since his horse was shot out from under him at Gettysburg.

"You were at Gettysburg, huh!" the old man exclaimed. The old man was off like a shot. He'd had two sons who fought at Gettysburg. One was killed, and the other had a minor leg wound. He turned out to be a talker. Both his boys had been with the artillery—the one still there, fifth artillery. Had Jim met him? Jim explained he was in the cavalry. He learned the old man's name was John Allison, and he raised tobacco and cotton on his hundred-acre farm. There were lots of men named John, Jim reflected—his own father and brother included though with a variation of spelling. Mr. Allison was afraid some of the Yankee deserters might steal his mules and milk cows. So he brought them up every night and corralled them and had his dog guard them during the night.

The food was simple, but excellent—corn pone with fresh butter, white beans fresh shelled from the garden, and freshly dug new potatoes. Jim hadn't brought in his bedroll and knew he'd better not go out to try to get it with the dog guarding the livestock. He mentioned it to Mr. Allison.

"You take Johnnie's room," Mr. Allison answered without hesitation. "There's sheets, blankets, everything you need in there. Just go to bed whenever you get ready." Jim felt a slightly choked-up feeling in his throat. The old man was treating him just like a son. And him a total stranger.

CHAPTER 34

The old man got out his pipe and lit it, and Jim followed suit. After puffing own their pipes a few minutes, Mr. Allison suggested they set out on the porch awhile. Jim agreed, leaving his carbine lying against the wall. His had his six-gun at his belt and figured that was all he'd need at night anyway, if there was trouble. After sitting on the porch, puffing their pipes a few minutes, Jim got out his mouth organ and started playing. He played "Sweet Evelina," and after he finished, Mr. Allison said, "You're pretty good with that thing, son." Jim thanked him and continued playing. He played "Soldier's Joy," "Dixie," and a variety of other tunes. After Mrs. Allison finished the dishes, she came out and sat with them. She apparently had been enjoying Jim's concert too. It seemed like all three of them were reluctant to go to bed. Jim would play awhile, then they'd talk awhile. Jim strangely felt more comfortable and at home than he had back at the plantation with Mama and Joanne. There were some mighty fine folks who lived in the South, he decided.

When they all three got so sleepy that they started nodding off, they went into the house and went to bed. Jim drifted off to sleep thinking how handy it was to have a guard dog that would watch the livestock during the night. He slept sound as a log until it came time for reveille to blow. Then he jerked awake and didn't remember where he was. Then he felt the soft mattress and the clean sheets and the warm blankets and remembered the night before and the warm hospitality of the old couple who had taken in a weary traveler. He rolled over and started to go back to sleep.

But he heard the clatter of pots and pans in the next room and decided to get up. He put on his uniform and pulled on his boots. He had brought his carbine in and laid it against the wall near his bed when he went to sleep. Mr. Allison seemed to think that was perfectly normal. He pulled on his boots and put on his gun belt and fastened it around his waist. Then he walked into the living room. Mr. Allison was sitting in a chair, sleepy eyed, with his brogans on the floor near him, packing his pipe.

"Come set, and have a smoke," Mr. Allison said by way of greeting. "Mama's got the coffee on.' Jim complied and thought again about how he felt so at home. He could learn to love these people very easily. "Mama'll fix us some coffee, then I'll go milk the cows while she's getting breakfast." He was assuming Jim needed to know the plan of the morning. Then he added as if he knew what Jim was thinking, "Don't worry about the livestock. Rover didn't let out a peep all night. That means nothing bothered them."

Mrs. Allison then came into the room, carrying three coffee cups. She returned to the kitchen and came back within seconds with a big pot of coffee. She poured the coffee, and Mr. Allison said, "Sugar's there if you want it."

Jim said thanks, but explained that he always took his coffee without sugar. In the Army they had sugar to go with the coffee so seldom that he had learned to like it just as well without sugar.

After coffee Jim decided to go out and help Mr. Allison milk the cows. He'd never milked a cow before. Since Jim brought his carbine along, Mr. Allison decided not to bother with his rifle. "One long gun ought to be enough," he said, and they walked out, each carrying a milk bucket. In the milk barn there were stanchions arranged, side by side, against the side of a feed trough. After the cow put her head through the stanchions to reach the feed, Mr. Allison moved a wooden bar over and put a bolt through a hole, which locked the cow's head. This way she couldn't change her mind about being milked after she'd finished her feed.

After the cow's heads were fastened, Mr. Allison let two calves in from an adjoining pen and let them suck.

"That's to make 'em give their milk down," Mr. Allison said. He made the calf suck all four tits just enough to get Ole Jersey's udder primed, then he let that one continue nursing while he went and took the other calf to Ole Brindle and repeated the process. Then he took a rope and made a makeshift halter and fastened it around Ole Jersey's calf's head and tied the calf off against a two-by-four that looked like it had been nailed to two of the barn studs especially for that purpose. Then he did the same with Ole Brindle's calf.

"Never milked a cow before, huh?" Mr. Allison observed. Jim had stood off to the side and just watched throughout the entire process.

"No, but I can learn," was Jim's reply.

"Well, you milk the brindle there," Mr. Allison said matter-of-factly. "She's real gentle. Just watch me for a minute, and you'll see what to do."

So Jim watched Mr. Allison get his milking stool, sit down, and start squeezing the cow's tits. Milk started streaming into the bucket, making a singing sound. Then Jim got the other milking stool and took the other milk bucket from the nail on the wall it hung from and sat down and started milking the brindle. He tried to imitate the motion of squeezing the tits like Mr. Allison did. It took a few minutes before he got the hang of it. Then he had milk singing in the bucket in a fashion similar to what Mr. Allison was doing—not as rhythmic, maybe—and within a few minutes his hands started feeling tired. He'd pause occasionally and straighten his fingers and then resume.

His hands were aching with fatigue when Mr. Allison got up, hung his bucketful of milk on one of the nails on the wall, and came over, looked in Jim's bucket, and said, "Pretty good for your first time." Then he went over and untied Ole Jersey's calf and let him resume his breakfast. "Now, let me finish her, you just rest your fingers," he said when he returned to the cow Jim was still attempting to milk in spite of his cramped fingers. It had reached the point that Jim's fingers were so tired, he could no longer squeeze them closed, so he relented without argument.

Mr. Allison finished milking Ole Brindle and hung the second bucketful of milk on the other nail on the wall. Then he turned Ole Brindle's calf loose so he could get any remaining milk Ole Brindle might still have in her bag and fashioned the rope halter on Jersey's calf and put him back in the calf pen. Then he did the same with

Brindle's calf. He shut the gate to the calf pen and released the cows' heads from their stanchions. Rover had found a place to lay on the dirt floor of the barn where he could look at his master in a loving fashion while the milking was going on. Mr. Allison opened the barn door and let the cows out. There were two barn doors—one that led into the corral and another that led directly into the pasture. He let the cows out directly into the pasture.

Then Mr. Allison carried both milk buckets back to the house while Jim carried his carbine. The dog followed them and started to take up station on the porch when Mr. Allison said, "Rover, go watch the horses." Rover immediately returned to the barn. *Wouldn't it be great to have a dog like that?* Jim thought.

Once inside the house they learned that Mrs. Allison had breakfast ready—eggs and bacon, biscuits and gravy, home-canned plum preserves, and plenty more hot coffee. Jim wanted to stay and adopt this family! But after breakfast he took his carbine back out to the barn with Mr. Allison in company to tell the dog to lie down so Jim could saddle up and make ready for his departure. Mr. Allison let his mules out to graze. His crops were laid by. He only got his mules up every night so nobody could steal them. He had some hoeing to do, he said, but he was going to go feed the chickens and gather in the eggs first. Jim got the name and outfit of his son first and wrote it down on a scrap of paper. He said he'd pay a call on him if he got a chance. Private Alfred Allison, he found out his name was.

Before Jim could pull out of the yard and onto the road, Mrs. Allison came out and handed him something in a brown paper sack. "Here's your lunch," she said. He felt choked up a little again and expressed his thanks. He put the paper bag in one of his saddlebags and pulled the carbine out of his saddle boot before he rode out into the road. He was overcome with a feeling of tremendous loneliness. He regretted this departure even more than he had when leaving Mama and Joanne at the front gate of the plantation the morning before.

CHAPTER 35

Back on Duty

Jim reached Richmond on the fifteenth of September. He always put his carbine in his saddle boot to ride through a town so he wouldn't appear as a threat to the local populace. On a few occasions he had been stopped by Confederate sentries and required to produce his leave papers. When it was determined that all was in order, he had been permitted to continue on his way. He had learned from one of the sentries that General Stuart's Calvary Corps was still up on the Potomac, near Leesburg. So Jim decided he had time to ride through Culpepper, since it wasn't too far out of the way. He had written to Vickie the second day after leaving the plantation and stopped by the nearest town to mail it. He knew letters were delivered by train, so he was sure it had reached her by now. He had told her he intended to stop by upon his return to Virginia if time permitted.

On the eighteenth of September, in the late afternoon, Jim rode up to the Allens' front gate. Vickie came to the door to see who it was and squealed with delight as she ran out into the yard to greet him. As soon as she opened the gate and ran through it, he reached down out of the saddle and grabbed her and pulled her up to hug her and gave her a big kiss. She was simply beaming with happiness at the sight of him. Then he let her back down to the ground and dismounted. She wanted to see the horses he had brought. She remarked that they were fine horses and walked with him to the back of the house where the stables were. She talked in an incessant chatter all the time he was unsaddling and feeding and rubbing down his two tired horses. After he'd finished rubbing the horses down, he let then out into the corral so they could go to the water trough when they wanted. There was a pump and well at the head of the water trough. He ran the pump enough to fill the water trough. Then he and Vickie headed up to the house. Mrs. Allen came and greeted him warmly with a hug. She had been sort of withdrawn before. He felt like he had just come home. Mr. Allen wasn't in from work yet, but Mrs. Allen wanted to know if he was hungry. He assured her he wasn't hungry yet and that he'd wait for supper with no problem. It wasn't much of a lie. He was a little hungry by then, but the part about he could wait for supper was the truth.

Mr. Allen appeared to be excited to see him too when he came in. It was like a homecoming all over again. For the next several days Vickie stayed home from the store to maximize the time she could spend with Jim. They talked about everything under the sun—except the war, that is. And Vickie had learned some new songs she wanted to teach him. They could be sung as duets with singing parts in which her harmony blended in beautifully with Jim's voice. He learned them first, using the mandolin (and, of course, the piano) as backup, then he learned to play the melody with his mouth organ. They enjoyed a very beautiful three days.

Jim decided he should make his departure on the twenty-second to give him a few days to ride up to the Potomac and find his regiment. When it came time to leave, he felt a sense of dread that he hadn't felt since the day he first joined the Army. On the day of his enlistment, it was mainly fear of the unknown. But the reckless, daredevil sense of youth had caused the feeling to pass quickly that day. This day it was no longer the fear of the unknown. He now knew what battle was like. But the feeling was compounded by the loss he felt at having to leave Vickie. She looked beautiful in spite of the sadness in her face when he saddled up Foxy and put the pack-saddle on Brownie in readiness to ride off. She walked with him out to the front of the house. Then he gave her a big hug and kiss. Then he mounted and rode off quickly. He glanced over his shoulder and saw tears streaming down her eyes that she was trying to hide. When she saw him looking back, she smiled through her tears and waved. He waved back and then turned down the side street toward the northern part of town. The feeling of dread and despair persisted as he rode. He just didn't want to go. He felt overcome with a sense of doom. But he had to go. He still knew that—just had to.

He made it to about five miles to the north of Warrenton before he stopped for the night. He stopped at a farmhouse and enjoyed the typical hospitality that he expected—supper, a place to keep his horses, and a good breakfast the next morning before heading out. They were near enough to the Confederate lines by now that he figured there wasn't that much danger from marauding deserters. He found his regiment on the evening of the twenty-fourth, and after showing a picket guard his leave papers, he asked him where his troop was camped. The picket guard told him, and he rode in the indicated direction until he found a campfire where someone was doing something to bread dough. He looked suspiciously like old Zeke. He rode up, and sure enough, it was Mess Number 9.

He dismounted, and when the men around the fire recognized him, a round of hand shaking and back pounding immediately resulted. After he'd shaken hands with everybody, he pulled loose and told them he had to care for his horses. They all wanted to look at his horses. After his two four-footed friends had been shown to everyone who wanted to look at them, he led them down to the creek and watered them, then took them back to the picket rope, and picketed them. He put a feed bag with some oats that he had left on each of them and let them have their feed while he rubbed them down with a piece of old gunnysack. After they finished eating, he took the feed bags off and stuffed them in one of his saddlebags and carried the saddle with all its trappings in one hand and the packsaddle in the other and walked back to the fire.

He found a tree with some unused branches and hung up his canteen and cup and laid his saddle and bedroll at the base of the tree. He walked to the fire to find that everyone was already eating. He got the rest of his mess gear out of his saddlebags, retrieved his tin cup from the tree limb on which he had put it, and got himself a helping of the food. The fare this night were beans and corn bread, with pieces of salt pork cooked in the beans. It was delicious, and Jim became aware that he'd missed Zeke's cooking while he was gone. Monday and Sam were both back, fully recovered from their wounds. He learned to his dismay that Jones and Marion had both been killed at Gettysburg. But on the positive side, Joe Williams had been promoted to corporal. Also there were some new faces.

Privates Jack Smith, John Neighbors, and Dal Walgreen were men he didn't know, but who'd been in the troop all along. There were also three new recruits, Privates Asa Johnson, Jonnie Wade, and Buck Songson. Jim then learned that Sergeant Adams had been promoted to orderly sergeant for D Troop, and Lieutenant Hanson had been promoted to first lieutenant and moved up to the position of troop adjutant. The new troop sergeant was Sergeant Waggoner. So many changes had occurred while he was gone!

But there were enough of the old troop left that it still was like a homecoming. Jim got the feeling he'd been collecting homecomings lately.

After supper when Joe got out his mouth organ to play music, Jim got out his and played along with him on a couple of them. When Joe saw Jim's mouth organ to his mouth, he immediately switched to playing harmony and allowed Jim to play the melody. It sounded like they'd been playing together all along. All the men were impressed with the musical ability Jim exhibited that they didn't know he had. Joe was especially proud because he remembered when Jim had first started learning to play the mouth organ. Joe and Jim either played together or took turns until both of them ran out of wind. Several of the men demonstrated their vocal talent by joining in on the chorus in several of their songs. Jim finally exhausted his repertoire of songs, but Joe would continue, playing background to songs that others in the group would sing. Jim joined in on the singing of the songs he knew. Finally, everybody seemed to have sung up all the songs they could think of, and then Jim learned they now had a poet in the troop—Dal Walgreen! At least he could recite poetry. And there was also a storyteller in the group, Jonnie Wade, who took over the entertainment after Walgreen ran out of poems. Many of his stories were humorous, and he knew how to play the clown while telling them, so he managed to keep everybody laughing most of the time. Jim figured he could just about make it with a gang of guys like this. Everyone finally was overcome with exhaustion and rolled up in their blankets to sleep.

Next morning, Jim reported to troop headquarters that he was back from leave. He knew he needed to get that on record so they'd know he hadn't deserted. Then he went back to Mess Number 9 to resume his duties, helping Monday chop wood. Joe came and told him that two of the new men had taken over that job. He wanted Jim to take a couple of the new recruits down after breakfast and show them how to care for the horses. So after breakfast Jim took Asa Johnson and Jonnie Wade down to the tethering rope to take the horses to water.

When they walked up to the tether rope, Private Wade walked up behind a horse and startled him and got kicked in the leg. Private Johnson took a quirt he was carrying and started whipping the horse.

"All right, knock it off," Jim scolded at Johnson. Then he checked on Jonnie Wade. He found out his leg wasn't broken, but he knew he'd have a bruise the size of a frying pan on his thigh. Joe had told him they were new recruits, but he didn't tell him they were raw recruits or that they were this stupid. Jim didn't see how anybody could grow up without learning something about horses—at least, enough not to walk behind one when he wasn't expecting it. As far as whipping the horse, it wasn't against regulations to whip a horse for kicking, but you had to use some judgment about the thing. The horse was just startled; that was all. He didn't kick him out of orneriness. So he gave Johnson and Wade both a stern lecture about the basic fundamentals of handling horses and then walked up to the horse that had kicked Wade, approaching him slowly and talking soothingly to him. The horse settled down, and Jim went up and unfastened the tether rope. He then unfastened the tether ropes of two additional horses, jumped on the back of the first one, riding him bareback, and told the other two to do likewise. Then he rode the one horse, leading the other two in the direction of the creek. He looked back over his shoulder to make sure Wade and Johnson were following instructions. In two trips they had finished watering the horses. Jim noticed he wasn't the only one who had managed to bring along a spare horse this time. Also he noticed that several of them had the U.S. brand on their left hip, indicating they were the result of some raid or battle with the Yanks.

After he finished watering the horses and had them all hooked back up to the tether rope, Jim showed his two helpers how to put the right amount of corn in the feed bags and put the feed bags on the horses.

After the horses had had time to finish eating, Joe told him that as soon as he and his two men had stowed the feed bags, they were going to saddle up for drill. Jim mentioned to Joe that he had lost his saber at Gettysburg and wondered if he could get another issued to him.

"They don't use sabers like they used to," Joe explained. "Since everybody has six-guns now, they're considered to be the standard cavalry weapon—six-guns and carbines."

Now that was the very opposite of what Sergeant Adams had taught him four months previously, and Jim said as much.

"I know. I was with the troop back then too as you well know. But you can get lead into a charging cavalryman a long time before he gets close enough to use his saber on you. So the tactics that are taught now have changed. Some of the guys still carry sabers, but we don't stress them as the primary cavalry weapon anymore."

Well, that was a new one on Jim. He and his two helpers went down to take the feed bags off the horses. Jim carried his saddle and bridle down with him, leaving his saddlebags and bedroll under the tree he had chosen to stow his gear. After the feed bags had all been pulled off, he saddled up Foxy and got ready to fall in for drill.

CHAPTER 36

Winter Quarters 1863–1864

The month of October was a very boring month for Jim. They were camped so that the picket riders were frequently in sight of the enemy picket riders, so each man had to stand his two-on-four-off, twenty-four-hour guard duty every other day. The alternate days were spent either drilling to get the new recruits up to par or taking care of camp chores. Scouting patrols were redundant since everyone knew the location of the enemy. But it wasn't practical to try to get leave to go see Vickie because of having the duty every other day. It would take more than a day to ride down to Culpepper unless he wanted to take the chance of killing a horse.

Jim heard that in some cases the Rebel pickets would trade tobacco to the Yankee pickets for coffee and sugar. They'd even get to know one another by name. Tobacco was raised in the South. The South was mainly agricultural rather than industrial, but there were tobacco-processing plants in both Virginia and North Carolina that Jim knew about. There probably were in other states as well. Since the Southern ports were all blockaded, things like coffee and sugar, which had to be imported, were especially scarce in the South. So a flourishing trade began to spring up among the picket watches of the two armies. When the brass heard what was going on, they issued strict orders not to fraternize with the enemy and threatened court-martial to anyone who dared violate the order.

In the middle of November they got ready to move to winter quarters. The cavalry was normally moved to the rear of the Army while at winter quarters because they were expected to care for their own horses and, likely as not, that of the artillery as well. Readiness was made for a march to the rear. Since Jim had a spare horse, he didn't throw away his packsaddle as he normally would have had to do. He packed all his gear and saddled up when they received the order to get ready to march. They formed up as a squadron under Lieutenant Colonel Thompson, who was still the squadron commander, and rode south, the mess wagons falling in behind. Jim had been told they were moving to the rear, but Jim wasn't sure what that meant. He didn't know how far you had to travel to get to the rear in an Army of more than fifty thousand men that required about five thousand campfires just to cook their rations.

After a half a day's march they passed near Warrenton, and Jim's spirits perked up. Would they winter near Culpepper? He hadn't seen Vickie in over a month. But after they passed Warrenton, the mounted mass of soldiers swung westerly.

After several days the cavalry corps was halted. They had just passed the town of Sperryville. When Jim got a chance, he consulted his map of Virginia. He had bought another map for his ride north from home a few months previously and kept it in one of his saddlebags with his writing paper. He found out that Sperryville was only about ten miles or so from Culpepper! Sure enough, they received orders to start repairing a rail fence around a huge pasture. They were at the foot of the Blue Ridge Mountains. The foothills were covered with timber. The horses were all herded into the pasture where they could graze the tall grass, and the men went into the foothills to fell trees to trim and split and make into fence rails. Enough riders were chosen to guard the horse herd to keep them in a big, loose bunch so they wouldn't stray off. Jim had his turn at both guarding the horse herd and logging for fence rails.

After the rail fence around the huge pasture had been built, the horses no longer had to be herded. Work then began building the corrals to make it easy to capture the horses again when they were needed. When the facilities for the horses were completed, including small buildings to serve for storing corn for horse feed, the men were permitted to start work on their winter shelters. The men would split up in groups of two, three, or four, each group to build a log cabin that they would share during the winter.

Jim threw in with Joe and Sam to build a small log cabin. It had a dirt floor, of course, and no windows. There was only one door. They built bunks out of split planks, three levels of them, one on top of the other. Sam built them a fireplace of rocks mortared with clay. The chimney was made of split logs with a thick layer of the moistened clay laid inside all around. When it dried, it would dry as hard as concrete.

A few horses were kept in the corral at all times, but most of them were permitted to roam in the huge horse pasture. The huge pasture held the horses of the entire squadron, which amounted to about three hundred horses plus, probably, at least a hundred and fifty mules. The cabins had been arranged in rows on three sides of the pasture. The pasture was about three miles long and one mile wide. A creek meandered through the middle of it, so water wasn't a problem. When the snow came, the horses could paw through the snow to reach the grass, and they could easily break the ice on the creek with their shod hooves when it became frozen. *So this is how you rig for winter quarters,* Jim thought. When he thought of how each regiment had three or four squadrons and there were probably from two to four regiments in a brigade, he could only imagine how many acres the entire Army took up just to have sufficient winter forage for their horses. They no longer had a mounted picket watch like before. They still had to stand guard duty, but guard duty was stood holding your carbine over your shoulder, with several pairs of socks (if you had them), overcoat, and gauntlets, and you still shivered while walking your beat through the snow. The hip-length riding boots became popular for the warmth they afforded even though they weren't designed for walking.

The first snow didn't fall until the last week in November. Because of the work going on, Jim hadn't had time to request a pass to go see Vickie. They worked from dawn till dark to make sure they were all settled in by the time the snow fell. But by the middle of

December Jim finagled a weekend pass and saddled up Foxy to make the trip. He had made sure that Foxy was one of the horses that were kept in the corral for utility use so he'd have a mount for the purpose. Part of the routine for winter camp was to ride the fencerow a couple of times a week to make sure it was in good repair. Another detail was to count the horses and separate out any that appeared to be sick and run them into a smaller hospital pasture where the camp veterinarians could provide special care for them. Jim usually volunteered for this duty, and Joe made a habit of always including him when he sent a detail out to check fences and horses.

Before Jim left to ride to Culpepper, he felt of his face and noticed that peach fuzz had started to be noticeable again. He couldn't have that. People hadn't made reference to his age or lack of it in a while. Since he'd lost his razor at Gettysburg (they were in his saddlebags), he borrowed Joe's razor and shaving soap and shaved before he saddled up Foxy and rode out.

Jim had been writing to Vickie a minimum of once a week and had notified her of his plans to come up. On the day he was to arrive, he rode up after dark on Friday night. It took about four hours to make the ride in the snow. But travel at night was easier than usual because the reflection of moonlight and starlight on the snow made it almost as bright as day. Vickie ran out into the yard to meet him. She heard his horse snort as he rode up. He got down off Foxy to give her a hug, and she walked around back with him to the stable in spite of the cold.

Jim stomped the snow off his boots at the door when he followed Vickie into the house. He had a blue overcoat. It was actually a Union overcoat from captured supplies, but with Confederate insignia on it. The regulation Confederate overcoat was blue too as was that of the Union uniform. A gray cape was sometimes worn over it to avoid confusing it with the enemy colors though Jim didn't have a cape.

Mrs. Allen had saved back some supper for Jim because she knew he'd be hungry. Vickie immediately started warming it over for him. Jim felt the warm, happy feeling he always felt when he was at the Allen house. And Vickie smiled often, like she used to do, showing off her dimples at anything Jim said.

Jim and Vickie played music after Jim finished eating as usual. Jim always carried his harmonica in his pocket—how convenient to have an instrument that you could keep on your person at all times!

Man and horse, both well-fed and rested up, headed back to the Army camp the following Sunday afternoon.

Many of the men played cards to amuse themselves while at winter quarters. Jim and Joe, of course, played music with their harmonicas every night. When Jim returned from his weekend in Culpepper, he found out that Sam, who had also managed a weekend pass, came back with a guitar. Sam decided that with two bunkies who were musicians, he'd just have to develop some musical talent too or, at least, find out if he had any. He couldn't play a lick, but had bought an instruction book and was learning. He'd practice by the hour when he wasn't on duty, much to Jim and Joe's chagrin. But times when Sam was on guard duty and Jim had nothing to do, he started reading Sam's instruction book and started learning how to get a few chords.

After about a month or so, Sam was good enough on his guitar that he was able to play background for Jim and Joe on several of the songs that they played. Jim was already as good as Sam by now on the guitar, but he never played it when Sam was around; he stuck to his mouth organ instead.

Jim spent a very enjoyable Christmas with the Allen family in Culpepper. Mr. Allen's brother and his wife came over on Christmas Day, so Jim made the acquaintance of Vickie's aunt and uncle.

On Christmas morning they opened their presents, and Jim's present from Vickie was a beautiful bridle, with a shiny steel bit and genuine silver studs on it. The gift he received from Mr. and Mrs. Allen was a brand-new pocketknife. Jim had racked his brain, trying to think of a proper gift he could get for Vickie that he could afford. When she opened her present, she discovered the final result of all that brain energy he used up. He had carved a small horse, saddle, and all about six inches long or so out of wood, and a cavalryman with a saber held high, making a cavalry charge. Jim had taken up carving as a hobby when he was about ten years old and had nothing better to do at the time. So his carvings were pretty good. He had scraped the wood smooth with the edge of his carving knife since he had no sandpaper, of course, whetting his knife frequently. Then he had finagled some varnish, and before he was through, he found he had created a work of art. Vickie was absolutely delighted.

"Jim, you shouldn't have. It must have cost you a fortune!" she exclaimed. Jim didn't know whether to be insulted or flattered. She obviously didn't think he had the artistic ability to create such a work. She cooed over it probably five minutes before it dawned on her to ask him if he'd carved it himself. The look on his face gave her his answer without him saying a word, and she reached over and hugged him, smothering him with kisses.

The next day after Christmas Jim had to head back to camp so he'd be there to stand his scheduled watches the following day. He managed to get a two-day pass every week or so to go visit Vickie for the duration of the winter. Jim couldn't remember ever having a happier winter in his life.

Rations were short in camp, and before the winter was over, there were days when there were no rations at all. The gnawing hunger did get to you. At first Jim thought maybe it was something you could get used to, but it never happened. It seemed like the longer you were hungry, the more obsessed you became to find something to eat.[2] They'd take corn they had stored to feed the horses and parch it in their fireplaces and eat it. They'd just toss it in the fire, shuck and all. After a few minutes they'd roll it over with a stick and let it cook on the other side. Then they'd let it cool, finish rubbing off whatever part of the husk hadn't burned off, and shell the parched corn into a pan. It was hard on your teeth, but it was better than nothing. They kept running out of coffee, but the men would write home to relatives, explaining the desperate need for hot stimulate, and they'd receive a package of coffee in the mail in a few weeks. Coffee and

[2] If a person does without food completely for several days, the digestive juices stop secreting, and you'll no longer feel hungry. If you get just a little bit to eat each day, then you stay hungry all the time.

sugar became the most precious commodities in camp and tobacco though tobacco wasn't as hard to come by as coffee and sugar. Of course, the shortage of rations made Jim appreciate his weekly trips to Culpepper all the more.

In February a flu epidemic struck the camp, and the Army surgeons and medics were overworked trying to prevent loss of life from this new invisible enemy. Sergeant Waggoner was one of the ones stricken, and in the first week of March he developed pneumonia. He kept getting worse and then finally died. Several of the men took sick including all three of the new recruits, but they all managed to pull through.

With Sergeant Waggoner gone, Joe Williams was promoted to the rank of sergeant and took Sergeant Waggoner's place as troop sergeant. When Lieutenant Sorenson asked Joe to name his replacement, he chose Jim. So Jim was promoted to corporal and sewed two chevrons on his sleeve. He decided he had something to write home about.

The spring thaw came in April, and there was a spell of pretty weather. The order came to prepare to leave winter quarters and join the main Army. Just about all the comforts of home that they had accumulated during the winter had to be left behind. What they could carry in their saddlebags and tie behind their saddles were all they kept with a few exceptions. So they formed up to start their march. General JEB Stuart's cavalry started moving eastward to take their position with the Army of North Virginia.

CHAPTER 37

Finding the Enemy

Lieutenant Sorenson was ordered to send a scouting detail north on a scouting mission and locate the enemy forces. He consulted Sergeant Williams, who recommended they have Corporal Bennett pick a detail from the troop. So Lieutenant Sorenson sent for Corporal Bennett right after breakfast.

Corporal Bennett went to Lieutenant Sorenson's campfire and told him he had reported as ordered. Lieutenant Sorenson explained the mission to him and asked him how he'd go about handling such a mission. Jim explained to him that he'd take two men with fast horses—the fewer, the better to make sure they weren't spotted by the enemy. Then as soon as enemy forces were spotted, he'd send one of the scouts back as a courier immediately to report the enemy position. He and the other scout would observe the enemy from concealment for several hours and gather any details they could about enemy strength, number of artillery pieces, direction the enemy appeared to be traveling, and such like, and Jim would then send the second scout back as another courier with the extra details, coming back himself by a different route. Chances were, one of the three would make it back unscathed with the needed information. Lieutenant Sorenson liked his plan and told him to pick his two best men and start immediately.

Jim picked Private Smith and Private Neighbors to go with him. He had determined during the last few months that they were reliable men, and both had fast horses. But mainly, they knew how to be quiet. He knew they'd be patient and could wait for hours waiting for something to happen without getting restless and making needless noise.

So Jim sent Smith to draw five days' rations for three men. They saddled up and headed north, staying away from roads whenever possible and camping in the cover of the woods. They had to camp without a fire, which meant no coffee. He allowed them to smoke their pipes only if the wind was from a northerly direction and he could be sure the scent of the smoke wouldn't carry in the direction in which he suspected the enemy to be. But a campfire made smoke you could see for miles away. And at night it made a beacon that could be seen from several hundred yards away and make it possible to find an otherwise well-hidden camp. Even a well-covered fire could sometimes be seen for miles off from some unsuspected angle if the trees weren't as thick as they looked. So Jim insisted on playing it safe.

When they came near a farmhouse, Jim would leave his two men hidden in the woods, and he'd ride in and ask the farmer if he had seen any sign of Yankees. He decided it was worth the risk to trust the loyalty of a farmer for the chance of getting information that it might otherwise take days to gather. But in each case the farmer had said no; they hadn't seen a sign of a Yankee since the previous fall. The third morning after they had started their scouting mission, they were near the Rapidan River. When they got up and broke camp and started getting ready to resume their search, Jim saw smoke to the north—small trails of smoke rising above the tree line of the horizon on the north side of the river like you'd see from many campfires.

Jim scanned the opposite bank of the river and spotted enemy picket riders patrolling the opposite riverbank. They had seen no evidence of Yankee presence on the south bank.

Jim consulted his map, wrote his report of the enemy location on a piece of paper, handed it to Smith, and told him to push his horse as fast as he could without killing him and take the report to Lieutenant Sorenson. And if Lieutenant Sorenson was out on scouting patrol or otherwise not where he could find him quickly, Jim told him to the take the report directly to the troop commander, Captain Wilson. Then Smith headed off to the south at a fast gallop.

Jim figured the next thing they'd do would be to wait and see if the enemy had plans to cross the river or to remain encamped where they were. So he and Neighbors finished saddling their horses and rode upriver far enough that Jim guessed they'd be out of the path of the enemy should they cross the river. Then they loosened their cinches and tethered the horses in some lush grass after taking the bits out of their mouths so they could graze. After that they settled down under cover of some trees on the riverbank to wait.

Since they hadn't had breakfast yet, they pulled some hardtack out of their saddlebags and started chewing on it. At about 9:00 a.m. by the sun, Jim saw some mounted horsemen come out of the woods on the opposite bank and start wading the river. It looked like about a dozen men. Jim just put his index finger beside his nose in a gesture to Neighbors, and they continued to wait. It might just be a scouting patrol crossing the river. But it could also be the advanced scout for a major march. They waited for about two hours, and then Jim saw a man on the south bank about half a mile to the east, waving a flag up and down. Pretty soon he saw another man on the north bank, waving a flag in a similar fashion—semaphore signals! Shortly after being promoted to corporal back during the winter, Jim had been taught that signaling with semaphore flags was a method of communication sometimes used by the Union Army, and he had been taught to recognize the signals for the characters of the alphabet and the numeric digits. It was something all noncommissioned officers had to know. He didn't expect to be able to decipher it; he was sure it would be in some secret code, but he wrote down the characters he recognized.

Within thirty minutes another cavalry unit started wading the river. It looked like an entire troop. Jim got a good idea of the position of the enemy's right flank by now and decided that Neighbors and himself might be spotted if they remained where they were, so they tightened the cinches on their horses, refastened the bridle bits, and rode upriver another half mile or so, being careful not to be seen. Jim and John Neighbors watched the enemy Army spend the entire day crossing the river. After the cavalry screen were all across, the artillery pieces were hauled across the ford. Jim counted them. Then the infantry started wading across.

Jim decided he'd seen enough. He and Neighbors led their horses on foot at least another mile to the west before they mounted and started riding south. Jim wrote a report for Neighbors to take to Lieutenant Sorenson and told him to ride as hard as he could without killing his horse to deliver it. He reminded him to take the message directly to troop headquarters if Lieutenant Sorenson wasn't immediately available. Neighbors pocketed the message and spurred his horse into a gallop. He quickly disappeared around a clump of trees.

Jim wasn't quite ready to ride back to the Confederate lines himself yet. He wanted to establish the direction of enemy travel first. So he rode wide on the enemy's right flank, making sure he was far-enough away from where the enemy cavalry screen would be that he would not be spotted and then put Foxy into a gallop so he could get well ahead of the advancing enemy. Then he found a place to lie and wait. By evening he saw a Yankee cavalryman—apparently, the right flank of the cavalry screen. He waited until he passed and decided the direction the Union Army was headed was toward Winchester. When the Yankee horsemen were out of sight and he made sure he didn't see another, he slipped off, got some distance between himself and the Union forces to the west again, and put Foxy in a lope south-ward toward where he expected the Confederate Army to be.

According to Jim's map the Confederate lines should be about forty miles from his present position. He knew it would be more like fifty actual miles traveled. It was his intention to keep Foxy at a run all night if he could handle it. Foxy was in fairly good shape since he hadn't had to do any hard running during the past few days. Jim hadn't had any corn to feed him in several weeks, but he figured he was good for fifty miles. Jim didn't try to avoid the roads. There was no moon, but enough starlight that they could still see how to make their way easily along the white caliche roads. He knew that traveling the roads would be riskier, but faster than trying to stick to cover.

After a couple of hours, Foxy was covered with lather, and when his sides started heaving in a fashion Jim knew to be a warning, Jim pulled him down to a walk and kept him at a walk for about a half hour while he caught his breath. He figured he probably was halfway to his destination. After Foxy had a good blow, Jim urged him into a gallop again. Shortly after midnight Jim was challenged by, "Who goes there?"

Jim answered and gave the countersign. Then he asked the picket guard where Lieutenant Sorenson's camp was and said that he had an important message for him. The sentry obviously was from some other troop because Jim did not know him.

Jim went up to the place and saw a tent that he figured was Lieutenant Sorenson's tent. He'd never awakened a commissioned officer before, but he was going to do so now. When he called, "Lieutenant Sorenson" into the open tent, he got a gruff, "What do you want?"

Jim identified himself, and Lieutenant Sorenson immediately came out of his tent, fully clothed except for his boots. He recognized Jim's voice and told him to wait a minute while he put on his boots. After putting on his boots he strapped on his revolver and told Jim to come with him. They woke up Captain Wilson so Jim would be handy to answer any questions he had while giving him his report.

Jim found that Smith had made it back at dawn that morning, and Neighbors had ridden in late in the afternoon. So both his men got back. Jim answered all the questions he could about enemy strength, location, and direction of travel. He also gave the captain the piece of paper with the semaphore signals he had written down. When he was finished and Captain Wilson dismissed him, he saluted and went back out to Foxy. Foxy had recovered his breath by now, and the lather of sweat was starting to dry. In spite of his fatigue, Jim took time to rub him down after he unsaddled him. He had a piece of gunnysack he kept in his saddlebags for the purpose. He needed to give him at least an hour to cool off before letting him have water anyway. When he finished rubbing him down, he tied him to a bush and packed his pipe. He hadn't had a smoke all night. He waited until he thought about an hour had passed since he first rode in, and then he led Foxy down to the creek so he could drink. He brought him back and tethered him. He'd find Mess Number 9 in the morning. He just gratefully rolled up in his blankets and was asleep instantly.

CHAPTER 38

The Wilderness

The next morning after breakfast Jim had his men check their weapons as the first order of the day. He told them to make sure they were loaded and that their spare cylinders for their revolvers were loaded if they had any and to replenish the ammunition in their ball pouches and powder flasks and paper cartridges if they had a carbine that used standard ammunition. They had paper cartridges for the .58 caliber, so Jim made sure he had a separate cartridge pouch at his belt for his carbine. He was carrying more on his belt than he preferred, but he didn't intend to be caught unawares without his arms on his person and warned the men likewise. He insisted they wear their revolvers at all times and keep their carbines handy whether caring for horses, chopping wood, or whatever. He left Monday in charge of the wood-cutting detail and assigned Johnson and Wade to help him. He had Privates Songson and Walgreen help Zeke with the cooking since they'd follow the tyrannical old cook's orders without argument. He put Privates Sam Blake, Jack Smith, and John Neighbors to the task of watering the horses and changing their tether rope to a place where there was fresh grass for them to graze. Jim knew the importance of keeping the men busy. That way they wouldn't have time to think of meanness or worry about the battle that Jim was sure was shaping up.

Joe came by and told Jim to have the men check their weapons, and Jim explained he had already done so first thing that morning.

"You're ahead of me as usual," Joe said with a smile.

206

For the next two days the routine of camp was very monotonous to Jim. He pulled his duty of being corporal of the guard on the fourth of May. Since he was now a noncommissioned officer, he didn't stand picket watches, but every third day he had the duty of being corporal of the guard, which was worse. It was his responsibility to wake up each picket guard during the night and make sure he went on watch on time. And you had to ride around and check on each picket guard and make sure he was awake and alert and doing his job.

On the morning of May 5, Joe came and ordered Jim to pick a detail and get them saddled up and ready to move. *So now it comes,* Jim thought. He gave the order to saddle up, and when they were ready to mount, Joe rode back on his horse and told them to form up. Jim lined up his men in a column on the right of the other two columns. Private Jack O'Henry, the guidon bearer, was up front with Lieutenant Sorenson and Sergeant Williams. But Jim noticed they were pointed south, not north. *What was this?* he thought.

When they finished forming up, Lieutenant Sorenson explained that they were being sent to the rear and would be in reserve for now. The infantry and artillery were getting in position to meet the enemy. This was new to Jim. Always before they had managed to get up to the front and participate in the fighting. But he followed orders.

They rode south for two hours, mostly through thick brush. The small town called the Wilderness was nearby, and Jim could understand how it got its name. Finally, Lieutenant Sorenson called a halt and told the men to dismount, loosen their cinches, but be ready to tighten them again on a moment's notice. They were permitted to light their pipes since secrecy was not a matter in question. Sergeant Williams came and told them to take the bits out of their horses' mouths so they could crop grass and fasten a tether rope around their necks, but not to drive stakes in the ground—just hold the ropes in one hand so they could mount quickly if the order came. They waited there until about noon when they heard the sound of cannon fire start up. After another thirty minutes or so the sound of small arms started blending in with the sound of the cannon.

Lieutenant Sorenson rode up and told them to tighten their cinches and prepare to mount. They replaced the bits in the horses' mouths, removed the tether ropes, and put them in their saddlebags, tightened their cinches, and stood by their horses. Lieutenant Sorenson rode off toward the rear a little ways, and within a few minutes, Sergeant Williams came riding up and told them to mount up. They mounted and followed Joe over to the west to a place protected by brush that overlooked a clearing. They were ordered to dismount again, take their carbines, and lie down in a thin line of brush in a fashion such that they had a field of fire overlooking the clearing. Jim ordered his men to tie their horses to a tree near their position, but to leave their cinches tight. Then he took his carbine and got in position himself.

A few minutes later he heard Lieutenant Sorenson's voice from behind telling them to pay attention to the colors they saw. "If you see gray uniforms, by all that's holy, hold your fire. They'll have Yankees chasing them, and wait until you see the Yankees before you shoot. We'll provide a covering fire for our boys if they have to retreat." Then from the back of his horse, he went on, "If you see blue uniforms, let the first wave get three fourths the way across the clearing, then fire at will, make every shot count, and be ready to mount up quickly."

Then they were back to waiting. The sound of small fire seemed to be getting closer. Jim made sure his cartridge pouch was where he could reach it easily. He felt a sense of dread—a deep sinking feeling. *Now what was going on here?* he thought. He never felt afraid at the verge of battle. He didn't know it, but he was feeling the feelings of a veteran soldier rather than those of a daredevil teenager. The sound of small-arms fire kept on getting stronger, and the cannon fire ceased. Then he heard thrashing in the bushes across the clearing and men in blue uniforms, rushing out, bayonets fixed. So they *had* broken through the Rebel lines! Jim put his sights on a blue uniform and waited. They weren't halfway across before someone fired, so he fired too. Dozens of men in blue uniforms faltered and sprawled headlong into the dirt. Jim pulled down the lever of his carbine, got a cartridge out of his pouch, shoved it in the breech, pulled the lever back up, and put in a new primer disk. It had a cutter that cut off the tail end of the paper cartridge automatically as he closed the breech. The soldiers in blue were close enough, he could almost see the whites of their eyes when he brought his carbine up to his shoulder and downed another Union infantryman. He reloaded his carbine again quickly. By the time he got it back up to his shoulder, he saw the Yankees reverse direction and head back into the thicket from which they had emerged, leaving several dozen dead and wounded in the clearing. Then he heard Lieutenant Sorenson's voice behind him.

"Mount up! Hurry! Get ready to fall back!"

But we just got through repelling their charge! Jim thought. He quickly fastened a primer disk to the nipple of his carbine, moved it to half cock, and swung up on Foxy. He made a quick count of his men while they were mounting and noticed he had no losses. He led his detail in pursuit of Lieutenant Sorenson's gelding, and they made their way through the dense brush, threading their way wherever they could find a trail. They kept moving south for a couple more hours. Then they halted again in a line of brush overlooking a clearing.

Jim heard cannon fire again, this time much closer than before. So at least the cannon were in position to fire again, but look at all the ground the enemy had gained! Jim wasn't used to this. He knew the enemy had them outnumbered about two to one

But he didn't think Yankees should be pushing Southerners back like this in battle even with those odds. Jim still possessed a little of the Southern arrogance that had motivated the South to undertake this war to begin with. The process of disillusionment was in its infancy; Jim thought it was incredible that Yankees could push them back this vigorously. In fact, Jim was sure they'd turn the tables on them and start gaining ground again before the day was over.

The sun was getting low over the horizon when Jim heard movement in the brush across the clearing, and he pulled his carbine up to his shoulder and got ready. As soon as he saw several men in gray uniforms emerge from the brush, he heard Lieutenant Sorenson's booming voice, yelling at the top of his lungs, "Hold your fire! Hold your fire!" The clearing was soon filled with men in gray uniforms, running toward them for all they were worth. They rushed past them, some of them stumbling over the cavalrymen in the cover of the brush when they reached the south side of the clearing. When most of the men in gray were behind him, he heard officers yelling at them to halt.

"Halt! Goddamn you! Prepare for counterattack!" Jim heard an especially verbose sergeant yelling. But the men didn't halt.

"Get ready to fire!" he heard Lieutenant Sorenson's booming voice again. Sure enough, there was a commotion in the thicket again, and this time a mass of blue uniforms rushed out into the clearing. Their mad charge was halted by the withering fire of the waiting cavalry troopers in a fashion very similar to the one earlier that afternoon. This was a totally different kind of battle from what Jim was used to, but when he saw the soldiers in blue, rushing back toward the cover of the thicket they had just left, he just put another cartridge in his carbine and got another primer disk out of his primer pouch and put it in place. He decided not to worry about it if it worked.

Next Jim heard a commotion in the brush behind him again, and this time he saw men in gray in a long line abreast moving toward them. So the officers had managed to rally the men for a counterattack after all. The infantry didn't stumble over the prone cavalrymen this time. They knew they were there. They just worked their way through the thicket, grim faced, and sprinted out across the open field in pursuit of the retreating Yankees.

Now this is more like it, Jim thought. This was more like what he expected. Now all they had to do was keep chasing the Yankees and keep pushing them back till they ran them clean across the Potomac where they came from. Jim felt much better now. Then it occurred to him that he should check on his men and see how they had fared. He found out he had two men wounded, Smith and Johnson—Smith in the shoulder and Johnson in the hand. Blake was bandaging Smith's shoulder, and Monday Mane was trying to stop the bleeding on Johnson's hand. His hand looked badly mangled. Jim walked up and said, "Bandage it tight. That'll stop the bleeding." It felt a little strange telling Monday what to do. Monday was at least thirty years older than himself. But Monday did fasten the bandage tight enough to stop the bleeding.

"Take a casualty count," he heard Joe's voice behind him.

"Two wounded," Jim replied very quickly.

"Very well," was all Joe said as he moved off to check on the casualties for the rest of the troop. Jim made sure his two wounded men were as comfortable as he could make them. Then he went and asked Joe about going down to check on the wounded in the clearing. Joe told him to hold off for now. There were men moaning and asking for water. Jim figured he could at least have his men take their canteens down and give them water. But he told his men to stay put.

CHAPTER 39

Before dark some men with stretchers arrived, led by one man carrying a flag of truce. Lieutenant Sorenson came and gave the men permission to go and help the medics all they could.

"When the enemy medics show up with a flag of truce to evacuate their wounded, be sure you honor it," he cautioned.

So Jim took his detail down with their canteens and gave the wounded water while the medics bound up wounds, moved men onto stretchers, and started carrying them back toward the rear. The dead were left where they lay. There was no time to attend to them now. But Jim saw his men taking rations out of the haversacks of dead Yankees and scrounging weapons and cartridge boxes while they went from man to man on their mission of mercy.

When the Yankee medics showed up under their flag of truce, the pilfering stopped. The wounded Yankees were bandaged up and hauled off in stretchers too. When all the men still alive had been removed from the battlefield, Jim and his detail retired to their original position in the cover of the brush. It was full dark by then. The medics had come and put Smith on a stretcher and carried him to the rear. Johnson refused to go to the rear. He insisted he still had one hand to fight with—that his injured hand was his left hand, and he could handle his revolver just fine with his right. Jim knew the real reason was that he was afraid the Army surgeons would want to amputate his hand. As bad as his hand was mangled, he was sure that they'd do that. So Jim asked Joe for some laudanum for his one walking wounded, explaining that he had a minor wound and could still fight, but needed something for pain.

Joe told Jim he'd see what he could do. He came back about an hour later with some laudanum. Jim had sent Monday with two men to find water. It seemed like Monday could find water when no one else could. They had just returned, all three of them loaded down with canteens, all of them full. Jim had had his men loosen the cinches on their horses and tie them up somewhere so they could graze. He had no idea how long they'd be guarding this clearing full of dead soldiers. He mixed some of the laudanum in a tin cup of water and gave it to Johnson to ease his suffering. He obviously was in severe pain. He had Monday change the bandage on his hand and tie it looser. It was too dark to look at his hand, so Jim had no idea how bad it really was.

Jim went and found Joe and asked him if the men were supposed to make camp, and Joe told him, "No, but stay ready to move." At about midnight they got orders to mount up. Jim hoped they'd be moving north to reoccupy the ground they had regained with such difficulty, but to his surprise and disappointment, found out they were riding back to the south again. They continued riding until the Big Dipper showed it to be about 5:00 a.m. or so. Then they halted. Lieutenant Sorenson briefed them to loosen their cinches, let the horses graze, but keep them tied near them so they could move out in a hurry if the need should arise.

In a short while Joe came by and told Jim to deploy his men in a nearby thicket covering a clearing in the customary fashion. When Jim asked him about rations for the men, Joe replied that rations would be available sometime during the morning. He'd be notified when. So with no sleep, Jim and his men either sat or lay in the thicket, depending on the cover available, until about ten o'clock. He heard some of the men snoring. *So what?* he thought. *Let 'em grab some sleep while they can.* He'd wake them if he heard the enemy coming. It was 10:00 a.m. before Joe came back and told him he could send a couple of men to the mess wagon for rations. He reprimanded him for letting his men sleep at their post, so Jim woke them up and told them to stay awake. They'd had a couple of hours sleep by then, so he knew they'd be much more alert than they would have been if they'd fought to stay awake the whole time.

They weren't allowed to have a fire. Rations were hardtack and dried peas. The hardtack went down okay. The dried peas weren't very palatable. Most of the men decided to save their ration of peas until they got a chance to cook them. They remained there in the thicket all day long, listening to the cannon fire and small-arms fire in the distance.

At dark Joe came and told Jim to post mounted picket watches in the thicket on the other side of the clearing.

"Give them orders to fire three quick shots in the air with their revolvers if they hear any movement from the north and then rush back here," Joe told him, then turned his horse, and rode off.

Jim selected two men for the first picket watch and briefed them as ordered. Jim got very little sleep that night. He had to wake the oncoming picket watch every two hours, and he rode across the clearing occasionally to make sure the pickets were on their horses and awake. He finally went to sleep at 4:00 a.m.

Jim awoke with Joe shaking him. "Rouse up, man, and get your men ready to move," he said. Jim jumped up.

"Yessir," he said a little sheepishly. He hadn't intended to sleep so soundly. He turned and told his men to tighten their cinches and get ready to move. The ones who were dozing, he shook awake. Then he rode across the clearing to tell his pickets to return to camp.

They mounted up and headed south again. The horses hadn't had water for two whole days, so when they crossed a creek, they stopped and let the horses drink. Then they went upstream and filled their canteens. They stopped at about noon and were told they were permitted to have a fire and could draw rations—pork and hardtack. It was the first hot meal they'd had in days. The ones who had saved their dried peas put them in their tin cups and set them in the coals to cook. Then they were ordered to post pickets again and settled in to wait again. They could still hear the cannon fire in the distance, but no small arms as yet.

They waited there all day, the sounds of battle not getting any nearer. The sounds of firing stopped when it got dark. They were permitted a fire again that night and received rations again, this time flour included. The supper of broiled pork fat and Zeke's biscuits tasted really good, but there was no coffee. And they missed the coffee.

The following morning Jim noticed that Foxy was getting rather gaunt and went to the mess wagon where the spare horses were kept and took Brownie's tether halter off and swapped bridles and saddles. He rode Brownie back to the campfire and left Foxy with the spare horses to recuperate. He'd have done this sooner if he had been able to finagle the time.

Joe came by and told him to get his men ready to mount up. Then shortly afterward came the order to mount, and they moved out. This time they headed due east. Lieutenant Sorenson picked them a clearing to defend as usual, and they dismounted and waited under cover, carbines ready. The sound of cannon and small arms started. As the morning wore on, the cannon fire started getting louder. Apparently, the cannon were being moved closer to them. Then they got so they could hear the cannonballs striking trees. The sound of the cannon died down a little while, then it came back even stronger.

Then Jim heard, "Hold your fire! Hold your fire!" from Lieutenant Sorenson's booming voice as he saw the clearing fill up with retreating Confederate infantrymen. Jim got ready for the expectant Union infantry, which he was sure would follow. But after what was probably hundreds of retreating Confederate soldiers who ran past, the clearing was then empty. He heard cannon fire again—louder than ever. He saw the cannonballs burst in the clearing ahead. Jim looked back to make sure Brownie was securely tied. He was. Everyone hugged the ground. Cannonballs struck behind them; more struck in front. Jim heard a horse scream and what sounded like the screams of a man. Then in minutes the barrage lifted, and cannonballs started whizzing over them.

Jim immediately checked to see if he had any men hit. Two horses were down, killed instantly by a cannon blast that landed between them. There was one man killed and two wounded by shrapnel. The one killed had been Private Buck Songson. The two men wounded were Privates John Neighbors and Jonnie Wade. Neither of the wounded were bad off. Neighbors had a minor facial wound where a piece of shrapnel grazed his cheek, and Wade had his leg cut in a couple of places. Apparently, the Yankee cannoneers didn't know they were there because the guns were now elevated to fire beyond them.

Captain Wilson decided to charge the guns. He rallied the troop, and they mounted, sheathed their carbines per Captain Wilson's order, and drew their revolvers. Then with Captain Wilson leading, they rode at a fast gallop toward the sound of the cannon. They rode through the thicket on the other side of the clearing then through some more thick brush. It seemed like they rode another hundred yards or so when, suddenly, they came upon the guns. With a piercing rebel yell they swooped down upon the cannoneers who were still firing their cannon. When Jim got within about twenty yards or so, he reined Brownie to a sudden halt, pointed his six-gun at a blue target, and fired. He reined Brownie over to the side while he thumbed back the hammer and sought another target. With five shots, he saw four men fall. He quickly pulled out the cylinder and pulled his spare cylinder from his pocket and changed cylinders as quickly as he could. When he got ready to resume firing, he saw the blue-coated soldiers disappearing through the brush.

"Limber up those guns! Hurry!" screamed Captain Wilson. Jim had never worked with artillery before, but he figured he must mean to get the teams of mules harnessed up and the guns ready to move. He saw some men leading mules toward the guns. So they had captured the mules.

"Chase the Yankees! Cover these men while they limber up the guns" he heard Lieutenant Sorenson yell. He saw Lieutenant Sorenson pass him, and he spurred Brownie in hot pursuit. He heard more firing ahead and spurred Brownie again. He was missing out on something! Then he came to a clearing and saw Lieutenant Sorenson halt his horse and turn around.

"Now head back the other direction a little ways," he yelled. "Just cover the men moving the guns." So they moved back south a little ways and halted, waiting to see if there was to be any counterattack. After a few minutes they turned and rode south some more, staying close to the guns, ready to respond to any attempt to recapture them.

It seemed like they kept riding for a couple of hours, halting occasionally to listen for any sounds of pursuit behind them, then resumed their move south. They caught up with the guns a couple of times, and Lieutenant Sorenson halted them to wait for the guns to get farther ahead. Finally, they halted and set up a picket watch around the guns to the north in a semicircle. Lieutenant Sorensen told them to dismount and loosen their cinches. They'd stay here for a while.

While resting the horses, Jim found out that they had captured four cannon, complete with mules and ammunition caissons. They halted there for the night. Jim learned they were on the outskirts of the town of Spotsylvania. Shortly after dark, men from the Confederate artillery came to get the guns. They were to be moved to where they could be used at best advantage on the enemy the next morning. They were ordered to camp without fires that night since the whereabouts of the enemy were not certain.

CHAPTER 40

The next morning Joe came and told Jim to send some men to the mess wagon to draw rations and told them they had permission to have a campfire. Much to everyone's surprise coffee was included in their rations, along with flour and beef. After breakfast Joe came by again and told them they were expected to hold their position the rest of that day. So Jim assigned Sam and Walgreen the task of watering the horses. He learned that he was one horse shy now. Walgreen's horse had been one of the horses killed by the cannon blast the day before. The other horse killed had been that of Private Songson, who was also killed by the same cannon blast. Walgreen had missed out on the attack on the cannon because he was afoot, but rejoined them on their return. He had caught a ride on one of the caissons while the guns were being moved south. It would have been impossible for him to keep up on foot. So after the horses had been cared for, Jim took Dal Walgreen with him to the mess wagon where the spare horses were kept and told the guard he was picking up his spare horse. He untethered Foxy and led him back to where the horses were tethered. With several days past without being ridden, Foxy had perked up somewhat, but he was still rather gaunt. He'd have to do, Jim decided.

"How about your saddle?" Jim asked Walgreen.

"I brought my saddle," Dal explained. "When I saw the captured guns and caissons coming, I took the saddle and bridle off my horse and caught a ride. I figured they'd stop wherever we stopped."

Jim commended him on his cool thinking and told him he'd use Brownie until further notice. So Jim removed his saddle from Brownie so Dal could put his own saddle on him. He put his saddle on Foxy. He didn't bother to swap bridles. They were the same. But his saddle fit pretty good, and he didn't want to part with it.

So all his men were mounted now again. His losses had been pretty heavy so far. The only ones left were Sam Blake, Monday Mane, Zeke Dally, Dal Walgreen, and Asa Johnson, who had been wounded in the hand and refused to report it to the surgeons. Out of ten men to start with, he had only five left. Private Jack O'Henry was included in Mess Number 9, but he was the troop guidon bearer and actually worked directly under Lieutenant Sorenson and Sergeant Williams. He didn't take orders from Jim. Jack Smith, Asa Johnson, and Jonnie Wade had been evacuated by the medics to wherever the field hospital was though he expected Wade back in a couple of days since he had only a minor leg wound.

They wound up holding their position for three days before they got orders to move again. They heard cannon fire in the distance periodically each day and sometimes small-arms fire. The battle was obviously in progress, but no activity in their little niche in the woods for now. This gave the horses some much-needed rest. They'd been kept on the move almost every day for about two weeks now with only short periods for rest and grazing. All the horses had lost a considerable amount of weight. But Jim knew that the day's rest they were now getting would help a lot. He had been afraid he might have horses dropping dead from exhaustion there for a while.

When Jim thought about how Wade would probably rejoin them in a few days, it occurred to him he could have let Walgreen use Wade's horse while he was gone. But he'd still have to use Brownie to keep all his men mounted after Wade returned, so he figured it was just as well. If they got orders to move before Wade returned, he'd put Wade's horse with the spare horses.

Wade did return four days after he received his wound and insisted he could sit his horse. He still had a bandage on his thigh, which showed through the torn cloth of his pants. The entire troop were pretty much in rags by now. It was the continually moving through brush that was hard on uniforms. The hip boots they wore were a godsend; they protected the leg from about midthigh on down, but everyone in the troop had numerous rips and tears in the arms and upper legs of their uniforms by now.

Along about noon on the twelfth of May they got orders to saddle up the horses again. They moved south, toward Richmond. Then Jim figured it out! The capital of the Confederacy was being threatened! That's why they kept moving south—to get in position to better defend the capital!

By May twenty-third they crossed the North Anna River, still heading toward the south. Jim hoped they'd hold the enemy now and start pushing them back. The horses were starting to get a little gaunt again, and rations were still rather skimpy. But they had ammunition, at least. If they still had ammunition, they could fight.

On May twenty-seventh, Jim's regiment found themselves on the bank of the Chickahominy River at a railroad bridge—the Central Railroad, Jim had heard someone say. The railroad was in Confederate hands, and it was desirable to keep it so. But they fully expected the railroad to be attacked and were ready. Pickets were stationed in a big, wide semicircle on both sides of the bridge. There was one convenience associated with being close to the railroad. The train could be used to deliver rations and ammunition to the troops. Rations had almost been adequate for the past several days. They were camped near the riverbank on the north side of the river—probably, a mile northwest of the bridge.

They could still hear cannon fire in the distance. Scouting patrols had been sent out to determine how near the Yankees were. They were far enough away that it didn't seem like the bridge was threatened yet.

On the morning of the twenty-eighth Jim heard three warning shots fired by one of the picket watches. Everybody sprang for their horses and saddled them as quickly as they could. The pickets came galloping into camp and reined their horses to a rearing halt. They reported that they saw the enemy cavalry approaching. Jim hurried his men while they were saddling and getting mounted up. He could already hear small-arms fire at the perimeter of the Confederate encampment. Jim yelled to his men to draw their carbines, and they raced to meet the onslaught of Union horsemen. They rode to the first open area, and Jim saw the blue-coated riders racing toward them. He pulled Foxy to a halt so he could get his sights settled on a blue target and squeezed the trigger. He saw the rider's horse swerve as he fell from the saddle. Jim sheathed his carbine, undid the flap to his holster, and pulled out his revolver—no time to reload his rifle now. He reined Foxy back and forth while he picked out another target. He intended to be hard to hit, so he kept Foxy moving. He wanted to be a moving target for whoever was shooting at him. Bullets were certainly whizzing all around him. The enemy soldiers were still firing at them with carbines, and they hadn't stopped to reload! They had pulled back out of range of six-guns and were still shooting at them with their carbines! They'd make a funny downward motion with their hand just below the trigger guard and then fire again. Jim heard the bugle blowing retreat, and they raced back to the cover of timber they had just left. They were ordered to dismount and fire from the cover of the trees. Jim holstered his six-gun and took his carbine back out of the boot and reloaded it to get ready in case there was another assault. The Union horsemen had withdrawn also, back to the trees they had come from. Repeating rifles—Jim had never heard of such!

They heard small-arms fire nearby. Apparently, there were other units in the regiment still engaged with the enemy. Another troop was put in position, covering the same clearing that Jim's men were covering. Pretty soon they saw riders in blue emerge from the trees and start across the clearing again. Jim heard Lieutenant Sorenson's voice bellowing, "Wait until you can see the whites of their eyes, wait until you can see the whites of their eyes." Nobody waited until they could see the whites of their eyes, but they waited until the Union cavalrymen were within about fifty yards or so before they opened up. Jim hit one rider and knocked him out of the saddle. The sheer numbers of the D Troop and E Troop combined broke the back of the charge, and the Yankee cavalry retreated back to where they had come.

"Reload quickly, and mount up," Lieutenant Sorenson yelled. "Get ready to move." They rode to a position closer to the railroad where they could strike the Union flank if they should charge again. They dismounted and found positions to fire from cover, but the

Union cavalry didn't come through the clearing again. The sound of gunfire made it clear that they were fighting somewhere nearby though. That was all the action D Troop saw that day, but the sound of firing continued sporadically until nightfall.

The pickets were posted that night. Jim assumed that the fight would resume the next day. After supper Jim decided he was going to visit the clearing where they engaged the Union cavalry that day. He needed to go check on the picket watches anyway.

He went afoot so he wouldn't be detected and walked to the clearing where the Union men had charged them. There was no moon, but his eyes were well-adjusted to the dark, and there was enough starlight that he could see the forms of the dead horses and men on the field. They would have picked up the wounded by now. Jim walked carefully out onto the field, and when he came to a dead soldier, he looked for something lying on the ground shaped like a long, straight stick. He saw what he was looking for. He went over and picked up the rifle the dead soldier had dropped. He went to the dead soldier, who was already starting to smell, and untied his belt. He slipped it over his shoulder—revolver, cartridge box, and all. Then he snuck back to camp.

The next morning before breakfast he looked over what he had found during the night—a .56-caliber lever-action Spencer carbine. Exploration showed that it fed through the butt of the stock. Checking the gear on the dead soldier's belt showed that there was a cartridge box full of *metal-case cartridges*. Jim worked the lever a few times and found out that that was how you ejected them. Then pushing cartridges through the hole in the butt of the stock was obviously how you loaded it. He learned that it held seven cartridges. There was also a revolver with the gear he had scrounged very similar to the one he already had with a spare cylinder. He went to his saddle and found a way to fasten the revolver to the right side of the saddle fork. He put his old carbine in the saddle boot. He took his old cartridge box with the paper cartridges and put it in one of his saddlebags and replaced it on his belt with the box of metal cartridges. He counted them—twenty-two cartridges besides the seven that were in the gun.

After breakfast when Joe came by to see how his men were getting along, he saw Jim holding the Union carbine. Jim was in the habit of carrying his carbine with him wherever he went even when hanging around camp. But Joe noticed something different about that carbine. He showed it to Joe and showed him how it worked.

"Man, I could do with about a thousand of these," he remarked as he handed the carbine back to Jim. "Where did you find it?"

"I just kind of stumbled across it while checking on the picket watches last night." Jim didn't know if Joe could tell if he was stretching the truth or not.

Jim hadn't had any losses the day before. He counted himself lucky. There had been about twenty men killed and wounded from D Troop in all the previous day.

On May thirtieth, Jim learned that General JEB Stuart had been killed near Totopotomy, not too far from Yellow Tavern. A dark sense of foreboding came over Jim. Everyone in camp was much quieter that night. General Stuart was something like a deity to them. They had always been glad to follow him anywhere and had always had confidence that he would lead them to victory. Jim felt almost the same sense of loss that he had felt when he had heard about the deaths of Papa and Jonnie.

May the fifth was Jim's birthday. His birthday had come and gone without his even thinking about it because of the heavy fighting over the past several weeks. In fact, he didn't remember his own birthday until the mail from the troop finally caught up with them and he got a letter and package from Vickie. When he opened the package, he found a new pair of spurs and her letter wishing him a happy birthday. She remembered his birthday when he himself had forgotten it.

Trench Warfare

Jim was tired. In fact all his muscles ached with fatigue. And he was hungry. For the last three days all he had had to eat was parched corn. He was in a trench, digging. He had blisters on his hands. His cavalry gauntlets had completely worn out, and he had discarded them. They had so many holes and rips in them that it was too much of a chore to keep them on to try to do any work with them. So now he had blisters to add to his misery—also the hot sun. It was mid-July, and the sun showed no mercy. You could still sometimes hear cannon fire in the distance.

There were other men in the trench, digging too, of course. But they were all so miserable that they worked silently. They didn't have anything to say to one another—just stomping their shovel in the earth and pulling it up and tossing it on the side of the trench away from the heart of the city. The ridge of dirt on the side of the trench was what they were using for a breastwork. They could stand and lay their rifles on the top of the ridge of dirt and fire at any attacker without showing anything, but the top of their heads.

The horses were even thinner than two weeks ago. You could see their ribs. Jim was thinner, even than two weeks ago. You could see his ribs. You could see them easily in the tears and rips in his shirt. His uniform was rags. Also his boots were almost worn-out—not his cavalry boots as they were too hot to dig in, but the boots he had bought the previous summer when on leave, the ones that fit. Jim learned that there was nothing that would wear your boots out like digging. Foxy and Brownie had both developed saddle sores from the rigorous use they had been subjected to in June. They were healing slowly in spite of the medicine he had put on them that he had received from the regiment vet.

Several of the men had started digging caves back from the trench to get away from the sweltering heat. Sam had dug a cave back far enough to provide a place for himself and Jim to sleep in.

They were on the outskirts of Richmond and were obviously under siege by the Union forces. After the Wilderness Campaign was over, there wasn't really anything for the cavalry to do, so they were put to work helping the infantry build fortifications to defend Richmond. Jim's first responsibilities as a noncom were, of course, supervisory. He still made sure the men took the horses to water every morning. Then they'd tether them in a different spot each time, trying to find a spot where the grass wasn't already grazed too short for them to grip with their teeth. This was getting harder and harder because there were many other cavalry units trying to find forage for their horses too.

After the horses were cared for each morning, the men were assigned the tasks of working on the breastworks. There were two main arrays of trenches. The outer system of trenches were being constructed by the infantry. Several hundred yards behind them were the ones being built by the cavalry so they could be closer to their horses. They wanted to keep the horses closer to the outskirts of the city where some grass were still left. At least two weeks ago there were some grass left. After taking care of the horses each day, the men started digging. Jim's main job was to make sure the men each did their share of the work and that no one shirked. But after that was done, it didn't seem right to just stand around and watch the men work, so when he hadn't anything else to do, he would get down in the trench and help dig.

At first Jim kept his Spencer carbine with him when he was digging. But it was in the way of their digging if he kept it in the ditch or tried leaning it against the walls of the trench. It would get covered up with dirt if he laid it on the side of the trench. They hadn't been attacked in two weeks, and most of the cannonballs and mortars didn't reach this far. The infantrymen in the front trenches caught most of it. So Jim just started keeping his carbine rolled up in his blanket. But at night he slept with it beside him. He wanted it with him if the enemy did attack, and besides, he was afraid somebody would steal it. He had given to Walgreen his Sharps breech-loading carbine he had bought the last time he was home. Walgreen's carbine had been wrecked by a Yankee bullet in one of the skirmishes with the Union cavalry while defending the Central Railroad Bridge a few weeks before.

There was no music or entertainment provided by local talent in the evenings anymore. No one was in the mood. They just gratefully retreated into their caves (unless they had guard duty) and collapsed to sleep on the cool, damp earth.

After another week passed Jim noticed that the blisters on his hands had turned into calluses, and he discarded his boots and just went barefoot. Probably, at least half the men were barefoot by now. But Jim still had his cavalry hip boots. He didn't wear them because they were too hot, and besides, they didn't fit. But they had protected his legs from many scratches and gashes from sharp tree limbs in the Wilderness Campaign, so he figured he'd keep them for use when they started functioning as a cavalry unit again.

Probably the hardest thing to bear was the hunger—something about always being hungry that worked on a man and undermined his resolve and his morale from within, a little at a time. But the effect continued to accumulate, so it made you keep sinking lower and lower and lower.

There was finally a mail delivery, however, the first in a month. There were eight letters from Vickie and four from Joanne. Vickie's letters showed progressively increasing concern about not receiving any mail from him. He found out the same thing from reading Joanne's letters. So Jim took time out and wrote, first to Vickie, then to Joanne and Mama, explaining to them that he was all right. He was helping build fortifications to defend Richmond. The horses were a little gaunt, but otherwise doing okay. He put his two letters in the troop mail sack and returned to his digging. He knew they'd censure the letters. They had been told not to seal the letters. The officers who censured them for any information to be protected from the enemy would seal them. After mailing the letters, Jim returned to his digging. Digging was more difficult when you were barefoot, he found out. Pushing on the shovel with bare feet really made your feet sore in a short period of time. He decided maybe he'd better put on his cavalry boots to dig after all. Most of the worst of the digging had been done by now anyway. The trenches were about three feet deep or so with about another mound of dirt three feet or so high tossed up alongside it, facing the enemy positions. Then indentations were made in the mound of earth just deep enough for a carbine barrel to fit in so you could stand and fire from cover should the enemy charge them.

At the end of August Jim learned that the cavalry had orders to move. They were going to go find some place with more forage for the horses. The horses would starve to death in a few more weeks if they stayed where they were.

They saddled the horses and formed up as a troop. It was really wonderful just to have a saddle under him again! Captain Wilson led them right through the heart of the city. Jim became aware of just how big the city was as they rode through. Toward the center of town the main street was as wide as two or three streets normally were. He found another column of cavalry turning into the street and merging with his own column. He didn't recognize the battle flags. The other column of cavalry was apparently content to share the street with them. Before long the young rider to his left called over to him and asked him what regiment he was from. He told him South Carolina, and a conversation resulted.

The other regiment turned out to be a Texas regiment. The young Texan said his name was Jack Watkins. Jim learned that he was nineteen years old and had been in the war since it first started three years previously. He apparently had enlisted at the same age as Jim. He seemed to enjoy talking about mean horses and mean cattle. He described the lean, rangy Texas cattle to Jim and described their long horns.

"The main thing I like about Texas," the young former cow-puncher drawled, "is that it's one place where you can make a living and never get out of your saddle except to grab something to eat or maybe to take time out to bulldog some old maverick you just roped to slap a brand on him."

Jim found the Texan very amiable and interesting to listen to. In fact it lifted him out of his depression just to hear his reckless, confident manner. He knew the Texans must have been through the same ordeal during the past couple of months as his own outfit, but he seemed unaffected by it. Jim enjoyed listening, and the Texan seemed to enjoy talking, so he just went on and on. He described the wide, open ranges and the fresh, clean air—plenty of room to move, he said. He described a world totally foreign to anything Jim had ever heard of. Of course he had read about Texas and learned something about all the states in the geography lessons the old tutor had taught him. But this was the first time he had made the acquaintance of a real, bona fide Texan firsthand. When they finally finished their ride through the city and the Texans veered off to find a place where their horses could graze, Jim felt like he'd lost an old friend—*Jack Watkins, hmm*. He figured he'd try to remember that name, just in case he ever saw him again.

They had to ride a good ten miles out of Richmond before they found a place where there was still grass left. Then they stopped and made camp. They stopped within about a hundred yards of a creek so they'd have a place to water the horses and then tethered them in a meadow where there were still some grass. It hadn't rained in several weeks, and the grass was starting to get a little dry, but at least it was long enough, the horses could get their teeth in it.

When Jim sent men to the mess wagon for rations, he discovered that two men were missing, Privates Asa Johnson and Jonnie Wade. When Joe came by for his nightly rounds, he reported it to Joe.

"They might have been separated in town," Joe reassured him. "If so, they should show up sometime tomorrow." Jim wasn't so sure. He had found it necessary to watch both of them like a hawk for the last month to keep them from sloughing off their duties. They did nothing, but bellyache and complain. For the past week they had been rather silent and sullen. They did their duties, but their reluctance was obvious, and they barely did what they had to.

But Jim was glad to see the horses eating with enthusiasm. He figured, a horse with an appetite was going to be all right. And rations did show up. Walgreen and Neighbors brought back flour and pork. So they had hot biscuits and broiled pork that night. It tasted really good, but Jim wished he had some coffee. At least they still had plenty of tobacco. Everyone had stocked up on tobacco when they guessed that supplies were going to become even more scarce than ever. Jim even entertained his men with his harmonica that night. It was the first time he had played his harmonica in over two months. Everyone's morale was higher than it had been in a long time.

The two missing men didn't show up the next day or the next. Jim assumed they had deserted. He had heard there had been a lot of desertions in the past month or so. They changed the tether rope each morning after watering the horses to make sure there was grass to graze. The horses regained some of the weight they lost, and the saddle sores had finished healing up. After two weeks they moved to a different camp because the grass was all gone in that meadow. They had to move on another ten miles or so to the west to find a spot of grass that wasn't already grazed short or not already in use by another cavalry troop.

Late in August two new recruits joined them—Privates Ash Sampson and Clint McNeil. They looked awfully young. They were from Richmond. But both the horses they rode seemed to be in good shape. Horses in good shape were about as important as the extra men.

C H A P T E R   4 2

Sherman's March to the Sea

As they went into September, they changed camp every couple of weeks to find forage for the horses to graze. Jim had heard that there had been some fierce fighting at Petersburg, south of Richmond, but it involved mostly infantry and artillery troops. As far as he had heard, cavalry weren't used at all.

Jim's two new men, Ash Sampson and Clint McNeil, turned out to be rather proficient foragers. They'd come into camp at least twice a week with some homeless pig they shot so he wouldn't starve to death. And sometimes they brought back homeless chickens. It was always an act of mercy, of course, but the extra rations were greatly appreciated. So the men regained lost strength as did the horses. It was good that they changed camp every few weeks, because some of the local farmers were starting to complain to Army authorities about missing livestock. But the farmers were assured that the Yankees were doing it.

They did get mail regularly, and Jim learned from Joanne that Mama had been sick, but was better now. Vickie's letters expressed appreciation for the fact that she was getting letters from him regularly again. Since he was always so good to write, she got especially worried when she didn't hear from him, she explained. "And would you be able to come up to Culpepper sometime soon?" she wanted to know.

By November Jim learned that the Shenandoah Valley had fallen to the Yankees, so he knew they wouldn't set up winter quarters up there like the previous winter. He learned that the cavalry had dispersed almost all over Southern Virginia to keep the horses on grass they could graze. But they were permitted to build log cabins again and corrals for the horses. The men now were herding the horses on horseback, however, instead of building a huge pasture for them as they did during the previous winter. This way they could range them over a larger area to make sure they could find feed. Many of the men's shoes had worn completely out, and they wrapped their feet in rags to keep them from freezing when cold weather came. Some captured Union uniforms had been distributed to the men to replace the rags that would no longer stay on their bodies. It looked funny to Jim to see his own men walking around in blue uniforms. The troop commander insisted that they still wear their gray caps so they could be distinguished from the enemy. Most of Jim's men also had acquired overcoats in the transaction and some new boots. They were especially grateful for the new boots.

Jim remembered Vickie's birthday this time. He had completely forgotten it the year before. But the fact that she remembered his birthday when he himself had forgotten it jogged his memory. She had told him her birthday—November 2. He still had no means of buying her a gift. He had no money even if he had been near a town. So he carved out a cannon with a figure of a man getting ready to fire it. It never dawned on him that she might not appreciate carvings pertaining to the war. It was just the only thing he could think of to make. His carving was pretty good. He mailed it to her and sent her a happy-birthday letter.

It snowed the last week in November, and the men settled down for a long, cold winter. Their duties rotated from standing guard to riding watch on the horse herd to gathering firewood. This required felling trees since all the brush lying on the ground had been long since picked up.

Jim got a letter from Vickie expressing appreciation of the wonderful gift he had mailed her. Vickie really and truly did like it. Jim's carvings had an artistic quality to them. But the fact that he remembered her birthday was what put her in overwhelm, and reading her letter, he could tell that his gift had really made her happy.

Jim wrote Vickie and Joanne several times a week and entertained Sam and Monday, his roommates, with his harmonica in the evenings. He still played mostly sad songs. That seemed to be the kind he most felt like playing and the ones his audience most preferred hearing.

The next day was Jim's turn to pick a detail to provide the herders for the horses. He rode out with his two men so he could check on the horses himself. He was riding Brownie so that Foxy could have his turn at resting and rustling some graze. Then he noticed that Foxy looked like he didn't feel well—as if he didn't have troubles enough. Jim and his two men gathered all the horses that looked sick and herded them back to the hospital corral. They didn't have a troop vet, but the medical officer had assigned one of the medics the task of doctoring the sick horses. He put Foxy in the shelter of the shed they had built at one end of the corral and put some corn in the trough, but Foxy wasn't interested in eating.

He got another letter from Vickie. She expressed regret that he couldn't come home for Thanksgiving and wanted to know if he'd be able to get leave to come up during Christmas. Since Culpepper was at least a hundred miles away, he knew it would be impossible. He wrote and told her so.

He checked on Foxy every day. He wasn't getting any better. He was so emaciated, his ribs were showing again. He still wouldn't eat. Then Jim came down with a cold himself. He figured he'd slough it off in a day or two. He normally didn't ever get sick. He still went about his duties, checking on the men standing watch periodically. He'd had Brownie turned loose with the other horses since they didn't have enough feed to keep any horses up that weren't absolutely essential. And they rotated them with the most able horses in the herd whenever they could so they'd get their turn at pawing for grass in the snow. He'd asked Monday to tell him how Brownie was doing periodically. He found out he had grown a long, shaggy coat and was as sassy as ever. After a week Jim's cold was worse. It had gone down into his chest, and he had developed a bad cough. Then one morning he simply couldn't get out of bed. His muscles ached all over. He decided he'd better go to sick call, but when he sat up in bed, he got dizzy. He asked Monday to take over his duties and keep Joe informed of anything he had to report.

A medic came in later that day and told him he had pneumonia. The hospital cabin was full of sick men, and there were no spare beds, so he told him to stay there and have Monday or Sam give him his medicine. He wanted to know what the medicine was and was told it was quinine. *No wonder,* Jim thought, *they always gave you quinine regardless of the illness.* He complained about his side hurting, and Monday gave him some laudanum. It was his left side, where the bayonet wound had been. It made him feel groggy, and he went to sleep. Joe came by to see him later that day. He was barely awake. He said he was thirsty, so Joe got him a dipper of water. Jim asked for a canteen. Joe got him a filled canteen. Jim held the canteen to his chest like a teddy bear. He slept with it held to his chest like a babe in arms all night. He'd wake in the middle of the night, dying of thirst, and take a pull of his canteen—cool, wet, blissful water. It felt so good going down his throat. He'd also wake up sometimes with spells of coughing and keep Sam and Monday awake. Monday would get up and give him some more laudanum to make him sleep.

For the next several days Jim was barely conscious. Monday would try to get him to eat, but he wasn't hungry. But Monday would insist, and he'd manage to drink some chicken soup. Jim wondered where they got the chickens from. Monday would feel of his forehead and find out he was burning up with fever. He'd bath his face with cold water. It felt so nice and cool, then Jim would doze off again.

Jim lost all track of time. Then one day in the middle of the day, he started sweating. His fever had broken, and he was hungry. Sam brought him some corn mush and told him Monday was sick and in the hospital cabin. Jim was up and around later that day, but still felt weak. Sam brought in rations that night of cornmeal and beans. After cooking the beans and making corn bread, they had a big feed, and Jim felt much better. Sam had just recovered from a bad cold himself, but he didn't get sick enough to go to bed.

The next morning he went by the field hospital to see Monday. He found out he'd been sick a week, and Sam had taken care of Jim during that time. And Jim didn't even remember it. He felt of Monday's head to see if he had a fever. He figured maybe he ought to nurse Monday awhile in turn. He felt sure Monday had caught his illness from him. Monday assured him he was already recovering. At noon Jim saved back his corn pone and took it to the hospital and gave it to Monday. Monday ate it with relish. He wanted to know if there was any coffee to be had, and Jim regretfully told him no.

Jim learned that Foxy had taken a turn for the worse and had died while his young master was sick. He had really hoped that he'd pull through. Foxy wasn't as big a loss as Blue Boy had been though.

Monday was up and around a few days later. So Jim felt better. There was so much sickness going on this winter—among the men and horses both.

CHAPTER 43

///

They made it through the rest of January. In February Joe got sick. Jim went to visit him every day and brought him part of his rations each time. Joe would refuse to accept them, but Jim would lay it on his bed when he left, knowing that he'd eat them later. After a week Joe took a turn for the worse. Jim knew there were medics to take care of him, and with so many men sick, his own duties demanded more of his time, but he still went and visited Joe as often as he could as did Monday and Sam.

Then Jim found out that Lieutenant Sorenson wanted to see him. He couldn't understand what about, but he went to Lieutenant Sorenson's shelter and knocked on the door.

The orderly sergeant let him in. Lieutenant Sorenson had a makeshift desk made out of split logs. Lieutenant Sorenson offered him a cup of hot tea, which he accepted. It wasn't coffee, but it was the next thing to it. It was, at least, hot. Then Jim noticed something different about Lieutenant Sorenson's shoulder straps. He wore a captain's insignia instead of those of a lieutenant!

"Congratulations, Captain!" Jim exclaimed and saluted. Lieutenant Sorenson smiled and returned his salute from behind his desk.

"That's my reason for asking you over for a visit. Captain Wilson has been moved up to squadron staff and was promoted to major. He's now the squadron adjutant. I'm now the troop commander. I asked you in here to ask you if you'll accept a commission as second lieutenant, subject to President Davis's approval, of course."

Jim was flabbergasted. "But how about Joe, I mean Sergeant Williams? He's senior to me."

"Army regulations prohibit promoting someone while they're in a sickbed. Besides, I've observed your work first as a scout, then your excellent handling of your men. You made an excellent account of yourself during the Wilderness Campaign, and I decided you're the man I want. In addition to that I like the way you led every cavalry charge at Brandy Station and Gettysburg. Will you accept?"

Jim recovered control of his vocal cords well enough to mutter, "Yes, sir."

Captain Sorenson explained that he expected it to take about two weeks or so to find out if his appointment to second lieutenant would be approved. But he could promote him to sergeant now. That didn't require presidential approval.

So Sergeant Bennet took inventory of the men in the troop. There were only a dozen men who weren't sick either in the field hospital or at least too sick to get out of bed. Lieutenant Sorenson had asked him to name his replacement. He named Monday and recommended him for promotion to corporal.

Jim spent time with Corporal Sawyer and the new men to get better acquainted with them. He already knew them, but had little contact with them recently.

Jim turned his updated muster report into Captain Sorenson. Captain Sorenson told him he wanted to meet with him daily for the first week. He said he just wanted a daily update on what was going on until he got grooved into his new role. When Jim finally got time, he sewed another chevron on his sleeve.

On the first of March 1865, Jim found out his commission as a second lieutenant in the Army of the Confederate States of America had been approved by President Davis. Jim moved his gear over to the log cabin with the other two officers and occupied the bunk that Lieutenant Sorenson had recently vacated. The other two officers were First Lieutenant Sol Jackson, who was now the troop adjutant, and Second Lieutenant Dan Dudson. They played cards all the time they weren't on duty. Jim didn't play cards. He and his buddies had mainly been involved in playing music, poetry, storytelling, etc. They congratulated him on his promotion, but Jim sensed they did so mainly out of politeness.

When Jim got out his harmonica to play awhile after supper, Lieutenant Dan Dudson just frankly said, "Can't you play that thing somewhere else?" Jim put his harmonica up and didn't play it anymore that night. But he didn't play cards with them either. Jim had always thought playing cards was boring. So he just got out his writing material and wrote a letter to Vickie.

When Joe recovered from his illness to the point he could return to his quarters, Jim would frequently go over to his cabin in the evenings, and they'd play their mouth organs just like old times.

There was still snow on the ground, and it was still cold. Monday reported to him that Brownie was still just as shaggy and sassy as ever. Jim found out his duties weren't a great deal different than they were before his promotion. He still mainly just walked around and checked and made sure the guards posted were on duty and doing their job, and he also got daily reports on the condition of the horses.

Sergeant Joe William's strength continued to improve each day, and he fully resumed the duties of troop sergeant.

Jim had written to Vickie and Joanne both and told them the news of his promotion. Within a couple of weeks he got letters of congratulations from both of them. Also Joanne expressed regret about the loss of Foxy. He detected a slight note of "I told you so" in her letter, but he knew that she shared the loss with him. Foxy had really been a good horse.

By the middle of March they got a warm spell, and the snow started melting. It was wet and boggy for the next two weeks. But by the end of March the snow was all gone, and the horses no longer had to paw for their feed.

Toward the end of March, Jim got some shocking news! He received a letter from Joanne with a return address from Montgomery, Alabama. The Yankees had attacked their plantation and burned it to the ground! They hadn't allowed Mama or herself to even take any food from the house. They had run off all the servants and had shot and killed Mose when he started to put up a fight!

What is this? Jim thought as he laid the letter down. *Are the Yankees now waging war on civilians? Women and children even?*

He resumed reading. They had stolen all the horses and milk cows, and she, Mama, and Emma had had to walk in the snow, hoping to make it to Florence without freezing to death. They had managed to put on their coats when the soldiers made them leave the house, but they didn't have any mittens or warm shoes. They surely would have frozen on the trek to Florence if a neighbor hadn't come by with his horses and wagon and given them a ride into town. He had heard of how the Yankees were burning everything in sight, and when he saw smoke from the farm to the south, he had hitched up his team and escaped with his family with blankets and what food they could pack hurriedly.

They had found a family to take them in when they got to Florence. She wasn't sure why the Yankees didn't burn the small town of Florence too, but thought maybe it was because it wasn't in their direct path. After the Yankees left, Mama and Joanne managed to catch a train to Uncle Ben's at Montgomery. She had heard that a stretch of the track had been destroyed the previous month, but railroad workers had already repaired it.

Jim was stunned! *Yankees making war against civilians! Burning the plantation to the ground in the middle of the winter and turning his mother and sister out in the snow to freeze.* And they stole all their livestock? That meant that they had stolen Blue Bonnet! His hatred of the Yankees sizzled even hotter than ever before. He wished someone would give the order to attack! He walked around in a burning rage the rest of the day. At nightfall he finally recovered from his anger enough to think about how grateful he was that Mama and Joanne had at least escaped with their lives and made it to Uncle Ben's. He could only hope that the Yankees didn't decide to burn Montgomery too!

CHAPTER 44

Appomattox

By the end of March the novelty of being promoted to a commissioned grade had kind of worn off, and Jim was bored again and hungry. Rations were still scarce, and even when the men would go foraging, they'd frequently return empty-handed. It was as if the countryside had been picked clean. So much of the time, they had only parched corn. They didn't feed any corn to the horses. They had grass to eat, and most of them weren't being ridden at all, so Captain Sorenson decided not to grain any of the horses for now. There were two things Jim decided he couldn't stand, and those were boredom and hunger. He was eager for the summer's fighting to begin. He remembered the wagon train they had captured on their foray up into Maryland two years previously. They had an abundance of food for several days after that. So Jim was eagerly awaiting orders to march—somewhere, anywhere, but just to do something!

Toward the winter Jim had noticed that facial hair had started growing on his face again except this time it wasn't peach fuzz. It was a regular, coarse man's beard. It helped to keep his face warm, so he didn't shave it off.

It started raining on the first of April to further add to everyone's misery. Then shortly after breakfast when he was starting to go out and make his rounds, Lieutenant Sol Jackson came and told him the captain wanted to see all the officers. So Jim followed Sol over to Captain Sorenson's cabin. Dan was already there. Captain Sorenson had a map on a tripod. He explained that a courier had arrived and notified him that the enemy had been sighted moving west from Richmond. He wasn't sure yet what their objective was, but he had orders to prepare the troop to move out. It was a fairly short briefing. Captain Sorenson showed them on the map their present location and the spot where the enemy had been sighted. It was about thirty miles or so northeast of their present location.

So Jim went and found Joe and told him to notify the men that they were going to prepare to march. So the horses in the corral were saddled, and men went out to round up the entire horse herd and bring them into the corral. The rain had stopped at least, but it was still muddy. Since many of the horses hadn't been ridden in months, they, of course, resisted the idea of being caught and saddled. But a smaller crowding pen had been built in a corner of the corral for the purpose, so they'd herd in as many horses as it would hold, whose owners would then get a bridle on them, then lead them out, and saddle them while another batch of horses were herded in, and the cycle repeated.

It was noon before all the horses were saddled with everyone packed and ready to move out. They were ordered to bring along three days of cooked rations, but this amounted to filling their pockets with parched corn. It was still drizzling rain. Jim still had his slicker though it had some rips and tears by now. He still had the Yankee overcoat as did many of the men, but by wearing the slicker over it, he was able to exhibit the colors of Confederate gray. Since many of the men still had only the blue uniforms they had acquired during the winter, there would have been some concern about being mistaken for the enemy. So maybe the rain was a blessing after all.

They rode northeast, mainly over open fields as there wasn't much timber along this stretch of country. But the rain limited the visibility to less than two hundred yards. Jim had two scouts sent out with orders to ride back quickly in case the enemy was sighted, but to otherwise ride in a big semicircle and return by nightfall.

When the troop stopped to make camp, the scouts returned to report that there was no sign of the enemy as yet. They had parched corn for supper and slept in the rain on the muddy ground. Jim slept in all his clothes, slicker and all. He had loaned his blanket and oil-cloth to a man who had neither an overcoat nor a blanket.

The next morning it was still raining. Captain Sorenson told Lieutenant Jackson to send out the scouts this time. They were to return at noon to report what they saw. The troop would hold their position either until they heard from the scouts or until the rain stopped. They let the horses graze until noon. The scouts returned and reported they hadn't sighted the enemy, but had learned from a farmer that Yankee forces had been sighted about twenty miles farther west the previous day. So Captain Sorenson told the officers to give the order to saddle up and prepare to move out. By nightfall they were within about five miles of Five Forks, which was about ten miles west of Petersburg. The rain had stopped finally. They camped for the night again.

On the morning of the third of April, they saddled up and rode out at dawn. They arrived in Five Forks to see the aftermath of battle. Bodies were strewn everywhere as well as the remains of burned wagons. Deep ruts from wagon wheels could be seen plainly. Captain Sorenson rode out front, following the direction the ruts indicated, which was northeast. It wasn't long before the trail turned north and then northwest. When they reached the Lynchburg Railroad, they heard gunfire in the distance. They rode into a cover of some trees, and Captain Sorenson halted the troop. By easing forward to the edge of the trees, they saw soldiers in blue uniforms, thousands and thousands of them, marching hurriedly toward the northwest. It would obviously be suicide to attack that force with only sixty men. Captain Sorenson decided to stay to the south of them and try to ride parallel to them without being seen.

They retraced their steps far enough to be sure the Yankees wouldn't spot them, then scouts were sent ahead to find the main Rebel force, which Captain Sorenson expected would be found in the direction the Yankees were heading. In the meanwhile the troop kept heading northwest as fast as they could without being seen. It was about 2:00 p.m. when the scouts returned and reported they had seen the main Rebel force, including both infantry and artillery, headed for the small town of Amelia. They hurried their horses in that direction. Captain Sorenson wanted to join up with the Confederate force and get his troop into the fight.

They rode for several more hours, and then they rode up over a hill overlooking a stretch of open country and saw several troops of Union cavalry getting ready to launch an attack at the rear of a retreating column of gray infantrymen. Captain Sorenson quickly told everyone to draw their carbines and get ready. Jim drew the .56-caliber Spencer from his saddle boot and looked around to make sure his men were all ready. When the Union cavalry started their charge, Captain Sorenson told his bugler to sound *charge,* and with the entire troop screaming at the top of their lungs, they attacked the left flank of the enemy cavalry and caught them totally by surprise. When they were within thirty yards or so of the nearest enemy rider, Jim swung his hand up and down as a signal for his men to halt and picked out a target with his carbine, squeezed the trigger, levered another cartridge into the chamber, found another target, and fired. He saw the first horseman fall from his saddle out of the corner of his eye while he was shooting the second one—same with the third and the fourth. Caught in a murderous cross fire from D Troop on their left and the Rebel infantry in the rear of the column who had turned around to meet the charge, Jim heard the Yankee bugle blowing retreat, and the Yankee cavalrymen turned their horses around and retreated out of carbine range as rapidly as they could, with D Troop chasing them. But they then saw that the Union cavalrymen were riding back to join what looked like the entire Union Army, so Captain Sorenson yelled at them to halt. They rode back to the Confederate infantrymen, who were apparently holding the rear guard for the retreating column.

Captain Sorenson decided they'd just assist the troops of the rear guard for now until they got orders to do otherwise. At least he had joined with what looked like a major Rebel force. The road seemed to be bearing to the left, and Captain Sorenson expected the action to be heaviest on the left side. Two scouts were sent back to keep an eye on the enemy and to ride back and report if they started closing on the Rebel force again. So the cavalry rode to the rear of the infantry column and guarded their flanks. Jim pulled four cartridges from the cartridge box and fed them into the magazine of his carbine, making a mental note to change the cartridge box to the right side of his belt as soon as he got a chance.

Jim didn't like this business of retreating. He'd rather attack. But while he had never met General Robert E. Lee, he felt like he knew him. Jim had resented the series of retreats during the Wilderness Campaign, but when he learned that Richmond was being threatened, he understood. General Lee was just deploying the troops in whatever fashion did the most good. And they didn't take Richmond last summer in spite of having twice the men as the Confederate Army.[3] So Jim figured General Lee was doing the same thing again. He'd get the Army in a position to strike a decisive blow to the enemy and then hold their ground and attack. But Jim wished he'd hurry. He hated the mud, was tired of always being hungry, and preferred fighting to running.

Then the scouts returned with some startling news. "They're bringing up two artillery pieces," one of them said breathlessly.

Captain Sorenson didn't hesitate; he quickly wrote an order and handed it to Jim and told him to send whichever man had the fastest horse to the head of the Rebel infantry column and deliver that message to the commanding general. Jim, in turn, handed the dispatch to Corporal Blake and told him to send Private Watson because he knew he had the fastest horse.

Then they settled down to wait. Within two hours he heard cannon fire from behind them. So the Yankee artillery was in position. It wasn't long before they had the range and had cannonballs landing and exploding among the rear guard of the infantry. Captain Sorenson told Lieutenant Bennet and Lieutenant Jackson to move the men farther away from the road so they wouldn't be hit by the cannon fire. There was nothing they could do, but wait. To attack the cannon with their small cavalry force would be suicide with the Union artillery defended by no telling how many thousands of Yankee infantry.

---

[3] Richmond did fall to the Union forces later when the Confederate forces started their retreat.

In about a half an hour, however, Jim heard cheers all along the Rebel infantry column. They were stepping out of the muddy road to make room for an artillery piece to rush to the rear of the column. When it reached the rear and turned about to unlimber, he saw another one! Within minutes they had them in position to fire, and with a couple of salvos, they had the range. Jim turned and looked toward the Yankee force and saw men diving for shelter as the cannonballs hit. The cannon duel lasted for at least an hour. Then the Rebel cannoneers relimbered, rehitched the mules, and with loud cursing and popping of their whips, headed them back up the road toward the direction the marching infantrymen had gone. Captain Sorenson told Lieutenant Bennet and Lieutenant Jackson to get their men mounted up and follow them.

CHAPTER 45

D Troop continued to guard the flanks of the infantry rear guard until night fell. After it was dark, they didn't halt, but the march continued. Jim noticed several of his men went to sleep in the saddle. He even dozed off a couple of times himself. Anytime a halt was called even for minutes, Jim noticed the men in the marching column would lie down and go to sleep in the mud and wouldn't stir until the officers and noncoms came and kicked them awake and insisted they get up and resume their march. The sun finally came up, and when they came to a creek, he had his men take time out to water their horses and fill their canteens. There had still been no chance to draw rations, but he had some parched corn in his pocket. So he filled his mouth with parched corn and chewed it gingerly. It hurt his gums. After the horses finished drinking, he insisted they remount and move on, following Captain Sorenson and Jack O'Henry, who was carrying the flag.

Captain Sorenson had directed Lieutenant Jackson to send two scouts to find out how far back the enemy were and what they were doing. In the meantime, they plodded on, hungry and exhausted and half asleep.

It was April 4, and they continued their march all day long, the cavalry squadron guarding the flanks of the infantry rear guard. The rain finally stopped, and the sun came out. Jim was grateful for that at least. At noon Captain Sorenson called a halt to rest the horses. He knew they could catch up later. The scouts came back shortly after noon with their report that the Union Army was still in hot pursuit.

After riding on the left flank of the infantry column awhile, they came to a ridge and dismounted. It would be an easy position to defend. The horses started grazing hungrily. The men lay down

245

on the ridge as if in ambush. Jim went and lay down next to Joe and asked him how he was doing.

"Okay," Joe said, "rather guardedly." Jim understood. Within a few minutes they heard snoring. With the exception of Jim and Joe, the entire troop was asleep!

Jim just grinned and said, "No need to wake them just yet. We'll be moving out in a little while." And when the infantry column was maybe a mile away, Captain Sorenson gave the order to mount up. So Jim told Joe to wake up the men and get them ready to move.

The infantry marched all night again that night. Captain Sorenson kept D Troop within a mile or two of the Rebel's rear guard. They caught catnaps every time they stopped.

The next morning Jim looked out and saw a long line of gray soldiers marching to the southwest. They stretched almost across the entire western horizon. Their slow *tramp, tramp, tramp* made it obvious how exhausted they were. Jim was concerned about the horses. They were getting rather gaunt and leg weary. But Captain Sorenson ordered them onward. They rode down near the infantrymen and found they had just crossed the Danville Railroad near the little town of Amelia and had turned southwestward.

A courier rode up and handed Captain Sorenson a message. Captain Sorenson read it and then turned and ordered Jim to take his detail to the front of the column and report to Colonel Hawkins, commander of the Fifteenth Regiment. Jim led his men in an easy long gallop down the line of marching infantry. The column was miles and miles long. When he neared what looked like the head of the column, he asked an officer where he could find Colonel Hawkins. The officer pointed over to the west. Jim told his men to ride parallel to the column where they were, and he rode over in the indicated direction. He saluted and introduced himself.

Colonel Hawkins explained he wanted his cavalry spread out in a screen up ahead, and he wanted scouts checking the country ahead with reports every two hours on what they saw. Jim rode back and explained to Joe and the other noncoms what was wanted. So the cavalry troop was deployed as an advance guard, and the scouts were sent ahead. This made sense to Jim to have the cavalry covering both the front and the rear.

Inside two hours one of the scouts returned with some disturbing news. Jim brought Private Ames, the scout, with him to report to Colonel Hawkins so Ames could answer his questions directly. It appeared like a huge Yankee force was dead ahead, no more than five miles, blocking their progress. Colonel Hawkins thanked him. He called a halt and decided to wait for word from the other two scouts before proceeding further. Jim could hear the men in the ranks, snoring within seconds after they halted. He was jealous of them.

After another half an hour the scout who had been sent to the west came back with a report that that direction was clear, so Colonel Hawkins ordered the regiment to its feet and proceeded to turn the column to the right to a westerly direction. Jim sent Joe out to pass the word to circle around to the right to conform to the movements of the infantry column. They found a road headed for the town of Rice and continued the march. It became apparent that the colonel intended to march all that day and continue through the night again.

Then Jim learned something from the scouts that woke them all up. The Union Army was turning them again. Jim sent a courier back to Colonel Hawkins with this news, and soon the same courier returned with an order from Colonel Hawkins to swing to the northwest.

So Jim shifted the advance guard toward the north to parallel the movements of the Yankee force, then veered to the northwest. On the sixth of April they passed through the town of Farmville. You could hear gunfire in the distance, so some skirmishing was going on somewhere. Jim rotated the scouts every half a day or so, more to give the horses the advantage of a periodic break rather than for the men. Scouting tended to use up horses.

From Farmville they followed the road northward up toward Raines Town. Men and horses both just plodded ahead like zombies. They were numb with exhaustion. They had been without food so long, they no longer felt the hunger, just weakness and exhaustion.

On Friday, April 7, they reached Cumberland church near Raines Town. A courier rode up with orders from Colonel Hawkins to turn back to the northwest. Jim adjusted his advance cavalry guard accordingly.

Private McNeil's horse dropped dead from fatigue. McNeil pulled his carbine out of the saddle boot and proceeded on foot, abandoning his dead horse. By nightfall none of them could go any farther. Jim rode back to see how far away they were from the infantry column. He saw that the infantry had halted. The men were lying in the middle of the road in the mud, sound asleep. They could go no farther.

Jim came back and posted picket watches and told the rest of the men to go unsaddle and tether the horses and go to sleep. He told Sam, who was assigned the duties of the corporal of the guard, to wake him if there was any movement in the infantry force.

When Jim woke at sunup, every muscle in his body ached, and he felt like he was too weak to stand. He managed to force himself to his feet anyway. He felt a little dizzy, but found a tree and hung on to it for a moment until the dizzy spell passed.

Then he looked down at the infantry force about four hundred yards to the east and saw they were still there. He did see a few campfires, however, so did they maybe have rations? He decided to walk down and find out, but first he decided he'd better check on the pickets. There were two picket guards on duty, one to the west and one to the east, and both of them were sound asleep. He kicked them both awake and told them to look smart. Then he headed down to what looked like the headquarters tent for Colonel Hawkins.

Jim found out they did have some coffee and also some corn for the horses. So he took the coffee and what corn he could carry back with him and woke up Zeke and told him to start a fire and make coffee. He told Joe to send some men down for some corn to parch. In thirty minutes every man had the first cup of coffee they had had in weeks and bacon and delicious parched corn!

It was Saturday, April 8, 1865, and they did not have orders to march. Jim sat on a rock and smoked his pipe. He was nothing, but skin and bones and hollow eyes. He wondered when they'd get orders to march again. He consulted his map and decided they must be camped near the town of Appomattox.

They were still camped at the same spot the following morning—still no orders to march. Jim went and checked on the horses. Their ribs were showing, and they had saddle sores even worse than before. He decided they were lucky they had lost only one horse; they were in such bad shape.

That evening a member of Colonel Hawkins's staff came and told Jim to announce to his men that General Lee had surrendered the Army of North Virginia to General Grant. They were to remain in camp until their paroles were properly issued to them.

Blond Hair, Blue Eyes, and Dimples

Jim was concerned about the condition of the horses. He knew they had saddle sores, some of them serious. He located some axle grease and had the men rub it into the horses' sores as a salve. Rations were issued by the Union Army, which arrived in the form of a herd of cattle that was butchered to feed the starving Southerners. There was nothing else but parched corn, but Zeke divided out the ration of beef, and each man broiled it over the fire, spearing it on either a saber blade or a belt knife. Jim tied his belt knife to a long stick so he could cook his piece of beef without burning his fingers. Jim turned down the parched corn this time because of his sore gums and teeth, but was glad they had coffee again. A big piece of beef and three cups of coffee and he was ready to smoke his pipe. He had given his blanket and oilcloth to one of the men during the march, so he used his slicker for a ground cloth and his overcoat for a blanket and went to sleep. It wasn't even dark yet. He slept sound as a log all through the night. He woke when he heard reveille sound. It was the first time he'd heard reveille in over a week. He got up and went to check on the horses while breakfast was being prepared. Brownie's saddle sores were beginning to heal. He was eating with an appetite, so Jim decided he would be all right. He looked the other horses over and saw they were recovering too.

After breakfast, Jim lit his pipe and sat on the rock again as the men took the horses down to water them and came back and tethered them at a new spot where there were still some grass left to graze. An orderly sergeant came by and notified Jim of an officers' meeting at 10:00 a.m. When Jim asked where, he was told, "In Colonel Hawkins's tent."

Jim arrived at the Colonel Hawkins's tent at ten o'clock and found out the meeting was held outside the tent on the grass. There were no seats, so they formed up and stood at parade rest. Then a major called attention, and Colonel Hawkins walked up and told them to stand at ease. He gave them a briefing on the terms of the surrender and the procedure they were to follow. He explained that each man would be paroled, and once he received his parole, signed by proper authority, he would be free to go back home. Commissioned officers would be permitted to retain their sidearms, horses, and personnel luggage. The men could keep their horses if they were their own private mounts. It would take several days for the paroles to be signed and issued.

They were dismissed, and Jim returned to the encampment of his men. They had three campfires, one for each mess. He called Joe and the other three noncoms together and explained to them what he had heard.

So the men had nothing to do, but cut wood for the campfire and care for the horses for the next several days until their paroles were ready to be issued.

That afternoon, Jim took a stroll along the creek bank. He presented the appearance of just checking to see how the horses' saddle sores were healing. He spotted a big oak tree and studied the top of it carefully.

That night after dark, he took the Spencer repeating carbine from his saddle boot, unloaded, cleaned, and oiled it with pork grease and counted the remaining cartridges he had for it—six cartridges left. They'd fit in the magazine. He loaded the six cartridges into the butt of the carbine and then walked down to the creek. He unfastened the saddle boot from his saddle and placed the carbine in the saddle boot. Then he went to the tree he had picked out, climbed it, and continued on up to the particular limb he had decided on while studying the top of the tree that afternoon. Then he placed the carbine on the backside of the tree trunk, the side facing the creek, muzzle down, with the muzzle resting on a limb. He tied it there securely with a piece of rope, then he climbed back down from the tree.

The terms of parole said that commissioned officers could keep their sidearms, horses, and personal baggage. Their saddle guns were not included. Jim did not intend to turn in that Spencer repeating carbine. He'd just come back for it later when he got a chance.

Jim checked to see if mail could be sent from Appomattox and found out that it could. He announced this fact to his men and got out his saddle to write on and wrote to Vickie and Mama and Joanne, letting them know the war was over.

Two days later Jim was issued the paroles to hand out to his men. His own parole was among them. They saddled up their horses and formed up as a troop, with the guidon bearer on one side of Jim and troop sergeant on the other side. They rode in formation through the ceremony of turning in the colors, dismounting, taking carbines, six-guns, and cartridge boxes, and stacking them as Jim had briefed them. Then they went back, mounted their horses, and rode on off. It was April 14, 1865.

Joe rode with Jim a little ways. He told Jim he figured they could ride together. Jim said that would be fine, but explained that he wasn't going back to South Carolina. He was going to Culpepper. Joe understood and rode with him until they reached the road where Jim headed north, and Joe headed south. Joe rode a little ways then, as if from an afterthought, stopped, turned, and saluted. He saw Jim just watching him. He hesitated for a minute then returned Joe's salute. Both men's eyes were moist.

Lieutenant Jim Bennett, with a dark-brown beard, a ragged Yankee uniform, and a gray Confederate cap, rode north toward Culpepper. He had told Vickie in his letter that he had expected to be at Culpepper in a little over a week. As he rode, he dreamed of blond hair, blue eyes, and dimples.

The End

ABOUT THE AUTHOR

///

Randell K. Whaley grew up in the Great Plains area, was a Navy pilot in Vietnam, has visited ten foreign countries, and has traveled extensively throughout most of the United States.

He has also been a cattle rancher and taught programming in college for twelve years.

He currently lives in Dimmit, Texas.

CPSIA information can be obtained
at www.ICGtesting.com
Printed in the USA
FSHW010623010421
79962FS

9 781662 432774